To Her_____ ____
a lovely friend and
colleague. Best wishes
always,
        Betty

    Elizabeth Noyes

ELIZABETH NOYES

Imperfect Wings

Imperfect Wings

© 2014 Elizabeth Noyes

ISBN-13: 978-1-938092-68-8

ISBN-10: 1938092686

Published by Write Integrity Press, 130 Prominence Point Pkwy. #130-330, Canton, GA 30114.

www.WriteIntegrity.com

Printed in the United States of America.

Dedication

To Paul
My husband, friend, biggest supporter, encourager,
listener, sympathizer, cheerleader,
sounding board, devil's advocate, and resource
and arbiter for all things male.

Acknowledgements

John Donne's famous line, "No man is an island," holds true across many facets of life, especially so in the birthing of a book. As the author I bore the brunt of the labor, but it took a team to deliver this baby!

It has been my privilege and honor to work with some very special people on this journey. My heartfelt thanks go out to everyone who encouraged me when I was down, reminded me to have hope, challenged me to look deeper and write stronger, made me laugh, made me cry, but most of all who believed in me when I didn't believe in myself.

To the girls in my critique groups who saw (and forgave) the really *rough* first drafts: Fay Lamb, Mandy Hawkins, Brenda Lowe, Deb Dulworth, Pamela Trawick, Martha Gorris, and Dena Netherton.

To my sweet friend and colleague, Yolanda Escutia, who showed me the beauty of the Spanish language.

To my "beta testers" – Brenda Curtis, my beloved sister-in-law, Barry Thomason, one of the funniest and most candid people I know, and Jan Welch, my dear friend.

To my editor and publisher, Tracy Ruckman, who took a chance on me.

Chapter One

From every direction the same cry echoed. "Don Castillo, *El Carnicero viene!*" Castillo, The Butcher, he comes.

Machine gun fire erupted, provoking a greater frenzy. The panicky villagers screamed and ran, deserting the village, fleeing with whatever they could carry.

TJ bucked the frenzied crowd, ducking into doorways and skirting the crowd. The path through the jungle, the one that led to the landing field, lay on the other side of the orphanage.

Ahead, the doors of the orphanage gaped wide. The children had gotten away. *Praise the Lord!*

She rounded the corner, ready to sprint … and almost crushed the cluster of little girls huddled against the side of the building. Six pairs of fear-filled, black-as-night eyes stared up at her.

TJ looked around, vainly searching for the older children who were supposed to lead the little ones to safety.

"*Por favor*, Tay-Sjay." Eight-year-old Gabriela touched TJ's hand. "Please. You no leave us?"

Her heart hammered. She couldn't leave them. TJ reached for Gaby's hand. "*Prisa niñas.* Hurry. Come with me."

The girls followed but when they reached the tree line, Gaby pulled back. "No, no. This way no good, Tay-Sjay."

"No, we have to get to the helicopter."

Gaby shook her head, the long black braid whipping across her shoulders. She tugged TJ in a different direction. "This way. I know."

TJ hesitated only a moment. "All right, go."

The other girls followed Gaby down a narrow track that seemed better suited for goats, each girl holding tight to a hand in front and one behind. TJ brought up the rear.

The soldiers wanted *her*. Why else would Castillo send men to ravage the village? He must know about the video. The bullet hole in the prisoner's forehead would forever be imprinted on her mind. Death came in many forms, but at El Carnicero's hands it would be a horror. "*Prisa niñas*. Hurry."

Seven days since she came to visit Señora Ramirez at the orphanage. A week since she paid the drunken pilot to fly her in and out of La Cruza. The three-hour flight saved a five-day trek by mule and flatboat, but even so, the turbulent hop had been one of the worst experiences of her life. She'd take it again without complaint today.

Sweat beaded on her brow, running in rivulets down her neck. Did they have enough of a head start?

The village of La Cruza lay at the edge of the rainforest, near the coast where Honduras bordered Nicaragua. Their trail wound through the Giant Kapok trees that towered above the rest of the jungle. Overhead, their foliage interlaced in a canopy so thick it muted the light of day, while underfoot, the ground seemed to writhe in a tangle of knotted vines and gnarled roots.

The youngest of the girls, four-year-old Ariella, scampered in front of TJ, her chubby legs working twice as hard. How much farther could the little girl go?

Ahead of Ariella, six-year-old Marisol tripped, tumbling the smaller child to the ground.

TJ scrambled over. "Shhh, *niñita*. It's okay."

The little girl made no sound, a sad indictment that one so young knew the danger of crying out. Ariella hugged her scraped knee as silent tears trickled down her cheek.

TJ sighed, readjusted her backpack, and lifted Ariella. She'd gotten farther than TJ expected. "*Vamos*! Let's go."

The shadows crept in. Time passed too quickly. It was all her fault. The need for justice ... no, her thirst for revenge ... had brought death and destruction to this poor village. All that mattered now was getting these little ones to safety. And giving the memory disc to the authorities. Justice might have an entirely different meaning down here, but the video clip would be difficult to ignore.

Ariella tightened her arms around TJ's neck. "*Gracias*, Tay-Sjay."

Ten minutes later, TJ's arms burned from her burden. When the path widened and a shaft of sunlight sliced through

the foliage, she dared breathe a sigh of relief.

"*El campo*, Tay-Sjay. The field." Gaby pointed.

The forest opened onto a barren landscape filled with broken trees and scorched stumps, one of many slash-and-burn cuts ripped from the rainforest to create farmland. The stench of fire still lingered.

On the far side of the clearing, near the winding river, the denuded tract was leveled, the soil turned and readied for planting. A perfect landing site—except no helicopter.

"Where are you, Rochester?" she whispered.

The girls hesitated at the edge of the trees, waiting for TJ's cue.

TJ shifted Ariella in her arms and led the troop to the center of the field. She lowered the little girl to the ground and turned in a slow circle to scan the tree tops.

Another spray of gunfire echoed through the jungle. The staccato rounds came less frequently now. What had happened in the village? When the soldiers didn't find her, they would look for her trail.

She studied the horizon, ears straining for the sound of whirling blades. She'd contacted Rochester by satellite phone more than an hour ago. He'd promised to come. Immediately. A glance at her watch didn't help. The drunken scoundrel could be full as a tick by this time of day, not that it would stop him from flying the piece of junk he called a helicopter. Whether he was soused or not, she'd gladly kiss him and the ground he walked on if he would just come.

Wisps of smoke appeared above the trees. For one grief-filled moment, TJ gave thanks her father hadn't lived to see his legacy destroyed. He hadn't been much of a father to her, but William McKendrick had been everything to these orphans. He and *Señora* Ramirez started the school—*El Camino de la Cruz*, the Way of the Cross—and like parents everywhere, the hardworking peasants brought their children. A collection of shacks sprang up like toadstools outside the tiny, one-room schoolhouse, giving birth to the village of La Cruza.

But then, Don Rafael Castillo came. *El Carnicero* took La Cruza for himself. The Butcher had no need for educated peasants, no need for teachers like her father.

TJ forced the memories away. She needed a way out and their only hope was the unreliable bush pilot.

The distinctive *whop-whop* reached her ears right before the aircraft poked its nose over the trees on the far side of the field. She turned toward the sound with renewed hope. They might make it out yet.

As the aircraft glided across the clearing, TJ studied the open cargo bay doors. The little spark of hope withered. "Oh, no."

The helicopter reduced speed and came to a hover before descending to the ground by slow inches. It resembled a glass bubble toy with skis on the bottom and a twirly bird hat on top. A relic from a bygone age. Spider web cracks filled the left

side of the windscreen. Rusty splotches created an ugly mosaic that ran the length of the boom and all but eradicated the bird's tail numbers. Worse, the open cargo door revealed huge wooden crates—filling the bay to capacity.

"Oh no," she whispered again.

The girls cringed, their hair whipped by the backwash of the rotor blades.

Grim resolve stiffened TJ's spine as the machine settled to the ground. She would pack the girls in like sardines if necessary, but none would be left behind.

The pilot, dressed in a shapeless, soiled jumpsuit and wearing a bug-like helmet that hid his face, hopped out of the cockpit on the right side of the helicopter and strode to where TJ stood.

Rochester himself, he of the bleary eyes, scruffy hair, and unshaven cheeks. A derelict contracted to fly her in and out of La Cruza and now a most unlikely candidate for white knight status. But he'd come.

He removed his helmet, yanked off the dark aviator sunglasses and—surprise of surprises—a clean shaven face greeted her.

"Ms. McKendrick." He acknowledged her and then nodded at the girls. "Who are these kids?"

"Your passengers, Mr. Rochester." TJ stuck her chin out, daring him to object.

His fierce blue eyes collided with hers.

Sidestepping him, she motioned to the girls. Not a good time or place for a battle of wills, especially so with six innocent lives in the balance. At least he didn't seem drunk.

"Ms. McKendrick."

Eyeing the straps that secured the cargo, TJ realized she and Rochester together couldn't move the massive crates.

"Ms. McKendrick!" Rochester shouted again. "What do you think you're doing?"

She had to shout over the engine noise. "Castillo is razing La Cruza as we speak. Now, are you going to help me get these children on board or wait for his mercenaries to find us?"

"They won't all fit. Can't you see the hold is full?"

For a moment TJ wondered if he would spontaneously combust. "Then make them fit, Mr. Rochester."

When she refused to look away, he continued to argue. "You paid for one person. You. I can't take all these kids."

She was pretty sure a tendril of smoke curled around his head. His teeth should crack any minute now.

The pilot turned in a full circle, took a visibly deep breath, and tried again. "Look, sweetheart. I can't offload all this …." He waved at the cargo hold. "Not without a winch. And I don't have a winch."

More determined than ever, TJ turned to the cockpit and yanked the co-pilot's door open. "Of course you can. Gabriela, *sientate aquí*." She nudged Gaby to climb in.

"Hey, you can't do that."

She turned, startled by how close he stood. She could feel the heat of his body. And good grief, he was big. The man moved like a wraith. She didn't recall being so intimidated when they first met in the shack where he ran his air ferry business. Of course, he'd been slouched behind a desk. With a whiskey bottle tipped up. And she'd kept her distance after slapping four hundred dollars on the table.

Undaunted, TJ jabbed a finger in his chest. "Back off, Rochester. Why don't you help me before you get us all killed."

He didn't budge.

Another burst of distant gunfire broke the standoff.

She clutched the pilot's arm, willing to plead if it would get the girls safely away. "Please. I can't leave them."

TJ knew the moment he caved. His scowl softened to unwilling acceptance, and the tension ebbed away. Rochester muttered under his breath, but returned to the cargo bay.

"We might squeeze one or two in along the bulkhead, but it'll be tight." He looked the girls over. "Maybe three. Won't be comfortable."

Prodding Maria, Carmen, and Marisol, TJ hurried them to the open door. "Living is more important than a little discomfort, Mr. Rochester."

He helped the girls into the narrow space, made sure they were snug, and then released the bay door to slide shut with a clang. When he looked over at the remaining girls, his voice grew soft, betraying a hint of western twang. "You won't all fit."

"I know." TJ lifted Ariella to Gaby's lap in the cockpit before turning to the last child. "Lucia, *aqui*."

Lucia hurried over and clambered inside. The two little girls snuggled on Gabriela's lap while TJ fastened their seat belt.

With the girls loaded, TJ took a deep breath, let it out, and faced the pilot again. The stony angles of his face spoke volumes, but Rochester's eyes told a different story. A muscle in his jaw twitched. He might hate leaving her behind, but he'd do it.

She really needed to rethink her perceptions of this man. "Does this overloaded bucket of bolts have enough oomph to carry me to the other side of the river?"

Rochester sized her up before nodding. "Wait here. I have something for you." He returned to helicopter and came back a moment later.

"You know how to use one of these?"

TJ pulled the handgun from its holster. Oh yeah. Trevian Jane McKendrick, daughter of Staff Sergeant William McKendrick, definitely knew how to handle one of these. Her father, a two-time Olympic marksman had taught her well. "Sig Sauer P226." TJ pulled the slide back and checked the chamber. "Full magazine." She looked up. "Nine millimeter?"

The pilot cocked one eyebrow, his tight-lipped expression

softening to an almost-smile. He nodded. "Yeah. If you have to use it, point the bad end at the biggest part of whatever's coming your way." He held up a plastic bottle, a spray can, and a small box before stuffing them in her backpack. "Water, insect repellent, and extra ammo."

The gun gave her a smidgeon of hope but couldn't dispel the bleakness of her situation. Paper targets didn't match up with flesh and blood. Sure, she could hit a bull's-eye most every time, but could she knowingly point the gun at a man and pull the trigger?

Rochester's expression grew intense. "Another thing." He unstrapped a leather band from his wrist and reached for her left hand. "This is a transmitter. It broadcasts a signal we can track. Do not take it off. Not for a minute." He shoved her shirt sleeve up and cinched the band tight around her wrist. "I won't be able to land on the other side of the river. You'll have to drop from the skid. Stay in the verge of the jungle, out of sight. Don't fire your weapon except as a last resort. Sound carries out here. Follow the river while you can see. Head east and be quiet. Do you understand?"

She nodded at his rapid-fire orders. "Got it."

Rochester was way more than the wastrel he portrayed. She hooked the gun holster around her waist. The belt rode low on her hips, pulled down by the weight of the gun. She'd have to stuff the holster inside the waistband of her cargo pants to keep it from flapping while she ran.

"Do whatever necessary to stay alive, Ms. McKendrick. I will come for you."

TJ frowned at the force of those softly uttered words, at the fire in his eyes. He meant it. Good. She needed something to believe in. With a pat on the gun at her side TJ said, "I like my odds a little better now, Mr. Rochester. Thanks."

"Let's go." Rochester nodded toward the helicopter. "Sit on the front left skid and grab hold of the strut."

TJ grinned and saluted, wanting to ease his concern. "*Gracias*, Mr. Rochester. Take good care of my girls for me."

Imperfect Wings

Chapter Two

TJ followed the river, staying within the protective cover of the jungle until she couldn't take another step without tripping. Sunset shed its crimson glory, gave way to taupe and then indigo as night lowered its curtain. She spotted a dying Kapok tree just in time. As a hiding place it offered little in the way of protection, but the burrowed hole in the base provided a semblance of shelter.

Impenetrable darkness surrounded her, blackness so complete all spatial perception disappeared. Poets called this time the dead of night or the darkest hour, but TJ claimed it as her own personal hell.

Sleep eluded her as the nocturnal cacophony filled the jungle—non-stop croaking tree frogs, small nocturnal animals rustling through the underbrush, and the distant howls of bigger animals—predators—on the hunt. She dared not close her eyes. And thank goodness she had insect repellent else the mutant-sized mosquitoes would've siphoned off her last drop of blood by now. The parents here must tie their babies down to keep them from being carried off.

A cat growled off to her right, closer than any she'd heard

so far. TJ squirmed deeper into her makeshift fortress until her spine rubbed against the interior wall. She pulled her knees to her chest and rocked. Would the night ever end? Her entire world existed in this moment, reduced to a microcosm of the space she occupied and nothing more.

In the jungle's quieting pre-dawn silence the past tried to crowd in. She whispered aloud, reeling off the girls' names, anything to ward off the memories.

She ran out of names and her childhood leapt to life. She hadn't thought about the dark place for a long time. Now, though, in the menacing jungle, the darkness seemed a million times worse than the tiny closet her mother had once banished her to.

TJ shivered in the warm air. Her shoulders and neck would be sore tomorrow from sitting in the cramped position for hours on end. Oh, who was she kidding? Fear had its hooks in her, pure and simple. Fear and guilt.

Had she fooled herself? Did she really come seeking justice for her father's murder? Or was it a clever disguise of her thirst for vengeance? Neither would bring him back, but removing Castillo would save others. Or was that rationalizing her actions?

A bit of wisdom floated up from the past, something her father said after her first boyfriend had cheated on her. "Be careful what you wish for," he told her. "There's an old saying, 'Before you embark on a journey of revenge, dig two graves.'"

The pitiful glow from her wristwatch pushed back the infinite darkness enough to reestablish a tether to reality. Five minutes past five. With a long steadying breath, TJ focused on the vacation cruise she'd considered. And the all-inclusive resort. Any place but Honduras.

Was the sky growing lighter?

She felt for the tree's opening and stuck her head out. Turning toward what she thought must be east, her eyes strained for the first hint of daylight. The sky bled through the color spectrum as the ebony palette gave way in time-lapse increments—darkest purple to violet, misty gray to the first rosy blush on the horizon. Dawn at last. Time to move.

TJ crawled from her hidey hole and dug through the backpack until her fingers located the postage stamp-sized plastic case. The horrifying moments when Don Castillo and his cohorts gloated over the man kneeling at their feet—right before they shot him in the head—all captured on video. Why hadn't she given the memory card to the pilot?

No matter now. She'd just have to survive to see justice served.

Justice. Such a bittersweet word.

Fishing the water bottle out, TJ twisted off the lid and took a swallow and then followed it with a bite of her only Hershey bar. She ate slowly, letting each bite melt in her mouth.

She licked the last of the chocolate from her fingers and stuffed the trash in her pack, careful to minimize the crackle of

the paper, and then finished off the water. When the waking birds fell silent, her senses tripped to high alert. The jungle and all its inhabitants seemed to hold their breath. She held hers, too. Slipping the backpack over her shoulders, TJ pulled the gun free of its holster.

A twig snapped off to her right. TJ whirled, thumbing off the pistol's safety. As she raised the gun, a shadow lunged for her, grabbing for her arm.

She swung high and cracked the barrel against his head but smashed her fingers in the process. She sucked in a breath with a hiss. Her fingers throbbed.

The attacker clutched at his temple and staggered back.

Not waiting for him to recover, she kicked out, intending to damage his knee, but the phantom twisted away at the last moment, taking the impact on his calf. He fell hard, holding his leg. And never made a sound.

Her kick had landed solid. What kind of man could take punishment like that without a whimper?

Adrenalin pumped through her veins, supercharging every nerve. Her attacker wore unrelieved black—shirt, pants, boots, ball cap turned backward, and some kind of heavy vest. Funny looking goggles covered his eyes.

Her mouth went dry as she noted his weapons—a long, wicked hunting knife strapped to one thigh, two holstered handguns at his waist, and a semi-automatic rifle slung over one shoulder. The vest pockets bulged with stuff she couldn't imagine. The man was a walking arsenal.

TJ bolted.

She made it five steps before a second shadow appeared out of nowhere and latched onto her gun arm. Letting her momentum swing her around, she ploughed into him with her free arm bent and raised high. Her elbow slammed up under his chin.

His head snapped back with the impact, loosening his hold on her arm a fraction. Enough for TJ to jerk free.

The jab to his chin sent a jolt of electricity radiating down to her fingers. Good. Pain would keep her focused. Keep her adrenalin high. Maybe he lost a few teeth.

She covered a dozen steps this time, almost reached the tree line when a third figure charged out of the shadows from the opposite side. He dove, catching her ankle in a shoestring tackle.

TJ hit the ground hard, oxygen exploding from her lungs. Everything hurt, but each moment could mean the difference between being captured—or killed—and getting away. Ignoring the pain, she rolled and kicked out with her unfettered foot. Her boot connected, catching the third assailant upside the head with a satisfying thunk. Using the gun like brass knuckles, she swung out and scored a bruising jab to his arm.

He grunted and scrabbled away, rubbing his injured arm.

TJ sucked in a ragged breath and took advantage of the momentary freedom. She lurched to her feet, holding the pistol

butt in a death grip, and took off. Four steps … eight … ten. A few more and she'd reach full sprint.

She broke free of the jungle where she could lengthen her stride without worry of tripping … and something that felt like a Sherman tank plowed into her from behind and slammed her to the ground. What little air TJ had managed to draw expelled with a whoosh.

Resting most of his weight on her back, this fourth attacker pinned her arms out wide and clamped tree-like legs around hers, rendering her unable to move. Face down in the dirt, under a half-ton of muscle, TJ struggled to breathe.

The tank's breath warmed her ear. "Let go of the weapon."

His growl held a hint of twang and a healthy dose of iron, but it was his words that surprised her. He spoke English.

TJ gripped the pistol as fog blurred her vision, black dots dancing at the edge. "Airrrr."

The weight on her chest eased a little.

"Let go." The big hand shackling her wrist squeezed.

Another shadow knelt by her head and gently removed the gun from her numb fingers.

The tank's weight lifted from her back, freeing her hands and legs. "I told you I would come for you, Ms. McKendrick."

TJ struggled to pull in enough air to get her lungs working again. It took several moments for his words to register. She pushed to a sitting position and turned to look at the man who'd taken her down. "Rochester?"

He wore the same black uniform as the other shadow warriors. "You don't play very nice, little girl. And here, we risked life and limb to rescue you from the boogieman." He made a tsking sound.

"I only know one way to play."

Several quiet chuckles came from behind her. How many were there?

Rochester rose to his feet in one lithe movement and extended a hand to help her up.

She looked around at the five huge shapes surrounding her as he pulled her to her feet.

One of them spoke. "Cowboy, we got tangos coming from the west. An even dozen. Fifteen minutes and closing. Gotta move."

Cowboy?

"Ice, Romeo. Take point."

Two of the men vanished into the morning mist before TJ could count their steps.

"Dingo, Casper, you got our backs." Rochester—or was it Cowboy?—jerked a thumb in the opposite direction and two more shadows faded away. "Dawg, you're with me."

He turned to TJ. "Can you run, Ms. McKendrick?"

She could finally make out his features in the weak dawn light. Black and green camouflage paint crisscrossed the fearless leader's face. He wore his cap backward like the others

and carried his own arsenal. Not a drunken, backwoods pilot hiding from the world. She'd misjudged him in a big way. "Is it Castillo? He's coming?"

"Yeah. We intercepted some radio chatter. One of the villagers spotted you outside the don's camp. What'd you do? We've been hanging here for months waiting for him to come out."

She shrugged.

"We'll discuss this later. Right now, there's six miles to cover and not much time. Stay close to me. Do what I say, when I say. Understand?" He took off at a jog, not waiting for an answer.

"Wait ... what about the girls ... are they ...?"

He called over his shoulder. "They're safe."

She sprinted after him.

Rochester gave them no breaks. Sweat darkened his shirt, spreading as the morning wore on.

Thank goodness she'd kept up her running after college, but six miles? In this heat? Hopefully, her legs wouldn't cramp up before they reached the finish line.

The two frontrunners slowed their pace, letting TJ and her cowboy commando catch up. One of the scouts might have been good-looking, but for the bloody nose and split lip he sported.

Satisfaction filled her belly. He wouldn't be playing Romeo anytime soon. All those self defense classes Dad put her through had paid off.

"Hey, beautiful, you need a breather?" The other guy, the one with intense emerald eyes that could freeze lava or set fire to an ice cube, had a pretty-boy face … and a noticeable limp. "I sure do admire a woman who can run like you." His gaze slid suggestively down her body.

She felt a little bad about injuring the one called Romeo, but this guy could use a few more knocks. If every muscle in her body didn't ache like a sonofagun, she might consider it. "No, thanks, Hopalong."

His jaw clenched. "My name is Iceman."

Oooh, he could dish it out but couldn't take it. Hands on her knees with her face dripping sweat, TJ managed to croak out an apology of sorts. No need to antagonize her rescuers. "Hey, guys, look … I'm sorry if I hurt you. I thought …"

Rochester-Cowboy cut her off. "That's what happens when you pull your punches, ladies. You get hurt."

TJ choked back a laugh and groaned instead, praying she wouldn't collapse. And yet the fearless leader of this wolf pack looked like he was out for a Sunday stroll. For that matter, the other three weren't breathing hard either. Their war paint wasn't even smudged.

Mr. Dawg, who'd run a few steps behind her, chuckled.

Romeo of the bloody nose stormed off.

Iceman snorted and hobbled after him.

"Let's take five," her rescuer called out.

Five minutes? That's it? TJ plopped to the ground, in a quandary about what to call her mystery man? Rochester? Sherman the Tank? Cowboy? Fearless Leader? Jerk?

"Drink?" He handed her a canteen.

The water, warm and flat, tasted like a little sip of heaven. Maybe not jerk.

"Thank you, Mr. Cowboy." TJ squinted up from where she sprawled and took in his long length. He sounded a little like a cowboy. Add a Stetson. Some chaps. Stick him on a horse … She choked on the water and coughed. The picture conjured up by those thoughts … the heat must've addled her wits.

The cowboy's lips twitched. Standing with his back to the sun gave him a halo, but angelic sure didn't fit him. He stood over her, not saying anything for the longest time.

Uncomfortable with his scrutiny, TJ started to get up.

"You can call me Garrett."

He could read minds, too?

Garrett. She liked that. Garrett Rochester? Uh-uh. Shades of Jane Eyre. Rochester must be his cover. None of the men wore insignia. Were they soldiers? Secret agents on a clandestine mission? Or a different brand of mercenary? They sure didn't get all their bad boy skills from your average neighborhood gang.

Garrett touched the com-link in his ear and turned away. "Speak to me, Maestro." A long silence followed while he stood still as a mountain. The next moment he sprang into action.

"Roger that." Turning to the others, he motioned them over and spoke into the com-link again. "Dingo, Casper. Check in."

TJ inched closer.

"I need you here double-time. Maestro says our secret's out. Ghosthawk spotted flanking action. We got twenty new tangos with heavy firepower coming in trucks from the north. Beach evac is a no-go. We are Plan B."

TJ stared at him with her mouth agape. "What? What's going on? Who's Ghosthawk?"

Garrett yanked her up from the ground. "Ghosthawk is a stealth helicopter tasked to support our mission, kind of an eye in the sky to feed us Intel on the enemy. And right now he's telling us to move out 'cause we got company coming fast. Let's go, angel."

Imperfect Wings

Chapter Three

Ice and Romeo, the same two who had taken the lead earlier, sprinted off again at a much faster pace than she could keep. TJ looked anxiously at the man they called Cowboy.

"How you doing, little girl? You have any giddy-up left?"

"And if I don't—Garrett?"

He smiled, a full out, teeth flashing, wicked grin that softened his stern features and revealed a boyish charm. "Why, I'll throw you over my shoulder and carry you—TJ."

Yikes! Okay, maybe not so boyish. He was such a contradiction, from slovenly alcoholic to unlikely white knight, menacing commando to audacious flirt, and all wrapped up in a too-hot-to-handle package of pure, masculine arrogance.

Her stomach fluttered, part fear and more than a little thrill. Garrett wasn't handsome by GQ standards. Handsome inferred a degree of softness, and there was nothing soft about this man. If she had a type, he certainly wasn't it. Nonetheless, something about him sure made her want to purr.

"Hmmm." She pretended to ponder her options. "In that case, I guess I might be able to go a little further."

He started to turn away. Was that disappointment in his

eyes?

"Um, Garrett? Before we hit the trail again tell me, who are you guys? I mean, I know now you're not a lush who hits the bottle too hard. It's obvious …" She waved her hand at the other men. "… you're from some government agency. Or are you military? Like the Black Ops in Clancy's books?" Her inner imp came out. "Or maybe John Wayne in the *Green Berets*?"

He rolled his eyes and grimaced, but that didn't deter her.

"Were you staking out Rafael Castillo? Did I mess up your plans?"

He said nothing, but a vein in his forehead pulsed.

"That's it, huh? You were in place, ready to take him out. But you didn't expect me. That's the only way you found me so fast? So, is the operation still on? Can you nail him? I have a video—"

He cut her off with a hand held up in the universal stop signal. "Whoa, sweetheart. We don't have time to chitchat right now. We gotta get moving again. I'll try to answer your questions while we run."

She fell in beside him, determined to not reveal how rubbery her legs felt.

"First off, as far as you're concerned, we don't exist."

"Yeah, yeah. Top Secret. Need to know stuff. Got it."

He gave her a sharp look before continuing. "Second, the answer is yes. We had a bead on the don. And then you came along and all h—heck broke loose. You should be grateful we didn't leave your ... uh ... leave you. What'd you do to rile him?"

TJ dropped her head, trying not to smile at his effort to rein in the salty language. She stopped running to wriggle out of the backpack, fumbled around inside it, and finally pulled out the memory card. Holding it up, she said, "This."

He stopped several yards farther on and looked back at her before returning in slow steps. When he reached for the tiny device, she tucked it in the pack again.

"Okay, angel. I'll bite. That's a memory card. What's on it?"

Sickness replaced her playful sass. "Justice. I saw Castillo and two other guys, Americans, I think, kill a man. They shot him in the head. At point blank range. While he knelt on the ground at their feet."

Garrett's ocean-blue eyes turned steely, shedding all warmth.

TJ shivered, imagining what it would be to have him turn all that fury on her. She had a feeling he never lost. At anything.

After a long pause, Garrett said, "Gutsy little thing, aren't you? Maybe our mission's not a bust after all. C'mon, little girl. Daylight's burning."

Sweetheart, angel, and now little girl? Really? Adding a kick to her pace, TJ caught up and matched him stride for

stride. She'd show him little girl.

An hour later, after a ten-minute climb up what felt like the Honduran equivalent of Mt. Everest, they reached a bluff overlooking the Atlantic Ocean. Sixty feet below in a straight drop, waves crashed against the sheer cliff face to send geysers of white froth spraying high in the air. TJ leaned down, hands on her knees, and gasped for breath. Her legs should collapse any moment now.

Dingo and Casper, the two running rear guard, arrived. Now all six of her bigger-than-life commandos were opening duffle bags, stripping off boots and shirts, and ...

Mother of Pearl! They were taking their clothes off! She whipped around, her face burning.

Garrett stood nearby—still fully clothed, thank goodness—and squirted a white lotion onto his palm. He dipped one finger in it, stepped toward her, and daubed a big glob on her nose. "Sunscreen. We're going in the water and your skin is too fair. After you strip down to your underwear, I'll smear some on your back and shoulders."

TJ choked. No way was she taking her clothes off in front of a bunch of half-naked men. "I don't think so." She smoothed the lotion over her cheeks and forehead.

Someone sniggered behind her. A solid thunk followed and then a "Hey!"

Garrett glared over her shoulder. When he met her eyes again, his expression softened. "Look, I know this is embarrassing for you, but we'll be in the water for hours. Clothes will weigh you down. Now get your boots off."

TJ flopped to the ground with a huff, removed one boot, and started unlacing the other. "How do we keep our stuff dry? What about the guns?"

Garrett tapped his duffle. "The bags are watertight with an inflatable bladder. Guns, clothes ... everything goes in. We'll divvy your stuff up among us."

"Are you sure it's waterproof? I mean ..."

In a blur he was leaning over her, nose to nose. "Clock's ticking, TJ. Your camera and the memory card will be fine. Now, do I need to shuck you out of your clothes?"

Oh, baby, what a visual! TJ stopped breathing for a moment, her eyes wide with near panic.

Another snicker burst from behind her, followed by another loud smack and a grunt.

"Can I at least borrow your tee shirt?" She thought she might die of humiliation.

"Skivvies, Ms. McKendrick."

"B-but my underwear isn't l-like yours. It's—"

"Now!"

All the moisture in her mouth dried up. She'd never undressed in front of a man and with her skimpy, barely-there, underwear, she might as well be naked. Worse, the pink, lacy lingerie would be all but transparent in the water.

She kept her eyes on the ground, confident she'd go up in

flames any second. Here she was, surrounded by six hunky men clad in formfitting boxer briefs—black, of course—and she blushed and stuttered like a school girl.

The men mostly ignored her, concentrating instead on breaking down their weapons and sealing the waterproof bags.

Garrett stuffed her socks in her boots and threw them to Ice. He tossed her backpack to Romeo. "I'm waiting for your clothes, little girl."

That did it. Rising to her feet, TJ deliberately turned her back to the other men and faced Garrett. With her eyes fixed on the ground, she slowly tugged her shirt from her pants. Did she hear him right? Did Garrett mutter under his breath? Something that sounded like, "too flipping young?"

She risked a quick peek, relieved to see him turn back to work on packing his bag.

She worked the buttons of her shirt free and slid the sleeves off her shoulders one at a time. She held it close and eased her arms out—a nearly impossible task—and dropped it on the ground.

Behind her, all the rustling movements and soft chatter ceased.

Her chest tightened. They were staring, she knew it. Could this get any worse?

Unbuttoning her pants and lowering the zipper took more courage. Shimmying the pants over her hips and down her legs, she stepped out of them. It had to be one of the hardest things she'd ever done. When she stooped to pick up her clothes, one of the men groaned. Another uttered something she couldn't quite make out, followed by a hiss that cut off in mid breath. It got worse.

She glanced over her shoulder and saw Dingo blanch, right before he jerked around in an about face. Romeo stood next to him looking dazed, his bruised mouth slack.

Garrett looked up at the sounds the men made and frowned. He looked from them to TJ ... and his jaw dropped. Three seconds later he'd snatched his tee shirt off and yanked it over her head.

Cheeks burning, TJ tugged the shirt down to her knees before looking up. She couldn't meet his eyes but didn't miss the tight line of his lips or the way his nostrils flared. "Thank you." She fought to hold back tears. These men were risking their lives to pull her out of a nightmare she'd brought on herself. She would not cry, not over something so ridiculous as modesty.

"You're welcome, angel," Garrett answered in a low voice.

She took a deep, shuddering breath and handed him the clothes she'd shed. "Okay. How do we get down to the water?"

Using one finger, Garrett gently forced her chin up until she met his look. His eyes were a darker blue than hers. Like an ocean. Eyes a girl could get lost in. His jaw clenched repeatedly, but then he relaxed and smiled. A devilish smirk.

One that promised something she was sure not to like.

Garrett nodded toward the men. "We jump."

In horrified fascination, TJ watched Ice grab his buoyant bag and take a running leap—out into nothing. Romeo followed seconds later and then Dingo. And Casper. When only Dawg, TJ, and Garrett remained, he turned to her. "Your turn."

"Uh, I don't think so, Mr. Cowboy. I'll sit this rodeo out. I'm sure I can find another way down." She backed away, both hands out to fend him off.

He stalked her. "Remember, take a big breath before you hit the water. Right yourself on the way down so your feet hit first. Feet first. Say it."

She shook her head, eyes wide. "You're crazy. You're all crazy." She looked to Dawg for help but found only laughter.

"Say it. Feet first."

Could the man be more domineering? "F-feet f-first." Her voice came out in a squeak as she continued to back away.

With a growl, Garrett pitched his duffle to Dawg and grabbed TJ, hefting her up and over his shoulder. The next second he was running full tilt for the edge of the cliff.

TJ screamed long and loud as they sailed out into emptiness. He immediately threw her as far away as he could to put distance between them as they plummeted. "Feet first!" he yelled again.

Somehow, TJ managed to right herself in the free fall,

angling her body feet down as he'd instructed. She even remembered to draw a deep breath just before the water swallowed her.

Cold was her first coherent thought, and then she was lost. Down, down she went, and then down some more. The force of the descent snatched at her tee shirt, almost yanking it off. The soft cloth wrapped around her head, adding to her disorientation before she could jerk it back down. Her hair came loose from the long braid, swirling as she sank. When her plunge slowed, the strands tangled around her face like seaweed. Trapped. Flailing in the frigid depths. Unsure which way was up.

Her lungs burned. She fought the panic hammering at her. And then pain lanced through her scalp. Someone tugged on her hair. The sting brought tears that mixed with the salt water. Another hand caught her wrist, and she was shooting straight up, toward the light. She burst from the water, gasping.

Garrett held her, keeping her head above the waves until she reclaimed her breath and wits. As they bobbed on the surface, TJ rested her head against his shoulder.

Yesterday she wanted to kiss him for coming to her rescue. Today, she was pretty sure she wanted to kill him.

"You can swim, can't you?"

Still panting, she wiped at her eyes. Saltwater stung the abrasions on her face and arms. "You ask that now? After throwing me off a cliff?" She pushed away and swam to where

the other men treaded water some yards away, trying hard to ignore Garrett's laughter.

TJ quickly realized as they headed for open sea that she would never keep up with these men. All of them were strong swimmers, moving through the water like otters. They looked ready to take on the world while she moved like a brick, laboring with each stroke. Her body rebelled, beyond weary, bone tired, and fading fast.

Garrett measured his pace to hers, never letting the distance between them widen. Before long, the rest of the team slowed their pace.

Dawg fell back to track on TJ's other side. He pulled a length of rope from around his waist and tied it in a series of loops and knots. "She's exhausted, man," he said to Garrett. "I'm amazed she's kept up this far."

Garrett took the rope harness from him. "Let me put this around you, baby girl. Lie on your back and I'll tow you. We've come too far to lose you now."

Too tired to argue, TJ let him slip a loop over her head and under her arms, cinching it tight enough to stay put, but not bind.

"Is a ship coming for us?" The coastline seemed a long way off now.

Dawg swam close to check her harness and winked. "Nah. No sissy ship. You got the dee-luxe adventure package."

She looked from him to Garrett, not comprehending. Their

camouflage paint was still intact. Did the Army issue waterproof makeup? What a stupid thought … She swallowed a mouthful of seawater and coughed.

Garrett chuckled as he pounded her back. "Just for you, blue eyes. Won't be long now. You get a water extraction."

"A water … what?"

"You'll see. Rest now." He pulled the other end of the rope over his head and set off with powerful strokes to catch up to the others.

Sometime later, Dawg took the rope from Garrett. And then Ice. She lost track after that.

TJ drifted in and out of consciousness, traveling through a nowhere land that rode the boundary between sleeping and waking. She snapped awake when a thunderous roar filled the air. A muscular arm held her upright in the water. Overhead, the wind beat down with unusual ferocity. She squinted up and saw two shadows hovering—helicopters. A moment later two rope ladders fell from the sky, one from each bird. Ice scampered like a monkey up one of the ropes, carrying two waterproof duffels.

"You're kidding. I can't climb that thing."

"I know." The amusement in Garrett's eyes belied the no nonsense tone of his voice. That's when she saw the big yellow horseshoe thingy being lowered from the helicopter directly above her.

Dawg snagged the horseshoe and swam over to her.

"What are you doing?" She tried to push his hands away when he snaked a strap between her legs.

Together, the two men got her strapped into the harness.

TJ stared at Garrett, who shook his head in disbelief. And then he leaned in to brush his lips over hers. So quick. Had she imagined it?

"Too innocent, man," Dawg mumbled behind her.

"I know," Garrett answered. "C'mon, off you go, angel."

She was sucked out of the water and rising upward at an alarming rate of speed, passing Romeo on the rope ladder. Strong arms caught her at the open door and pulled her inside the helicopter. A moment later, someone removed the harness and wrapped a towel around her.

A medic called out. "Bring her back here, Farmboy."

The crewman—Farmboy—nudged her toward the rear of the chopper.

"Rest easy, Ms. McKendrick," the medic said. "My name's David. I'm gonna check your vital signs. Make sure you're okay."

A few seconds later, Romeo climbed inside.

"Where's Garrett? And the others?" she asked.

"Cowboy and Dawg are on the ladder," he told her. "The others are on the second chopper."

"Boat coming up fast. Ten o'clock."

"Roger that. Everybody hold on."

"Incoming!"

Their helicopter veered sideways with a lurch. Curses blistered the air as everyone scrambled for something to hold on to.

TJ fell off the bench and slammed up against the hull. Fear, her constant companion for the past twenty-four hours, surged anew at the familiar sound of machine gun fire. Several metallic pings left her holding her breath as the chopper yawed again and sped away.

"What about Garrett? You can't leave them!" She clawed at the straps hanging from the wall and righted herself.

Romeo turned to her, his face ashen. "He and Dawg ... they fell."

Imperfect Wings

Chapter Four

Noxapater, Mississippi

"Janey!"

It took a moment for TJ to realize the short order cook, Aaron, meant her. Two years after Agent Fowler changed her identity and sent her into hiding she still balked at the new name, one of many fragments of her life she'd forfeited on this journey.

"What?"

"I said your order's up."

She'd have to go soon. Leave her new friends. "Hold onto your shorts or I'll tell the customers you dropped their food on the floor."

The glare he shot her way could flash-freeze Lucifer himself. Aaron might be on the far side of fifty, certainly old enough to be her father, but he defied the term 'senior citizen.' The man wore slabs of muscle while other men his age had grown soft around the middle … and here she was, prodding him.

TJ held her hands up in a mock defensive gesture.

"Kidding." She gave him a brilliant Hollywood smile, knowing he had a soft spot for her. She'd miss Aaron most of all.

Sure enough, the thunderous scowl slipped away.

Stella's Diner drew quite a breakfast crowd. Everybody wanted a stack of Aaron's special recipe hotcakes, said to be the fluffiest this side of heaven.

"Hey, Janey, can I get a refill over here?"

TJ turned and waved at Virgil Wagner, one of the regulars as well as the chief of police. For an older guy, the chief was easy on the eyes. Despite being bald. "Be right with you." She grabbed the three plates from the serving window, stacked them along one arm, and hurried off to serve the family in the booth near the door.

Noxapater, Mississippi, population four hundred and forty-one. It might be small potatoes, but the diner would give the Flapjack Shack down on I-20 a run for its money. Today proved no different except with Stella coming in late, TJ about burned the soles off her shoes trying to keep up with all the orders. Thank goodness the rush had ended.

As she refilled the chief's mug, the absentee waitress and owner came barreling through the diner's front door. Mid-forties, blazing red hair with just a hint of gray at the temples, and a figure that would make Marilyn Monroe proud, Stella's personality lit up the room. She tossed her purse under the counter, snatched an apron from the hook on the wall behind the cash register, and cinched it around her waist.

"Sorry, hon. Got here as quick as I could."

Stella had at least twenty years on her, but what TJ wouldn't give to have some of the older woman's curves. And half of her energy.

"Hey, Stel, you okay?" The chief's husky baritone carried from his usual spot at the far end of the counter.

"Flat tire," Stella answered without looking his way. "Spare, too. I had to wait for Eddie Jay to send one of his guys from the garage to fix it."

"You shoulda called me."

She turned and looked at him, eyebrows lifted. "Well, Virgil, last I heard, you wasn't in the tire repair business."

"And you might be surprised at what all I do for this town."

These two had been sniffing around each other for the last year, neither one willing to make the first move. If something didn't give soon, TJ planned to lock them up in one of the chief's cells until they came to their senses.

Today it was Stella's turn to throw down the gauntlet. "You mean like keeping Elsie Flanders from beating the crap outta her worthless husband when he goes on a bender? Or pulling old Matilda Wharton's ancient Cadillac out of the ditch—again—when you shoulda pulled her license ten years ago since she can't see ten feet in front of her?" She minced her way toward the chief until she stood across the counter from him.

"Or do you mean searching Bitsy Randall's house every time she calls?" Stella propped a hand on one hip, her voice rising in a prissy drawl. "Oooh, Chief Wagner, ah think there might be an intruder in mah bedroom. Would you bring your big, strong self over heah and take care of little ole me? You're sooo brave." Stella flounced away with a sniff. "Shameless hussy."

"Jealous much, Stel?" The chief raised his cup in a salute, not even trying to hide the smirk on his face.

TJ hid her own smile. Their banter ran a fine line between flirting and bickering and would only escalate from here. Stella and Virgil were adults, but darned if they didn't act like a couple of teenagers. TJ poured herself a cup of coffee and settled on a stool at the end of the counter near the register. Time to relax now that Stella had arrived.

She would miss them—Aaron, Stella, Virgil, and the others. But she sure wouldn't miss waiting tables. Waitressing was hard work. The meager amount she earned in tips didn't come close to being worth the long hours and fickle customers. Give her a computer and a calculator any day. Numbers might throw you a curve now and then, but machines could be turned off.

Did she really want to go back to her job at the accounting firm? The fifteen-hour days during tax season, with bad coffee and greasy takeout? TJ reached down to rub her aching instep. Time enough to worry about next steps after the trial. Eight weeks to go. If the judge didn't grant another postponement.

Coffee finished, TJ stacked her cup in the half-filled tub of dirty dishes inside the kitchen. The tomfoolery between Virgil and Stella had quieted. They'd moved to the front window and now stared out at something. Aaron walked up behind them, wiping his hands on a towel.

The family in the booth by the door got up. The father came to the cash register with the bill in hand.

TJ took his money, handed him the change, and thanked them for coming in, and then breathed a sigh of relief when he herded his family out. With all the customers gone for the moment, she joined Stella, Virgil, and Aaron at the window.

"What's going on?"

A black car sat at the curb down the street, outside Eddie Jay's Auto Repairs. The shiny sedan stuck out in a town where pickup trucks were prevalent and dust ruled, but the two men standing by the car made it a sure bet every eye in town had zeroed in on them. Suits, wraparound sunglasses, dark tinted windshield—everything about them screamed city.

TJ stumbled back from the window on shaky legs and fought an urge to hide. Her hand sought the necklace she always wore, one she'd donned almost two years ago and had never taken off. Her thumb rubbed over the knobby latch on the side of the locket. Agent Fowler hadn't called. There was no signal. Two years without a hint of danger. This couldn't be about her.

The gold locket came alive in her hand, buzzing and vibrating without pause.

"Ohhhh!" TJ released the whirring gadget only to have it quiver against her chest.

All three of her friends jerked around at her outburst.

"What?" Virgil demanded, taking a half step toward her.

Stella clasped a hand to her heart. "Gracious, Janey, you scared six months off my life." Her eyes narrowed. "What's wrong?"

Aaron's eyes bored into hers as though he could see into the depths of her soul.

TJ couldn't answer. Two years she'd waited for this. Two years she'd spent preparing for the worst to happen. And now it had.

Castillo had found her.

The chief's radio crackled to life. He turned his head and spoke into the shoulder mic. "Yeah, Billy Ray, I see 'em." He hitched his pants up, checked the gun on his hip, and moved toward the door. "Think I'll go see what those fellows are up to."

A hundred thoughts and as many emotions raced through TJ's mind, but one thing stood uppermost—those men were dangerous. She grabbed the chief's arm. "Please don't go out there, Virgil."

He exchanged a look with Aaron before peeling her hand away. "Don't you worry none, honey. Everything's gonna be fine." A moment later the door closed behind him.

"I got a feeling something's going on that I'm not seeing." Stella followed as Aaron hustled TJ to the back of the diner.

"Get her purse, Stella," Aaron barked over his shoulder.

To the older woman's credit, she didn't balk. Without a word, Stella hurried to the counter, retrieving the purse.

TJ's knees buckled. Unable to hold herself up any longer, she fell back against the wall, slowly slid to the floor, and pulled her knees to her chest. The locket continued to pulse.

"Easy, now." Aaron squatted in front of TJ, his big hands gripping both of her arms. "Open the locket, sweetheart. It's okay." Soothing assurances replaced the harsh tone he used with Stella.

TJ lifted the long chain over her head with trembling hands and thrust the locket at him.

"No, Janey. You can do it.

Her eyes fluttered closed as she recalled Agent Fowler's instructions, words he'd drummed in her head before sending her to rural Mississippi. "Keep the locket on at all times. Remember the two codes. One—go to a public place and use a pay phone to call me. Zero—drop everything and run as fast and as far as you can."

Aaron chafed her arms. "Take a deep breath. That's it. Now let it out."

"My name's not Janey. It's TJ."

"I know. Now open the locket. Clock's ticking."

She pressed the latch and the locket clicked open. A single red digit pulsed in monotonous rhythm—zero.

TJ's world tilted.

"Hold it together, girl. You trained for this." Aaron hauled her upright and manhandled her toward the back door, his voice harsh again and filled with urgency. He untied TJ's apron and thrust it at Stella. "Where's your scat bag?"

She blinked at his gruff manor. "In my car." She'd filled the emergency backpack—the scat bag—with everything Fowler told her she would need: clothes, toiletries, two different drivers' licenses with matching credit cards, disposable cell phone, and five thousand dollars in small bills the government provided. She'd added water and power bars, a phone charger, atlas, and the snub-nosed Smith & Wesson .38 special with extra ammo.

"You gotta leave, TJ. Now. We'll delay them." Aaron nudged her into the kitchen. "You know where to go. Stick to the back roads."

She took her purse, met Stella's bewildered look, and turned away. No time for explanations. No good-byes. TJ wiped her eyes and slipped out the door.

Her tired little Honda sat across the yard where she'd parked it before dawn that morning. She hurried toward it.

A dozen steps along, something hard jammed against the small of her back. A big hand clamped down on her shoulder. She stilled, knowing she'd have bruises in the morning—if she lived that long. Her runaway heart pumped fear-laced adrenalin through her veins.

"Scream and I kill you," the deadly voice whispered in a Spanish accent. "Unlock the car and get in. You drive. I tell you where."

How had he gotten so close without her hearing him? TJ fought a gut reaction to struggle. All her years of self-defense training took over. She'd worked hard to become the son her father wanted. And learned a hard lesson. You find the courage to live each day and deal with obstacles head on. And regardless of the outcome, you accept how it all falls out. But she was tired of not being good enough. Sick of running and hiding.

"Move." The gun jabbed a little harder.

Forcing a breath to calm her frantic heart, TJ assessed her assailant. Big. Too big to fight. He probably came with the men out front. More importantly, he hadn't killed her outright. That meant somebody wanted her alive.

Her shoulders sagged. She whimpered and took a tentative step forward. A second step. A third. If he shot her ... Well, she'd rather die here than face a slow, torturous death at Don Castillo's hands. Or Senator Farleigh's. They both stood to lose much more than a fortune if she testified.

She moaned again when the thug shoved her. She didn't have to fake the trembling. If he thought her helpless and frightened ...

They neared her car and TJ stumbled. The man's leather-soled shoes slid on the loose gravel, throwing him off balance. For a brief moment his painful grip loosened.

TJ jerked free. She dropped to the ground and pulled her knees into her chest, twisting as she fell. With a grunt, she kicked out as he lunged for her. Both her feet connected with painful precision.

He crumpled to his knees, retching.

Unfortunately, she'd either not put enough force into the blow or her attacker had an extremely high pain threshold. Before she could scramble away, he was on her again, roaring like an enraged animal.

TJ rolled, but he dove for her, one hand snagging her shirt.

She squirmed, clawed, punched, and jabbed, trying to evade his clutches. But then his meaty fist clipped her chin. A starburst of pain exploded through her head.

The would-be kidnapper lurched to his feet and yanked her up with him. Spittle sprayed as he cursed. Then he followed up with a backhand to her face.

The force sent TJ sprawling where she curled into a fetal position and waited for the next blow.

Chapter Five

The seconds ticked by. Sounds of a scuffle registered. A thud of something hard meeting flesh. Pebbles skittered. And then gentle hands smoothed her hair from her face.

TJ flinched as the gravel dug into her skin.

"Talk to me, girl. How bad you hurt?"

"Aaron?" He still wore his apron.

"Can you get up? I figure we got three minutes before the others find their way back here."

TJ latched onto his voice and willed away the nausea, shivering from the cold sweat that covered her body. She could do this.

Aaron helped her stand. "Where're your keys?"

"Purse."

He released her and collected the handbag from where it had fallen.

"Can you drive? Just a little ways? All you gotta do is follow me."

Did she have a choice? TJ nodded … and wished she hadn't. Her head throbbed. "Think so," she whispered.

"I shoulda stayed with you." Aaron half carried her to the

Honda and somehow managed to get her inside and the seatbelt fastened. "Listen up now. Nod if you understand."

She gritted her teeth and gave one quick nod.

"Stay on my tail. When I pull over, you do the same. We won't go far. Five minutes tops. Okay?"

Another nod left her fighting to not empty her stomach.

Aaron stuck her keys in the ignition. "Crank her up and stay alert."

TJ managed to follow his dented old Silverado from the parking lot and down a narrow road. She blinked, trying to stay centered on his taillights.

When Aaron pulled onto a grassy shoulder, TJ followed, shoving the automatic transmission into park. He helped her from the Honda and carried her this time, settling her in the cab of his truck.

"Still with me, girl?"

"Yeah." One-word answers worked better than nodding.

"I'll get your scat bag and purse and then we're out of here. Lay your head on the console and stay below the window."

TJ did as he said.

"Your phone in your purse?"

"Yes."

Awareness came and went after that. She woke when the truck stopped moving.

"Wake up, TJ." Aaron gave her a gentle shake. "I need to

see how bad you're hurt."

Her movements were slow and deliberate as she sat up and looked around. A Wal-Mart parking lot. A long way from the other cars.

"Where…?"

"Kosciusko. We need gas, food, and supplies." He got out and walked around the front of the truck to open her door. "Look at me, girl."

Aaron eased her legs around until she sat sideways on the passenger seat, facing him. Her legs dangled in the open door.

"Follow my finger." He moved his index finger in front of her eyes. "Good. Now, open your mouth and shift your jaw side to side."

She opened slowly while his fingers pressed along her jaw. Everything seemed to work the way it was supposed to, despite hurting like the dickens. Especially her cheek. "How do you know to do all this?"

"Soldiers don't always have the luxury of a doctor or a hospital." Aaron's long fingers probed her scalp. "I don't think anything's broke, but you're gonna have one heck of a shiner."

He uncapped a bottle of water from her pack, handed it to her, and then opened another smaller container and shook three tablets into his palm. "Ibuprofen. Take it and wait here while I go shopping."

"What about the man who …" Her fingers feathered over her swollen cheek.

"He won't hurt you no more. That's a promise." Aaron eased her legs back inside the truck. "I'm going inside to pick up a few things. Keep the doors locked. Lay down again if you want." He shut her door and took off at a trot toward the Super Center.

TJ downed the pills with a long pull on the water, unwilling to delve too deeply into what he said about her attacker. Why hadn't Fowler sent the alarm sooner? How much did Aaron know about her? She'd seen the look he exchanged with the chief right before everything fell apart. Did Virgil know as well? Was he okay? And Stella? From her bewildered look, TJ guessed she didn't know much, if anything. Why now? After almost two years, with the end finally in sight, how had Castillo managed to find her?

She stuffed a fist in her mouth. Crying would only aggravate her headache.

Twenty minutes passed before Aaron returned carrying several bags. He pulled a lightweight hoodie from one and ripped off the tags. "Put this on over your tee shirt." He guided her arms through the sleeves and zipped it for her.

A pair of sunglasses came next. "These will help hide the bruises, but we need ice."

A disposable cell phone and charger emerged next. "Here, plug this in." Aaron pointed at the outlet under the dash.

"Why do we need another phone? I have one in my purse and a spare in my bag."

"Not anymore."

"But …"

"Think, girl. They found you where they shouldn't have. Without much warning. I'm not taking any chances 'til we know more."

She started to ask another question, but he stopped her. "Let's gas up, get something to eat, and some ice. We'll talk on the road."

After a stop at the Quik Trip, Aaron pulled into the McDonald's next door. "Last chance for the ladies' room. C'mon. I'll help you inside."

In the restroom, TJ winced at her image. The bruise was already purpling. Her hair, usually worn in a tight braid, had loosened during the roll in the dirt and now curled around her head in a wild halo. Ignoring the assortment of aches and pains, she finger-combed her long mane into a somewhat respectable ponytail.

TJ splashed her face with cool water and dabbed it dry with paper towels. Donning the sunshades, she inspected the mirror again. Passable. If you didn't look too close.

Aaron, holding a bag of food and a cardboard tray with drinks, waited for her outside the restroom door. When they reached the truck he handed her their food and then climbed into the truck bed to dig through the toolbox. He returned waving a box of plastic sandwich bags. "I use these for my fishing lures. Keep them in a tackle box. Here." He opened one

and held it out. "Pour that cup of ice in and hold it to your cheek."

TJ touched the homemade ice bag to her face, careful to not press too hard.

Aaron wheeled the truck out of the parking lot and headed north.

"What's your role in this, Aaron? Do you work for the government? How did Castillo find me?"

He unwrapped one of the hamburgers and bit off half with one bite.

Was he trying to figure out how much to tell? Or not tell? Like all that "need to know" drivel her dad used to spout. TJ nibbled at her own sandwich and waited.

"I spent twenty-one years in the Army, TJ."

That seemed like an ominous start.

He stuffed the rest of the burger in his mouth and pulled another one from the sack. He took a smaller bite this time. "On my last assignment in the Army, I wound up in a bad place at a bad time," he said while chewing. "My team was dispatched to remove a hotheaded Sunni who'd become an undesirable influence in a critical area. We were ambushed."

She'd wondered about the slight limp he couldn't quite hide on rainy days.

"Kevin Fowler piloted the rescue chopper. When things got hot, word came down to abort the evac. He and his crew disobeyed a direct order to get us out of there." Aaron took a deep breath and let it out slowly. "I ushered out on a medical discharge later that year. Kevin left under less than pleasant circumstances."

After a quick sip of his drink, Aaron went on. "The FBI was waiting for him. He joined the bureau and eventually made his way over to Homeland Security, and then the Bureau of International Intelligence. We stayed in touch and every once in a while, I'd do special projects for him."

"Am I a special project?"

Aaron tapped the new Tracfone where it lay in the cup holder. "See if that thing's charged yet."

TJ picked up the phone and set it back down. "Half full." He hadn't answered her question. "Why the new phone?"

"I tossed yours back where we left your car."

"What ... why?"

"Because you got a thirty-second warning."

TJ set the ice pack on the seat, her face blessedly numb. "You think Fowler...?"

Aaron snorted. "Not even. Last minute or not, he got the warning off, didn't he? No, somebody higher up than Fowler must've gotten your info."

Her case file had been breached once before. Castillo didn't have the means to get the top secret information, but a senator could. "Farleigh?"

"More likely somebody on his payroll. You sure stirred up a hornet's nest."

Imperfect Wings

A weight settled over her shoulders. Would it ever end?

"I never meant this to happen. An unknown assailant murdered my father in Honduras. Two teachers and five children died with him, gunned down in the middle of a school day. I went there to find the truth, to find justice. But I really wanted vengeance. My foolishness destroyed La Cruza and who knows how many lives."

"I'm sorry about your father, TJ."

She laughed at his words, a bitter, mirthless sound. "I lost him long before he died. Dad was already married to the Army when my mom got pregnant. A boy might have been more tolerable, but he didn't have much use for a daughter." Her fingers mangled the hamburger she still held.

Her throat constricted. "He didn't come home often, but when he did, I'd beg him to teach me Tae Kwon Do or how to shoot. Anything for a little attention. I earned a black belt despite his skepticism and showed him I could hold my own on a gun range, too. But it was never enough. After mom died, he couldn't take me with him to Afghanistan, and there was no one stateside to pawn me off on, so he chucked an eighteen-year career to stay home until I finished high school."

"How'd he wind up in Honduras?"

"Got involved with a local church. Went on a couple of mission trips. He put the house up for sale the day I left for college. A month later, I had a bank account in my name with enough money to finish college. He took off for Honduras.

Christmas cards and a birthday check came every year, but I never saw him again."

Aaron let the silence drag out before saying, "That why you went down there? To see what the big draw was?"

TJ's voice broke a little when she answered. "Yeah, I guess so. Pride plus stubbornness with a splash of naiveté make a deadly combination."

Aaron covered her hand and squeezed. "Are you so sure your dad didn't care about you? Crusty old soldiers find it hard to express their feelings."

"Pretty sure. I have a whole lifetime of firsthand experience. Some things can't be forgiven, and some wounds won't be healed."

"Only if you won't let them."

She stuffed the remains of her food in the sack. "All my good intentions and I'm the one running—from a monster who wants to torture me and a politician who wants me dead. For someone who's not very ambitious, I seem to be number one on a lot of lists."

She turned the air vent to blow in her face and help stem the lurking tears. "I don't know if Señora Ramirez got away. Or what happened to the girls. La Cruza's gone. Garrett's gone. Dawg. The girls. Maybe Stella and Virgil. How many more?"

"I don't know about any Señora, but I'm pretty sure Virgil and Stella are doing fine. When I left, he had a dozen shotguns trained on those two suits. And I know for a fact the one who

took you down won't be getting up no more."

TJ's eyes narrowed as his meaning sank in.

"As for the girls, they landed in an orphanage in Atlanta. Cowboy and Dawg, well, let's just say they took a detour, but both of them made it home." He looked over and winked.

The girls were safe. Garrett and Dawg, too. A heavy weight in her chest eased.

She hadn't known their names that fateful day when Don Castillo shoved a gun in Alex Krieger's hand. When he wrapped the man's shaking fingers around the handle and coaxed him forward until the muzzle pressed against the kneeling man's head. Krieger pulled the trigger that killed the DEA agent, but Castillo orchestrated the atrocity. And she'd captured them both on video, their faces plain to see. Indelible images in her mind.

Unfortunately, the third person in the video remained in the background, his features too obscured for a positive ID. The best forensics specialist couldn't enhance the image enough to identify him, but there was enough circumstantial evidence to cast suspicion on Senator Edwin Farleigh. Krieger's boss.

TJ shivered. A crazed drug lord or one of the most powerful men on Capitol Hill—who would find her first? They both stood to lose if she testified, and with the weight of the evidence against Krieger and her eye witness account, there was little doubt the jury would convict him. The district attorney in Virginia had asked for the death penalty, hoping to force Krieger into a plea bargain. Lethal injection or a life sentence for fingering his boss—not much of a decision.

If Farleigh went down, the drug pipeline that ran through the senator's home state would topple. And that would place Don Castillo in an extremely vulnerable position with the South American cartel who supplied the uncut cocaine. Agent Fowler doubted he'd last a week if that happened.

"Aaron, do you think Memphis is safe?" The old familiar panic waited in the wings. "If they found me in Mississippi, it's possible they know about the safe houses."

"We'll call Fowler in a bit and get his take."

"Are you sure about Fowler?"

"Yes, I am. Kevin's been after Castillo for years. The undercover team in Honduras had enough intel to extradite him, but the Washington link remained elusive. We all knew who it was, but Kevin wanted the proof. That's when you waltzed in, took that earth-shattering video, and turned the whole area into a war zone." Aaron's laugh filled the truck. "When Cowboy showed up with a helicopter full of kids and without you … I've never seen Kevin lose his cool like that."

The memory didn't hold the same humor for TJ.

Seemingly unaware of the way his words affected her, Aaron continued, "You know, he refused to send the extraction team after you? Cowboy threatened to tear his head off. Said he'd go in alone. That's when I reminded Kevin of another

time when right and wrong collided. When another soldier rebelled against an abort order."

"You were in Honduras?"

"Yeah, I'm the one pulled you inside the chopper, dripping wet and looking like a sea nymph."

Increased traffic, strip malls, gas stations, and fast food chains gave up the first hint of Memphis. Aaron pulled into a Kroger parking lot and cut the engine. "You remember Fowler's number?"

She nodded.

"Does he answer or someone else?"

She tilted her head and frowned. "I've only called him twice. He answered both times."

Aaron inclined his head toward the new phone still plugged into the charger. "Punch in his number and put it on speaker."

TJ dialed the agent's number.

A series of tones crackled on the line before the call connected. A crisp female voice answered on the fourth ring. "Agent Fowler's office."

Aaron reached over and pressed the disconnect button before TJ could say anything. "I was afraid of that." He pursed his lips, looking lost in thought. After a few seconds, he opened his door and tossed the brand new Trackfone in a trash can near the shopping cart corral.

Not knowing what to say, TJ stared at him.

Several miles down the road, Aaron made a call from his own cell phone. He put the call on speaker, looked at her, and whispered, "New plan."

"Hello," a pleasant male voice answered.

"Sawbones, how ya doing, man? Farmboy, here."

"Farmboy, is it really you? Where you been? I haven't heard from you since our Caribbean cruise. I thought we had true love, man."

Aaron snorted at his friend's words. "You wish. I got my own little dove sitting beside me. You might even remember her from our last time together. Little thing got shoved outta the nest, and now her momma's gone missing."

TJ frowned at the curious conversation.

"I remember your dove. She squawking much?"

"Naw, she's dinged up, but good for now. Got a hunch there's a cuckoo involved. Can you get her some fresh feathers while I go sightseeing?"

"Sure thing, buddy. What's her count, and what's your twenty?"

"Ten and a Bee." He glanced over at her. "Better make that a Cee. We're paddling around the bottom of Elvisville. You in the same tent?"

"You remember. You do still love me."

Another snort. "Cut the smooch crap, lover boy. And get my dinner ready. I got things to do." Aaron disconnected the call.

"Okaaaay." TJ pursed her lips. "Who was that and what did you say? In English, please."

"And here I thought you were a smart one." He gave her a sly grin.

"I got most of it. I think. Sawbones is the medic on the helicopter?"

Aaron nodded.

"And I'm the dove, banged up but not dead. Fowler must be the missing momma bird."

"Go on."

"Then Farleigh has to be the cuckoo."

He nodded again.

"You think we're safe. For now. He can expect us around dinnertime, after which you plan to do some snooping."

"Reconnaissance."

TJ snorted. "I know from cop shows on TV that twenty means your location. What I don't get is the feathers and count."

The sun hung low on the horizon, highlighting Aaron's face.

She watched in disbelief as his cheeks turned red. "Spill it, soldier."

"Well, you need clothes…and he needed the size."

Now it was her turn to blush. "For your information I'm an eight, not a ten."

A sassy, impudent grin stretched his mouth wide. Still

embarrassed but trying to cover it, he responded. "Yeah, but we need to hide your assets as much as possible. Nobody notices a woman in dumpy clothes."

Imperfect Wings

Chapter Six

High on a bluff overlooking the Mississippi River, somewhere on the north side of Memphis, TJ sat in a rocking chair, staring at the night.

Jasper, the big chocolate lab, ambled up the front porch steps, returning from one last romp before bedtime. He lumbered to her side and nudged her leg with his nose, demanding affection.

The River City sparkled in the distance, a majestic diamond in a crown of twinkling stars. She searched the heavens and located the Big Dipper … and there, the Little Dipper.

David "Sawbones" Sallijay and his wife, Carrie Anne, had carved out their own little niche of paradise. Much as she envied them, soothing and peaceful as it seemed, TJ couldn't quite let go of the edgy apprehension that kept her looking over her shoulder.

The darkness reminded her too much of Honduras, of the night she spent in the jungle. It was there she'd learned to survive, taking each moment as it came. Perhaps after the trial she could move beyond this fractured life.

"Good boy." She scratched behind Jasper's ears and smiled at his doggie rumble of appreciation. When he settled to the floor at her feet, TJ set the rocker in motion again.

With nightfall, the Tennessee countryside traded the day's frantic pace for tranquility. Honeysuckle filled the air, the fragrance sweet. She could be happy here, given half a chance. She could be happy most anywhere, as long as people weren't trying to kill her.

The screen door scraped open behind her. She glanced over and smiled at Carrie Anne.

"Lean forward so I can drape this shawl around you. It might be summer, but the nights can get a bit cool. 'Specially up this high."

TJ adored the genteel drawl that marked the other woman as a true southern lady. Carrie Anne's words flowed like the sweetest honey.

"Thanks, Carrie Anne. I love the view. It's spectacular."

"You know you can stay here, TJ. Stay with us, I mean. As long as you want."

A pang of regret tolled somewhere deep inside TJ's soul, a yearning for a home and family of her own. "That means a lot. But you know I can't." She'd already put them at risk by coming here.

Please, Lord. Don't let anyone else get hurt because of me.

She seemed to be praying a lot more these days. More

than she'd done since Mom died. Was this the Lord's way of drawing her back to the fold?

"What did you do before ... I mean, did you have a job?" Carrie Anne sat in the other rocker.

"Before Honduras? Yeah, I worked for a large accounting firm in Atlanta."

"Think you'll go back someday? To Atlanta?"

Going back seemed pointless, not knowing if she had a future. Getting to the trial was proving difficult enough. "Probably not. I don't have any ties there." Truth was, she didn't have ties anywhere.

The conversation lulled as the two women rocked in companionable silence. A short while later, David came out and squatted beside his wife. "You're awfully quiet."

"Have you heard from Aaron?" TJ glanced at her wristwatch, surprised to see it knocking on midnight. She understood Aaron's need to keep her safe, but his absence made her uneasy. She wasn't used to depending on someone else.

"Naw, nothing yet. Why don't you go on to bed? Dawn will be here before you know it."

She stifled a yawn and then laughed with them as she tried to hide it.

"C'mon. Let me show you the clothes I got for you." Carrie Anne tugged TJ toward the guest bedroom.

After a quick look at the sweats, jeans, and serviceable

underclothes, and an even quicker shower, TJ packed all her things into the rolling suitcase David provided. She offered up another prayer for Aaron's safety and climbed onto the soft mattress, exhausted but knowing she wouldn't sleep a wink.

She stirred sometime later to the sound of her name being called. "Go 'way," she mumbled.

Hands shook her. "Wake up, TJ. It's time to go."

"Wha...?" She sat up. "What time is it?"

Carrie Anne yanked the covers back. "A little after four. Get up, sweetie. We gotta get moving."

"Is Aaron back?" She didn't like Carrie Anne's frown.

"No, but he called. Said to get you outta here as soon as possible and not wait for him. Now use the bathroom and get dressed or knowing my husband, he'll toss you in the car as you are."

TJ took the clothes Carrie Anne thrust at her and hurried to the bathroom, hesitating before she closed the door. "What about you and David? Are you coming, too?"

"C'mon down to the kitchen when you're ready." Carrie Anne left her standing there.

Five minutes later, dressed and packed, TJ sat on the bed jamming her feet into sneakers.

David knocked on the open door. "Ready to go?" He took her bag.

"What's going on, David?"

"Grab your backpack and come get some breakfast. I'll fill

you in."

In the kitchen, Carrie Anne held up three paper bags. "Hope you like bagels and orange juice. I thought they'd be easier to handle while you're driving."

TJ stilled, knowing she wouldn't like the information to come. "Why would I be driving? I don't have a car. Is Aaron okay?"

"Aaron's fine."

She took a seat at the kitchen table.

"He called about twenty minutes ago," David said. "He cased the safe house you were heading to but backed off after seeing it was compromised. And Fowler's disappeared."

"Where's Aaron now?"

David rubbed the back of his neck. "He picked up a tail. Couldn't chance leading them here, so he's drawing them away. Don't worry. He'll lose them. But he wants you gone."

"Where? If the safe houses are all compromised…"

David slid an envelope across the table. "Aaron left this. In case he couldn't get back. Said you should read it alone."

"He thinks they'll find me here, doesn't he? What about you and Carrie Anne?" Her pulse sped up as the grim truth set in. Once again, her enemies had tracked her down. And once again she'd brought peril to innocent people.

"My link to Aaron is buried a long way back. It's unlikely they'll connect the dots, but just in case, Carrie Anne and I will head out, too—only in the opposite direction. Now, let's get moving."

He led them from the house toward the detached double-car garage, with Jasper trotting at their heels. Much to TJ's surprise, instead of raising the door, David led her around to the back where a Jeep sat. He opened the driver's door, tucked her suitcase in the backseat, and handed her the keys.

"I picked this beauty up some months back but never got around to changing the registration to my name. It drives like a dream, has new tires, and a full tank." He nudged her to get in behind the wheel.

TJ settled into the seat, bottom lip quivering.

"At the bottom of the drive, turn left. The road winds around, but eventually you'll come to a major intersection. It doesn't matter at this point where you go, TJ. Just get as far away from Memphis as you can. There's a road atlas and a new cell phone on the passenger seat. I put your gun in the glove compartment. Aaron said not to read his note until you got some distance behind you."

Carrie Anne leaned in to give her a quick hug and handed her the bag of bagels and juice before hurrying off with Jasper.

"You trust Aaron. Do what he says and you'll both get through this."

"David, these people are evil. If they find you, they'll hurt you. Hurt Carrie Anne."

"Not your problem. In the long run, you'll save more lives by testifying, so take care."

Maybe so, but the short-term costs kept mounting. A tear broke free. How much more could she endure?

"Don't worry about us. They won't get near my wife." He patted her shoulder. "Now, crank this baby up, and let's roll."

He left her, and a moment later, an engine crooned.

TJ drove down the long drive with David and Carrie Anne not far behind. She turned left as instructed. David turned right and, just like that, she was alone again. Sometimes it seemed she'd been alone her whole life.

She came to the major road David described. The sign pointed north to St. Louis, or south—to Memphis? North it was.

With help from a country music station, she avoided all thought of what had happened since she fled Stella's Diner. Was it only a day ago? Keeping to the secondary roads in Tennessee and for the short distance through Kentucky, she finally approached the Mighty Mississippi at Cairo, Illinois. Dawn broke the horizon behind her as she drove up the steep inclined cantilever bridge and crossed over into Missouri. Misty plumes stretched up from the water below before dissolving under the morning sun's scrutiny. Three hours later she hit the outskirts of St. Louis.

Her body rebelled at the long confinement in the Jeep. She squirmed to relieve cramped muscles and started thinking about a bathroom stop. That's when the gas indicator light came on.

Several blocks ahead on the right, she spotted a gas station, one of the mega chains. Perfect. She could top off the tank, use the facilities, grab a sandwich and something to drink, and get back on the road in no time. Her stomach rumbled as she pulled into the station.

TJ spent the next several moments trying to locate the gas tank release and decide whether to use one of the credit cards Fowler had provided. Aaron's warnings came to mind. The emergency cash seemed the better option.

With sunglasses covering her black eye, TJ went inside to use the restroom, buy food and water, and prepay the fill-up.

A half-mile down the road, she pulled into a strip mall to eat her sandwich. She opened the plastic-wrapped pimiento and cheese sandwich, took a bite, and pulled the road atlas into her lap. Time to figure out where she was going.

Hidden beneath the map book all these long hours, the envelope Aaron left for her slithered off the seat. How had she forgotten it?

She retrieved the note from the floor, ran her thumb under the flap, and pulled out the single sheet of notebook paper.

TJ, if you're reading this, it means I didn't get back. And that means you have to get far away from Memphis. Don't go to any of the safe houses Fowler listed. Don't contact Homeland. I'm not sure who we can trust there.

I know you're scared, but you're also smart. And strong. I want you to head to Idaho. Call Sheriff James Evers in

Hastings Bluff at the number below. He's a friend and someone I trust with my life. More importantly, I trust him with your life. James is expecting your call. Drive safe and be careful, but get there as quick as you can. I'll contact you when it's safe.

Turning her attention to the map book again, TJ looked over the best route to get from Missouri to Idaho—and groaned. Sixteen hundred miles. That would shave a few days off her wait for the trial. She reread Aaron's note, committed Sheriff Evers's number to memory, and tore the note into confetti before depositing the pieces in a nearby trash can.

She punched the numbers into the new cell phone. "Hello? Sheriff Evers?"

Imperfect Wings

Chapter Seven

Triple C Ranch, Hastings Bluff, Idaho

A single bead of sweat trickled down the side of his cheek. Garrett wiped it away with the dirty kerchief from his neck. He'd eaten enough dust in the past week to plant a garden. Dirt caked his clothes and every inch of exposed skin, not to mention crawling into places it shouldn't. The only time he could remember being filthier was the year-long assignment in Honduras, posing as a drunken bush pilot. Not bathing for days on end and then only a quick dip in the river. It took six months to cure the jungle rot that left his feet raw and bleeding. Yeah, he'd ride trail behind a herd of horses any day over that.

He looked around at the mountains surrounding the valley. Open ranges, wild horses, and the freshest air in the world— what more could a man want? Even worn out after six long days driving the herds to higher pastures and dirty enough to shame a bucket of mop water, there wasn't another place he'd rather be. Took him long enough to realize nothing was more important than family and heritage. He loved everything about the Triple C Ranch. Couldn't imagine leaving it again.

A long hot shower and a gallon of iced tea waited for him

back at the house, and not necessarily in that order. Maybe he'd take a ride over to Challis later. See who was hanging out at the Broken Keg. Friday night meant Ladies Night and he'd been in a long dry spell.

He stretched in the saddle, trying to loosen the knotted muscles in his back. Maybe he'd ask Rascal for some of that cure-all snake oil he mixed up. Yeah and the longtime ranch foreman would never let him hear the end of it. Worse, he'd smell awful for days. Horse sweat had to be one of the primary ingredients. Something the long-legged cuties at the bar wouldn't appreciate.

"Jo," he called to his youngest brother who lagged behind.

When Jonas didn't answer, Garrett twisted around to find his brother's big dun stallion twenty yards back. Jonas slumped in the saddle like a sack of millet, his chin down.

That boy could sleep anywhere, anytime.

Eyes rolling, Garret yelled. "Jo! Wake up before you fall off."

Jonas jerked upright. "What?" He looked around, resettled his hat on his head, and prodded the horse forward.

"I'm too tired to haul your carcass home, and you know Mom will have a fit if I leave you for the buzzards. Now get on up here."

Dad would've left him. Their father had never coddled them, even as kids. But Dad wasn't here. This was the first drive he'd missed in forty years of ranching.

Hard to think of his parents getting old. At sixty-five his dad remained fit and strong, but Cody Cameron had handed the reins of the ranch over to Garrett and his brothers. Claimed it was time for the next generation to step up. Claimed he wanted to spend more time with his bride.

What a pair. Married the same year they started the ranch. Still fought and made up like they were twenty. At one time, Garrett had wanted a relationship like theirs. Now he knew better. Not many women like his mom out there.

The four hands who'd worked the drive with him had turned off a ways back. They'd be at the bunkhouse by now. Garrett and Jonas had another mile to go before reaching home. Dad always said it was wrong to mix family and work. The sprawling two-story ranch house where he'd raised five children sat atop a small knoll, facing the three big working barns and bunkhouse across the valley. His way of ensuring separation.

Jonas trotted up alongside Garrett wearing a sheepish grin. "I sure am glad this drive is over. Can't remember ever being so dirty. I swear we used to think herding horses was fun."

"I know what you mean. Too bad we didn't find that cat that's been stalking the herds. So tell me again why Wade couldn't join us?"

"Hit a snag with the Bar M contract. They wanted to expand the scope of the security project, which threw all his calculations out the window."

"That's the same excuse he gave last year with the Wilson Ranch down in Texas. You think he's gonna bail on us? Focus full time on the security side?"

Jonas stretched one arm across his body and then the other, flexing his shoulders. "Probably. You can blame Dad for Wade missing the drive this year. He sold his old rodeo buddy Andy Milligan on Wade's security system. Andy owns the Bar M."

Garrett whistled. That explained it. The Bar M supplied rodeo stock, both horses and bulls, to all the larger rodeo associations and most of the smaller circuits. Milligan's operation would be a big win—and a huge endeavor.

"If you ask me, Sarah's leaving was a good thing. He might be gut-punched and shorthanded, but he's better off in the long run. And once word gets around about how good his security programs are, he won't have time for the ranch."

Garrett didn't see the attraction of sitting at a computer for hours on end, but he understood Wade's need for control over every aspect of the business. His brother's former partner and ex-fiancé had kicked him to the curb. Now he struggled to hold his fledgling business together.

"You know where Rascal keeps his smelly liniment?" Jonas stretched his arms again and grimaced. "Not much of me that don't hurt, ache, scream, or moan. And since I already stink to high heaven, a little more smell-bad can't hurt."

Garrett grinned, his face feeling tight with the unfamiliar

effort. He didn't laugh much these days. When he caught Jonas gaping, Garrett let his features settle back into a scowl. "What?"

"You smiled. The family all thought you'd lost the knack. Half the town, too."

Once upon a time, Jonas would have run from Garrett's glower. Now his little brother stood an inch taller and carried the same weight. Jo didn't intimidate so easily anymore.

"Seriously, man. It's been like forever since you showed any sign of life, any indication that my crazy, fun-loving big brother still existed." Jonas's grin stretched wider. "Seriously, it's okay to have fun. And I know just the place to play. We can—"

They rode side by side, near enough that Garrett drew back and punched his brother's arm.

"Yeeeooow! What's that for?"

Garrett nudged his horse to a faster gait.

Jonas sulked the rest of the way home.

When the ranch house came into view, they made their way toward the long barn that sat off to one side. On one end they kept the family trucks, cars, four-wheelers, and their mom's golf cart. The other half served as a stable for the horses the family rode. Garrett and Jonas dismounted outside the big double doors and led their mounts inside.

On the Triple C, like any other ranch, caring for your horse came first. He'd had it pounded in from the time he could

put a foot in the stirrup. Garrett and Jonas tugged their mounts
into adjacent stalls and removed the dusty saddles, blankets,
halters, and bridles. Settling into an easy rhythm, they used
damp cloths to wipe down the animals, picks to clean their
hooves, and then currycombs to clean the sweat and trail dust
away.

Halfway through, Jonas stopped and propped both arms
on his horse's back and stared.

Annoyed, Garrett finally looked up. "You got a case of
hero worship, or did I sprout a second head?"

Jonas's impish grin reappeared, a trace of the mischievous
boy who'd terrorized their sisters. He cocked his head to one
side as though choosing his words carefully. "Mom and Dad
went off on another"—he made air quotes with his fingers—
"honeymoon. Embarrassing, don't you think? I mean, the way
they're always sneaking around like nobody sees them
smooching in the corners. Parents aren't supposed to act like
that."

Garrett suppressed another smile and waited. Jonas hadn't
gotten around to what was on his mind yet.

"Anyway, I wondered if you'd … uh … come out with
Wade and me tonight. We're gonna grab some barbeque at the
Taste-T-Pig and then head over to Sidewinder's to check out
the scene. It's Friday night, which means half-priced drinks for
the ladies. The joint will be rocking, what with the rodeo in
town. How 'bout it, Gare? Been a long time since we turned

this town upside down."

An invitation for a night out on the town was the last thing Garrett expected. His brother was right. It had been a long time since he'd done anything besides get up, work himself into a stupor, eat, and go to bed, and then do it all over again the next day.

Siggy, his big roan stallion named for his gun—stupid teenage choice of a name—whickered and bobbed his head, seeming to approve the idea. "I don't know. I got stuff to do."

"C'mon, Garrett. It's been more'n two years. Allie's gone. Let her go, man. I want my big brother back."

Ahhh. The old "pick up the pieces of your life and move on" sermon. Garrett didn't know whether to be relieved Jonas had finally spoken up or concerned that he'd done so. Of their whole family, his youngest brother always seemed to understand him best. Now Jo had to go and jump on the bandwagon.

Garrett frowned. Had he really gone sour? Fallen in a rut so deep he couldn't see his way out? "We'll see." Garrett dumped a cup of oats in Siggy's feed bin. After topping off the horse's water, he strode from the barn.

Jonas hollered after him. "I'm meeting Wade at his office in town at seven."

A long, hot shower didn't keep him from thinking about how good a cold drink would taste at Sidewinders. That got him thinking about the seedy little bar on the outskirts of town,

not to mention all the hot cowgirls sure to be there. He glanced at his watch—six fifteen.

He tossed aside the plain black tee and chose a white western shirt with pearl snaps instead. After tucking the shirttail into jeans that fit just right and stamping his feet into a pair of Tony Lamas, he grabbed his good black Stetson and tapped it on his head before heading out.

In the barn, his brand new toy—a fully loaded, molten red, Dodge 2500 Power Wagon with a 5.7 liter HEMI V8 engine and six-speed transmission—sat waiting. And some people called it a truck.

The drive into Hastings Bluff, population three thousand twenty-one, took less than fifteen minutes. Big town or little city, it was large enough to boast several decent restaurants and quite a few specialty stores but small enough so the people who lived there still looked out for one another. And nosed around everybody's business. The thought dredged up another smile.

Garrett glanced at his wristwatch. Fifteen minutes early. He left the truck in the parking lot behind the Taste-T-Pig and walked the few blocks down the street to Wade's office. His brother's 1967 fully restored yellow Mustang convertible sat in front of the office building next to a dusty jeep. No sign of Jonas's truck.

CSS, or Cameron Security Services, occupied the second floor of the Palmer Building. At the top of the stairs, Garrett paused in front of the etched glass door. He opened it, not surprised to find the reception desk empty. A lot of things had fallen by the wayside since his brother's ex-fiancée left.

Whirring sounds came from an office down the hall. Rather than call out, he decided to surprise Wade.

Garrett walked softly down the hallway, taking care to not let his boot heels thud. He could move like a ghost when he wanted. He peeked in the first office.

A woman sat at the desk with her back to him, the chair angled to face the window. Intent on a stack of papers, her fingers tapped out a steady rhythm on an adding machine. Long whiskey-colored hair fell in a cascade halfway down her back.

Garrett's lungs seized. "Allie?"

He hadn't seen his former girlfriend in two years. Not since he came home to stay. Not since she gave up on him and stormed away. And lost the baby.

She whirled around and the vise in his chest eased. Allie Vincent had soulful brown eyes like melted chocolate. The eyes staring back at him now were the color of a warm Caribbean sky. Over Honduras. Unforgettable eyes.

He'd never thought to see TJ McKendrick again.

Imperfect Wings

Chapter Eight

Garrett's jaw dropped. Any similarity to his former girlfriend vanished the moment TJ turned around. In contrast to Allie's carefully contrived appearance, TJ's fair complexion looked freshly scrubbed with only a trace of pink lip gloss.

The last time he'd seen her, a helicopter was pulling her out of the water—and right out of his arms. He'd never expected to see her again, especially given her involvement in the high profile indictments that followed their Honduras adventure.

Mesmerized, his steps carried him from the doorway to the edge of the desk. He wanted to relearn every soft curve of her face—the dimple in her chin, the apple cheeks and … Ah, there they were, the faint scattering of freckles on her nose. Like grains of brown sugar, they also kissed a trail across her shoulders. He knew. Had seen them. Garrett quickly quelled the memory of pink lacy underwear

"TJ?"

A slight discoloration under one eye marred her otherwise perfect complexion. A flare of anger ignited in his gut. Had someone hurt her? She sure wasn't clumsy. He'd seen this little

woman in action. All one hundred and fifteen pounds of fighting wildcat. She'd gone toe-to-toe with three of his men and set them on their butts. And then matched them step for step on a six-mile run through the jungle.

She tilted her head back to look up at him. Those gorgeous blue eyes held wariness and more than a hint of fear before widening with recognition. Her lips parted. "Garrett?"

He blinked. Her voice highlighted another disparity between the two women. Allie had a high-pitched voice, with a soft nasal intonation. TJ's voice was lower, like smooth jazz on a warm summer's night.

He decided it was her hair that initially brought Allie to mind. Both women wore their long wavy tresses loose, reaching midway down the back. They shared the same warm brown color—except when the tropical sun burnished TJ's locks into a halo of red-gold. Or the warm Caribbean waters darkened it to mahogany. She'd worn his tee shirt over …

Best not go there.

The image persisted despite the baggy gray sweats she wore now. At least two sizes too big. Why would she hide what he considered near perfection?

"Wha … what are you doing here?" TJ rose from the chair, reaching for every one of her five feet few inches.

"I live here. Hastings Bluff is my home." He crossed his arms over his chest. This couldn't be coincidence. No one came to Idaho without a purpose. "And since you're in my brother's office, the more pertinent question is what are you doing here? And what the devil happened to your face?"

"Wade's your brother?"

Before he could answer, a heavy shoulder bumped him aside.

Jonas, looking like a cat that found his way into the canary cage, planted himself in front of the desk. "Well, well, Garrett. Lookee what you done found." He leaned down, invading TJ's space. "Hey pretty girl, what's your name?"

Garrett didn't understand why his baby brother's exaggerated drawl and over-the-top flirtations made females of all ages turn gooey, but the boy had always attracted women. Like ants to a picnic.

When TJ backed away, Jonas edged around the desk and captured one of her hands. He tugged her forward, slowly drawing her hand up to his mouth.

TJ curled the hand he held into a fist and popped Jonas in the mouth.

"Ow!" Flinging her arm away, Jonas clapped a hand over his injured lips. "What was that for? Is that any way to treat a gentleman?" He backed up a few steps, glowering at her.

Garrett choked, trying to turn his laugh into a cough.

"What?" TJ rubbed her knuckles on her pants leg, all wide-eyed and looking innocent. "My hand slipped."

Turning to Garrett she said, "Let me guess—another brother. Are there any more Camerons I need to watch out

for?"

Unable to hold back his amusement any longer, Garrett grinned. "Twin sisters." In a courtly, old fashioned gesture, he swept one arm wide in a flourish. "TJ McKendrick, meet my youngest brother, Jonas Cameron."

TJ and Jonas glared at each other like a couple of junkyard dogs for several long moments before her head jerked up to look past them.

"What's going on in here?"

Before Garrett could turn, his middle brother shoved in between him and Jonas. "You said your name was Jane … Janey Williams." Wade's face looked like a thundercloud.

Janey? No wonder fury etched Wade's face. He'd been duped by a woman once. But TJ wasn't Sarah. Why was TJ here?

The guarded look returned, her eyes darting around the room. TJ pulled the desk chair in front of her and, with a nonchalance that belied the edge of panic in those beautiful blue eyes, she picked up a granite paperweight from Wade's desk.

"Easy, Wade." Garrett clamped a hand on his brother's shoulder.

She hefted the paperweight, testing its balance and increasing his apprehension. Not much in the way of a weapon, but in her hands that rock could do some damage. He had to defuse the situation before things got out of hand.

Cameron men were known for being big. He and his brothers stood well over six feet and probably outweighed TJ by a hundred pounds or more each. To her they must seem a formidable barrier to the room's only exit. And they'd backed her into a corner.

His brothers would never hurt a woman, but the pint-sized woman didn't know that.

Wade growled again. "I asked you a question—Janey."

His snide tone sent Garrett's blood pressure soaring. "That's enough." His fingers dug into his brother's shoulder. When Wade tried to shrug him off, Garrett squeezed harder. "I said back off. You're scaring her. It's not like you think."

The fierce warning got through. Surprise replaced Wade's scowl. He looked from Garrett to TJ and back again, and finally stepped back with his hands raised high. "All right."

Jonas took the hint, too. He flopped down in one of the chairs in front of the desk, one long leg draped over the arm giving him the look of a gangly puppy.

The pose didn't fool Garrett. He knew all too well how dangerous his little brother could be.

The tension in the room dropped tenfold.

In the same gentle voice he used to soothe skittish horses, Garrett spoke to TJ. "Why don't you sit down and...?"

A door slammed somewhere outside the office followed by a female voice. "Yoo-hoo. Janey. You still here?" Footsteps clicked along the hallway. "Please tell me Wade doesn't have you still working?"

Garrett groaned. His little sister, Mallory, the older twin by two minutes, sauntered into the now crowded office.

"Garrett? What are you doing here?" she asked before turning to TJ. "There you are. You were supposed … to meet me …" Mallory looked from TJ to Jonas, to Wade, finally honing in on Garrett. "What have you morons done?"

Without warning, Sheriff James Evers appeared in the doorway, his big smile fading as he took in the tension. "Jonas, out," he barked. "You, too, Wade."

Surprised, Jonas looked to Garrett.

He nodded.

Jonas shrugged, drew his lanky frame up from the chair, and sauntered from of the room.

Wade stuck his chin out. "Stick your nose somewhere else, Evers. This is none of your business."

Garrett sighed. His middle brother stood a couple of inches shorter, but he had weight—and muscle—over both Garrett and Jonas. He wouldn't be easily moved if it came to a battle of wills. "Do as he says, Wade. I got this. I'll fill you in later."

Wade looked like a thundercloud about to let loose. He took his own sweet time but finally left without another word.

The sheriff turned to Mallory and ran one big hand up and down her arm. "Sweetheart, would you mind keeping those two out of trouble while I talk to Garrett and TJ in private?"

That earned him a fierce frown. And what was the touchy-feely stuff about?

"Please, Mallory?" James asked.

Cassidy, Mal's mirror image, was the sweet one, while Mallory got all the prickly attitude. The girl wouldn't listen to anybody but Mom and Dad. James must be some kind of horse whisperer. She glared at him, but a moment later, she left. A bonafide miracle.

James shut the door behind her, shaking his head. "I'm gonna pay for that."

Garrett took the chair Jonas had vacated, intrigued by the interaction between his best friend and little sister. He nodded. "Probably. Never knew anybody who could hold a grudge like Mallory."

Garrett sneaked a peek at TJ, relieved to see her set the paperweight down.

James turned his attention to TJ. "You okay, honey?"

Garrett frowned at the endearment.

"Yeah. I'm good." She reached under the desk, pulled out a ratty old backpack, and looped it over one shoulder. "But I think my welcome is about used up here since someone ..." she stared pointedly at Garrett, "blew my cover. I'll be going now. Thanks for everything."

James moved to block the door. "Have a seat while I fill Garret in."

She went all stiff, and her face turned red.

"Please?"

There went that please thing again. Garrett waited to see if it would work this time.

TJ seemed to think about it for a moment and then, lo and behold, she dropped the backpack on the desk with a huff and plopped down in the chair. "Five minutes. Then I'm out of here."

Garrett tucked the little "please" nugget away for future consideration.

James's lips twitched once before he pressed them together in a firm line. "Garrett, you remember Aaron Hanson? Farmboy?"

Garrett nodded slowly.

"He called a week ago. Said he'd been trying to reach you."

"Jonas and I were taking the horses to the high pasture. No cell coverage that far out. What'd he want?"

James nodded toward TJ. "A place to stash our girl here. Aaron's had her under wraps for the past two years.

That explained the alias that had Wade in such a snit. "What happened that he had to hand her off?"

"Somebody tracked her to Mississippi. Got too close."

Garrett's eyes narrowed, drawn again to the discoloration under TJ's eye. "That how she got the shiner?"

"Nothing to do there, buddy. That one won't be bothering her anymore."

TJ turned away to stare out the window. Her hands trembled.

"What else, Dawg?"

She jerked around, her mouth falling open. She stared at the sheriff, slow recognition dawning.

Garrett rubbed his mouth with one hand to hide his smile. Interesting that she knew him but hadn't recognized James.

"Farmboy's been with her since Honduras. Said there are too many unanswered questions, like how they found her after all this time. Out in the sticks. Why Fowler barely got the warning off. And why he's gone silent. She needs a safe place to stay while Aaron digs for information."

"Fowler's her handler?"

James nodded.

The whole situation grew more and more curious. Fowler had wheedled his way into leading the task force sent to drag Castillo out of Honduras. And now he was missing?

She refused to meet his eyes when he looked at her. "Aaron sent her to me, huh?"

"No. When he couldn't reach you, he sent her to me. My deputies are all on alert, along with some of the other men in town. The question is—are you stepping up?"

TJ slapped her hand on the desk. "That does it. I've taken care of myself a long time. I sure don't need two hulking cowboys vying for the honor." She snatched up her backpack and started for the door. "Get out of my way ... Dawg."

James crossed his massive arms across his chest and leaned against the door.

Of all the tricks for fate to play, the last thing Garrett wanted was another woman in his life. Especially not one who was prickly, impulsive, too-young, headstrong, gorgeous, and didn't listen worth a flip. A little tease and tickle now and again worked just fine, thank you very much. No emotional vises. He'd be a fool to get involved with this one. She messed with his mind.

TJ confronted James with her hands on curvy hips—a modern day David and Goliath. "Get out of my way, Sheriff."

James looked at Garrett, eyebrows lifted. "Well?"

TJ's blue eyes snapped like a gas flame. If her glare got any hotter, she'd burn his hide to a cinder right where he stood.

Garrett held her fiery stare, daring her to look away first. And then he grinned. What an idiot. "Yeah. I'll take her on."

Chapter Nine

Somehow, without understanding how it happened, TJ found herself whisked from Wade's office to the Taste-T-Pig Restaurant three blocks down the street.

James followed the smiling hostess with the rest of their group trailing close behind. TJ found herself at a long table seated between Mallory and Garrett with her pack stuffed between her feet on the floor. A moment later, their waitress arrived and started handing out drinks.

"I took the liberty of ordering ahead since they're so busy tonight," James shouted from the end of the table next to Mallory.

TJ lifted her glass and cautiously sniffed the frothy liquid. "What is it?"

"Sarsaparilla," James said. "Every visitor to Idaho has to try it. State law."

"Does that mean you're going to arrest me if I don't drink it, Sheriff Dawg?"

James gave her a hurt look. "Hey, it's not my fault you didn't remember me?"

"You could have mentioned it."

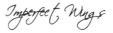

"What, and tell everybody we went swimming in our skivvies? That you wear lacy pink underwear?"

Mallory spluttered. Her jab to James's ribs earned her a grunt from the big sheriff.

Heat flooded TJ's cheeks.

Wade, sitting across the table from TJ, looked surprised. "I definitely want to hear that story."

James bumped Mallory with his shoulder. "Tell her to drink up, Mal."

TJ's stomach chose that moment to growl, a reminder that breakfast had come and gone a long time ago. When the food arrived, the rich aroma of slow-roasted meat and the tart and tangy smell of barbeque sauce made her mouth water. Her plate alone held enough smoked pork, baked beans, and coleslaw to last a week.

She ate with slow bites, savoring the food. After jumping at shadows for so long, to sit in a restaurant and enjoy a meal felt surreal.

The Camerons and James joked and teased each other, including TJ like she belonged. Would they be so accepting when Castillo found her again?

He would find her. He always did.

"Don't over-think this, little girl," Garrett whispered in her ear. "Aaron knew what he was doing sending you here."

Little girl? She set her fork down and dabbed her mouth with the napkin.

"What?" Garrett asked, lifting one eyebrow.

Mallory laughed at something Jonas said and threw a piece of roll at him. She ducked when he returned the favor. The doughy projectile struck TJ's cheek.

Her mouth fell open with a protest. "Hey …"

The others howled.

Garrett shoved a roll in her hand under the table. "Wait 'til he reaches for his drink," he said leaning down.

TJ smiled with wide-eyed innocence, all the while picking the bread apart to knead in a ball.

Finally, Jonas pushed his plate back and tipped his bottle up. He drained it in two long swallows, followed by a loud ahhhh.

TJ launched her bread missile and pegged the youngest Cameron male square in the mouth. Bull's-eye!

Jonas's dark blue Cameron eyes widened with surprise as he choked.

With a little fist pump, TJ hissed, "Yesssss."

Garrett grinned and gave her a high-five while everyone else, including a few of their dining neighbors, laughed. He signaled the waitress for the check.

While he took care of the bill, James leaned over to speak to TJ. "I'm taking Mallory home now. You know you're safe with Garrett, right?"

Mallory gave TJ a hug. "He can be a real pain, but none of my brothers would ever let anything happen to you. And we

are going shopping soon. These things," she plucked at the sweatshirt TJ wore, "are an offense to women everywhere. I'll call you in the morning, okay?"

Insulted and befriended, all in the same breath. Mallory's unique gift.

Jonas and Wade rose from the table at the same time, waving good-bye. TJ had declined their invitation to Sidewinders and the enticing Friday-Night-Drinks-Half-Price-for-Ladies. Now, she was alone with Garrett. Why did that make her nervous?

His hand, pressed to the small of her back as he guided her through the restaurant, left her insides quivering. How had she forgotten the raw magnetism of the man? She needed distance from the soldier-turned-rancher, and quick. Preferably before she said or did something really embarrassing. Men like Garrett Cameron didn't look at girls like her, at least not the way she wanted. And he called her 'little girl' for Pete's sake.

TJ sniffed. Twenty-seven years old and not a single date in six years. If she had a type, he sure wasn't it. But, oh boy, did he make arrogant and bossy look good.

Outside, on the sidewalk, twilight teetered on the brink of night. She turned to Garrett and smiled. "Thanks for dinner. I'm going to head off now." She adjusted the knapsack over her shoulder, gave him a finger waggle, and started off toward Wade's office and the nearby small apartment James had found for her.

Garrett stepped around her, blocking the way. "My truck's back behind the restaurant. C'mon. I'll give you a ride." His rough hand closed around her arm.

She pulled free. "Yeah, well my jeep's parked in front of Wade's office. I don't need a ride for three blocks. Good night, Garrett." She turned away.

"TJ?"

She paused. "What?"

"You need to fill in some blanks for me so I can determine how best to keep you safe."

TJ rolled her eyes. She'd survived just fine so far. And without his help, thank you very much.

"Please? Ride with me? Half an hour and I'll bring you back. Promise."

Her head argued for distance, but her traitorous body wanted to get a whole lot closer. Besides, she had a ton of questions, too. His 'please' did her in.

After a moment's hesitation, she took his outstretched hand. "All right but only for a little while."

Was that a smirk on his face?

In the parking lot behind the restaurant, she picked out his vehicle immediately. "The red truck, right?"

"How'd you know?"

"Easy. It's the biggest, baddest one in the lot." When he lifted one eyebrow, she added her own smirk. "A man's choice of vehicle is oftentimes an extension of his self-esteem. Add in

the alpha-soldier-cowboy-ego you got going on and ..." She shrugged and batted her eyelashes.

Garrett's eyes narrowed. He clicked the remote unlock that set the lights flashing and opened the passenger door of the big Dodge pickup.

TJ stared up at the seat, trying to figure out how to climb inside. Why did men feel the need for such large, gas guzzling monstrosities?

Garrett came up behind her. "Ego too big for you, angel?"

Before she could retort, Garrett lifted her so she could slide inside and closed the door behind her.

He walked around the front of the truck and climbed in behind the wheel, filling the cab's interior. "Buckle up."

The engine woke with a purr.

"I thought we'd ride over to the state park. There's a lighted picnic area and some tables down by the river. We can talk there in private. I'm sure you've got your own questions."

"Yes, I do. All this time, I thought you and Dawg ... er, James ... were dead. No one would tell me anything. I didn't know the girls made it to Atlanta until Aaron told me on the way to Memphis. I hope they found homes."

"You deserve to know after risking your life for them. As for me and Dawg ..." He shrugged. "Our first priority was your safety. Dawg got shot, and since he didn't have any family, I brought him home. We both got out after that."

There had to be more to the story, but men like Garrett

and James—and the rest of their team—held their secrets close.

"It's all part of the job. You worried needlessly."

"Yeah, well they didn't tell me that either." She didn't want to argue. "What happened to the rest of your team?"

"Some stayed in. Some got out. I can't imagine how difficult it's been for you these past two years. For your family, too."

Not very subtle, but she could roll with the diversion. And play his game. "I don't have any family. Have you lived in Hastings Bluff all your life?"

"Except for my time in the Army. You have no family at all?"

She shook her head.

"Tell me about it."

She could ask him another question instead, but for the first time in a very long time, TJ wanted to talk about the loneliness and grief. And guilt.

"My mom died when I was sixteen. I had my learner's permit and nagged her to let me drive. We got T-boned by a furniture truck. She died instantly."

Garrett didn't say anything.

"My dad was in the Army. He qualified for the Olympic Marksmanship Team twice. He had eighteen years in when Mom passed away. He gave up his career and stayed home with me 'til I finished high school." TJ kept her voice emotionless, reciting facts.

Garrett let the silence drag on for several minutes before prompting her again. "No sisters or brothers? Aunts or uncles?"

"Accidental only child. Mom had a sister, and my dad had two brothers, but we were never close. I don't remember them, much less where to find them."

The memories marched on, settling like a weight on her chest. Forcing a bright smile she quipped, "Hey, at least there's no one Castillo can threaten me with."

Not true. Faces came alive in her mind's eye—Señora Ramirez, Aaron, Stella and Virgil, David and Carrie Anne. And now the Camerons and the people of Hastings Bluff.

Garrett released her hand and turned down a narrow dirt road that opened into a graveled parking lot. Picnic tables and cook pits dotted the area, illuminated by a few tall lights. Nearby, water sounds gurgled in a soothing rhythm.

"Let's go down by the river."

TJ followed him along a winding path and sat across from him at one of the picnic tables.

"You know you're too darn trusting, don't you?"

She looked at him in surprise. Trusting? Hardly. Trust meant leaving yourself wide open, and she'd learned a long time ago where that led. And yet for some unfathomable reason, she trusted Garrett Cameron. Maybe because he saved her once before?

"So, where are we?"

"That's the Salmon River," he said, nodding at the

flowing stream. "You can get a good raft ride down it in places. There're a few decent waterfalls, too. It runs west to east across the state before dipping south here. Six miles that way." He pointed in the other direction. "It runs through our property. But this spot here is the best. My brothers and I used to come here to swim in the summertime before they turned it into a park." He sighed. "That was a few years back."

"Do people fish in the river?"

"Oh, yeah. Idaho's famous for salmon fishing."

She chuckled. "Guess that explains the name of the river. And the town I passed through on the way here."

He chuckled. "You ever fished in a river?"

"Nope. Went deep sea fishing once, though."

"City girl, huh? I'll have to see about expanding your education while you're here. Show you how life is supposed to be lived."

"I'd like that. My dad could hit any target you put in front of him, but hunting or fishing … not his thing."

"That how you learned about guns?"

TJ nodded.

"You took down three of my men back in Honduras. Without firing a shot. How'd you learn to do that?"

"Dad held a black belt in Karate. I begged him to teach me, but he never had time. So I took Tae Kwan Do classes."

"Must be a good student."

Her life had changed so much. She'd come to grips with

the bad times. Before Honduras. Now, she lived day-to-day, the upcoming trial her sole focus.

Garrett interrupted her reverie. "Tell me about the men who found you in Mississippi."

TJ rubbed her hands up and down her arms. The night had grown cooler, but her shiver didn't stem from the dip in the temperature. "Two men in a shiny black sedan. Really big guys. Wearing suits and black shades. If you can imagine a tractor driving through downtown Chicago during rush hour—that's how bad they stood out. They parked across from the diner where I worked."

"Go on."

"My locket—the signaling device Agent Fowler gave me—it went off. I had very little warning. Aaron shooed me out the back door. Told me to run. He went back to make sure they didn't follow me. That's the first I knew of his involvement." Another shiver, stronger this time, made her whole body shake.

"There was a third man hiding out back. He stuck a gun in my ribs. The weird thing was he didn't act like he wanted to kill me. At least not until I kicked him in ... uh ... well, that's when he hit me." Her fingers touched the fading bruise on her cheek.

Garrett reached across the table and pulled her hand away but didn't let go. "What happened then?"

"Aaron happened. He took care of the third guy and

hauled me out of there."

"You're a remarkable person, TJ McKendrick." He pulled her hand across the table and kissed her fingertips. "Let's go. The nights are nippy in the early summer months. You're cold, and I don't have a jacket to give you. I'll crank the heater in the truck and get some heat going."

TJ climbed out from the picnic table but didn't follow him right away. He seemed such a paradox—the hard lines of a face that had seen too much darkness were soft now, caring. His work-roughened hands gentle.

He stopped when she didn't follow, a questioning look in his eyes.

"You don't understand how risky it is for me to be here, do you, Garrett? Not dangerous for me but for you and your family. Your friends. This town. Don Castillo won't quit. Senator Farleigh has too much to lose if I testify. I'm running blind. I don't even know where the trial's supposed to be held. I have to move on before another innocent soul gets hurt." She despised feeling helpless. Hated being at fate's whim.

Garrett walked back to her and wiped away the single tear perched on her cheek. He pulled her into his arms and pressed her head against his broad chest. "You can drop that line of thought right now, little girl. There's no safer place you could be than right here. The good Lord brought you to Hastings Bluff for a reason."

There he went with that little girl stuff again.

Imperfect Wings

Chapter Ten

No doubt about it. The Camerons were a bossy bunch, with Garrett the most domineering of the lot. TJ stood on the front porch of the Triple C Ranch on Saturday morning and once again found herself overruled, overridden, and overwhelmed.

Irritated as she might be, though, a tiny smile emerged at the memory of Garrett's conniption fit the previous night. He'd insisted on escorting her back to the little apartment over the bakery but grabbed her arm when she started up the stairs.

"This is where you're staying?" he'd demanded.

She couldn't tell if he was surprised or angry.

"What the ... heck was James thinking? A ten-year-old could break in here. This lock won't keep a trashcan safe."

Other than being a bit small, TJ didn't think the place looked bad.

The maddening cowboy gave her ten minutes to pack. At eleven minutes, he hustled her to his truck and drove to the Triple C Ranch, overruling all of her objections.

Last night she hadn't minded so much. He made her feel safe. Today, though, while waiting for Mallory, TJ mentally

kicked herself for giving in. These people had taken over her life, and she'd let them.

A car flew down the mile-long driveway, a cloud of dust trailing behind. Mallory Cameron. Come to take her shopping for new clothes. Oh, joy.

"Here's my little sister, now." Garrett's deep voice came from just inside the screen door.

TJ gave him a dirty look. "Aaron got me these clothes. He said keep a low profile. I don't think a shopping spree is such a good idea."

Garrett chuckled. "I'm sure he also told you to try and blend in. Around these parts, feed sacks are not in fashion. You got everybody trying to guess who you are and why you're hiding."

Feed sack? She stared down at her attire in dismay. The baggy sweatshirt hung halfway to her knees. Paired with the too-big jeans and with her hair stuffed up under a baseball cap, she could pass for a boy. Wasn't that the point?

Lips pursed, TJ frowned at Garrett. He wore snug-fitting jeans that drew the eye of every woman in town, a starched blue plaid shirt neatly tucked in and sleeves rolled to show muscular forearms. She thought back to the previous night and Mallory in her cute little Capris and body-hugging tank top. The rest of the guys had looked pretty darn good, too. She, on the other hand, could pass for a vagabond.

Garrett was right. Maybe a few things in the proper size

wouldn't hurt. Hadn't Granny McKendrick always said, "Wear your clothes tight enough to show you're a woman, but loose enough so's people know you're a lady?" TJ wanted very badly to be seen as an attractive young woman and not a boy. Or a little girl.

Mallory's car cruised to a stop in front of the porch. She lowered the passenger-side window and called out, "Ready to go?"

TJ looked over her shoulder at Garrett, still unsure.

"Mallory knows not to leave Hastings Bluff, and James has his deputies on alert. If I know those boys, they'll be all over you like fleas on a hound dog. You're safe."

She whirled around with hands on her hips. "Oh no, you did not just compare me to a dog."

Garrett blanched. "Uh … that's not … I mean …"

Her chortle cut him off and now his face turned red. Score one for TJ. She climbed into Mallory's SUV, still laughing as they drove away.

She hadn't seen much of the ranch the night before. In the clear morning light, the view through the car windows revealed a paradise of rolling hills, green grass, and horses. Lots of horses. "How many are there?"

"The herd? I have no idea. Four or five hundred that my dad and brothers train and sell. But that doesn't include the wild horses. Last I heard there were three small herds of mustangs—maybe a hundred total."

"They don't train and sell the mustangs?"

Mallory's face lit up. "Noooo. Aren't many wild horses left these days. The open ranges are disappearing and too many farmers think they're nothing but a nuisance. When the Triple C first started up, Dad carved out a refuge for them. He and Rascal Sutcliff, that's our foreman, they bought up a bunch of what was then worthless open range backed up against the foothills. They fenced it off and created the Lost Trail Wild Mustang Refuge. There, wild horses are protected and even though their range is limited, the herds roam free and safe. You should get Garrett to take you out to see them."

The Hastings Bluff city limits sign came into view, saving TJ from answering. Intrigued? Absolutely. Alone time with Garrett? Not a good idea.

"Western World, straight ahead." Mallory indicated a store with a rustic frontage. "They have everything a cowgirl needs."

"Are you sure about this? I mean, I'm okay with the clothes I have."

"Well, I'm not. If you want to blend in, you should look good doing it." Mallory gave TJ a quick onceover. "After we finish, I'm taking you to the salon for a haircut and manicure."

TJ curled her fingers to hide the ragged nails. She couldn't remember the last time she'd pampered herself.

"Oh, look. There's James." Mallory slowed the car and yelled out the window. "Hi, there. Want to meet us for a late lunch at the diner?"

James stood outside his office, his usual stern countenance softening when Mallory spoke. Looked like something going on between those two.

He nodded and shouted back. "What time?"

"Two o'clock." She waved and drove on. "Okay now, spill. Tell me how Mr. Garrett Bossy Pants convinced you to move in with him."

TJ's mouth fell open. "I didn't move in with him."

"Then how come I had to pick you up at the ranch this morning instead of the apartment? Huh?"

Oh mercy. TJ hadn't thought of what people might say about her staying with three bachelors at the Triple C Ranch. Alone. "Last night … he, uh, insisted on seeing me back to the apartment … and then he sort of went ballistic. Claimed it wasn't safe and … well, some other not very nice things. It was just easier to go with him."

"I know exactly what you mean. Garrett thinks he's in charge of the world. All the Cameron men are that way. Funny, now that I think about it, James acts like that, too. He came home with Garrett after he got shot, and Mom and Daddy sort of adopted him. Probably learned the He-Man thing from being around my brothers."

Mallory looked far away for a moment. "So, what did my obnoxious big brother say about our esteemed sheriff?"

She certainly knew her brother well. "That James didn't

have the sense of a jack ... um, rabbit."

"Jackrabbit, huh? What else?"

"That he couldn't see past the blind end of a nearsighted ... er ... mule."

Mallory chuckled. "Gosh, it's hard being right all the time."

"What do you mean?"

"James thought you'd stay at the ranch with me, but I've been bunking at Miz Tillberry's this week. She's fresh out of the hospital after gallbladder surgery. Anyway, he didn't think it was a good idea to leave you alone at the ranch with Wade. Especially since you didn't know him, and he didn't know you. Wade's got a bit of a reputation, if you know what I mean. All my brothers do. And Garrett has more than a bit of a temper. Now that I know you two have a history, James's reasoning makes sense." She waggled her eyebrows at TJ.

"We do not have a history. It's just that a few years back, he and Dawg ... I mean James ... helped me out of a jam." She rubbed her temples. How much did Mallory know?

Mallory patted TJ's clenched hands. "It's okay. James told me what went down in Honduras. Anyway, I'm the one who suggested you stay in my sister's old apartment. Garrett hates that she stays there instead of the ranch when she's home. I think she does it for spite."

"If it's not safe, and Garrett hates it so much, why'd you stick me there?"

"You were never in danger, TJ. James's men have been watching over you night and day. I knew Garrett would spaz when he found out, but it had to be his idea to drag you off to the ranch. He's funny like that. It's the Tarzan gene. All the Cameron men have it."

Trying to follow a conversation with Mallory gave TJ a headache.

"Soooo, share the dirt—you staying in the guest bedroom next to Garrett ..." She did the eyebrow waggle thing again. "... or in his room?"

TJ closed her eyes and prayed for calm. "Neither. I'm in your sister's room. Alone. Garrett said she wouldn't mind. So, what kind of shops are we going to?"

Five hours later, the two women walked out of Fancy's Hair and Nail Salon. Mallory stopped to look TJ up and down. "You know, sometimes I amaze myself. You look spectacular!"

TJ ran her hands over her hips and the new low-rise Wranglers. They were tight and confining, especially with the legs stuffed inside a brand new pair of Ariat Crossfire buckskin boots. A simple white tank top teased the waist of her jeans. She tipped her new felt cowgirl hat back, stuck her thumbs in the belt loops, and said, "Yee-haw."

Mallory laughed. "You're gonna knock a few cowboys outta the saddle, and I can't wait to see it happen. That little sundress you got will be perfect for church tomorrow. I'll swing by in the morning around ten thirty to get you. Unless, of course, one of my brothers can be persuaded to give you a ride. Let's head on over to the diner before James sends a posse after us."

During the short drive to the Dixie Diner, TJ couldn't help but wonder if the new clothes would make a difference. Two-inch boot heels gave her some much needed height. Hopefully, the way she filled out the skintight jeans would make her seem less like a teenager. With her hair trimmed and layered and pink polish on her nails, she had to look a little different. Enough to change Garrett's little girl impression of her?

Shut it down, TJ. Not going there. Don Rafael. Senator Farleigh. The trial. Staying alive. That was her focus. Until she could put all this behind her, she had no future. And no right to dream up one.

She just felt so safe here.

"That brain of yours is gonna explode like a firecracker any minute now." Mallory turned the key, making the SUV's engine rumble. "Ease up and enjoy the moment."

TJ took a deep breath and let it out. Mallory was right. Trouble would find her soon enough. It always did. "So, how old are you and your twin? And your brothers?"

Mallory sent her a knowing look. "Garrett will be thirty-four in November."

"Okaaaay." TJ ignored the heat rising to her cheeks. "He's seven years older than me. Which is probably why he keeps calling me little girl."

"It's an excuse." Mallory glanced at her wristwatch. "I'll give you the Reader's Digest version of why Garrett is trying to keep you at arms' length."

TJ didn't know if she really wanted to hear it.

"He got involved with a girl in college."

"Allie?"

Mallory gave her a surprised look. "Yeah. How'd you know?"

"He thought I was Allie. Last night in Wade's office. Do I look like her?"

Mallory shook her head. "Not really. Maybe your hair. A little. Anyway, Allie wanted to get married. Her father's a town councilman, and her mother thinks she's the queen. They've been trying to hitch Garrett to their daughter forever. But all Allie wanted was to live anywhere but Idaho. Garrett had his heart set on joining the Army, with no intention of putting his neck in a noose—his words, not mine. Anyway, Allie pitched a fit when he took a commission after college. He still saw her every time he came home on leave. Made her hotter than a goat in a pepper patch when he'd leave again without giving her a ring. This went on forever—her demanding they get married and us holding our breath, praying he wouldn't. And then, a little over two years ago, she up and announced she was pregnant."

Something twisted in TJ's chest. She swallowed hard.

That Garrett had cared for someone else shouldn't matter.

"When Garrett found out, he resigned his commission. That's when he brought James home with him. My big brother is a do-right kind of guy and would've married Allie, but staying here didn't factor into her plans. I thought she might explode when Gare told her he'd come home to stay. It didn't take long for her to conveniently lose the baby and high-tail it out of town. Far as I know, he hasn't heard from her since."

"This was after Honduras?"

"Yeah. James didn't have any family to look after him, so my tough-skinned, softhearted brother brought him home to recuperate. James didn't stand a chance once Mom got hold of him."

"I didn't know. I couldn't get any answers about the men who rescued me."

"Of course not. It's all hush-hush. Anyway, that was the last we saw of Allie."

"You think she deliberately …"

"No. I don't think there was a baby."

"Does he still love her?"

"Don't know if love entered the equation. He didn't seem all that broke up about her leaving. Guess you'll have to ask him." They parked in front of the old-fashioned diner.

Inside, an assortment of cowboys in dusty jeans and boots sat at the counter alongside a few businessmen wearing short-sleeved shirts and ties. "I think we're about to reap the benefits of our shopping," Mallory whispered in TJ's ear.

Elbows jabbed and heads turned when the two women walked through the restaurant. Several men called out as they passed.

"Hey, Mallory. Who's your friend?"

"What's your name, darlin'?"

"Hey cutie, where ya from?"

"You and your friend wanna join us, Mal?"

Unsettling as she found their attention, the unexpected consideration gave TJ a boost of confidence. Men usually went for lookers like Mallory.

She followed her new friend to an empty booth by the window.

"Well, that was uncomfortable." TJ tried to make light of the gauntlet they'd run.

"I tried to tell you. The necessary attributes are there. All you have to do is showcase them."

TJ shook her head. "Guys aren't into short girls with brown hair."

Mallory looked past TJ's shoulder with a huge smile. "Well, hello, heaven."

A quick glance over her shoulder confirmed TJ's suspicion. The sheriff stood in the doorway looking their way.

James whistled when he reached the table. "You two should be locked up for your own safety, and I just happen to have a jail cell with your names on it."

Mallory groaned. "Cheesy, James. Save it for someone who might bite."

A shadow loomed behind the sheriff.

"You gonna show me your new duds, TJ?"

When had Garrett come in? She wanted to slide under the table and disappear. If he made fun of her clothes … If he called her little girl again …

"We picked up a few things." Mallory smirked. "Stand up and show him, TJ."

TJ sighed and slid out of the booth. With feigned confidence, she held her arms out and turned in a slow circle for them.

"Heeey," Mallory complained.

TJ glanced around to see her punch James in the ribs. "Reel your eyes back in, cowboy." She yanked his arm, pulling him down to sit beside her. To TJ, she said, "Show them the boots. They're kicking hot."

Garrett's eyes slid down TJ's body to her feet and then back up again. "You look good, angel. Real good."

At least he hadn't called her little girl again.

James started laughing. "You are one wicked, wicked woman, Mallory Cameron. Remind me to never cross you." He nudged her with his elbow.

Mallory gave him a smug smile. "You don't know the half of it, Jamesy."

"Thank you, Garrett," TJ murmured. She took her seat

again with Garrett easing his big frame down beside her. "That's very kind of you."

He looked puzzled. "Not kind at all. It's the plain truth."

After the waitress took their orders and brought their food, TJ waited until Garrett took a big bite of his steak sandwich. She'd come a long way today. Would it hurt to push her boundaries a little more?

"Garrett, Mallory invited me to church tomorrow. Rather than have her come all the way out to the ranch to pick me up … would you take me?"

Garrett choked.

Imperfect Wings

Chapter Eleven

TJ pirouetted in front of the full-length mirror in the bedroom, fretting over the new sundress. The pattern looked good—a multi-colored riot of embroidered wildflowers splashed across a white background. She couldn't wear this. Her hands reached for the zipper, but stopped when her eyes caught sight of the alarm clock on the nightstand. Garrett would be yelling any minute. And what else did she have suitable for church?

The mirror beckoned again. What was it about the little bit of soft cotton that made her uncomfortable? There was nothing improper about the dress. The scoop neckline was tasteful, the bodice a snug fit, but not too tight. The skirt flared out from a nipped in waistline, and when she turned, the hemline swirled about her knees. Perhaps the thin straps bared her shoulders too much?

She added the cornflower blue bolero. Better. Oh, who was she fooling? TJ McKendrick didn't dress like this. Why had she listened to Mallory? The girly fashion worked for the tall and thin sassy flirt, but she used clothes like a weapon. TJ wore them as a defense. Tight jeans were one thing, but this

dress … She didn't wear ultra-feminine things. Ever. Except for her underclothes. But nobody saw those.

TJ slipped into the new white sandals and looked again. The person staring back didn't even look like her. This stranger tossed her head and flipped a mass of long, wavy hair over one shoulder. Was she really going to do this?

"If you don't want to sit in the front pew, we gotta go," Garrett shouted from downstairs.

TJ's breath hitched. Something about his voice sent little pinpricks of awareness scuttling up and down her spine. Shoulders back. Chin up. Smile. Be polite. Keep it friendly but remain distant. If he made fun of her dress, she'd blame Mallory. Right.

TJ ran her hands over her hips one more time and tugged the little cover-up closer before leaving the bedroom.

Garrett stood at the bottom of the stairs, but there was nothing teasing in the way his eyes smoldered. He watched her descend each step, never once blinking.

Years had gone by without a single man triggering the slightest flicker of interest for her. Why now? Why, when her life resembled one huge disaster? And why him? Garrett Cameron didn't play in her league.

On the next to the last step, TJ stopped. She could almost meet him eye to eye. His cologne played havoc with her good intentions. "Hi."

Brilliant. Tongue-tied, cheeks aflame, and unable to meet

his eyes. Not a good combination. He probably wore that arrogant I-drive-women-crazy-and-I-know-it smile. At this rate, her cheeks would soon look like overripe tomatoes.

Reaching for a spark of anger, TJ tried to salvage her delicate pride. She firmed her jaw and looked up, ready to confront his smug look.

There was no smirk. No knowing smile. Only ... heat.

One eyebrow lifted right before he spoke. "Wow. You trying to roll me into an early grave, angel?"

All her insecurities about the dress vanished. The vise holding her tongue loosened. "Uh, thank you. You look nice, too.

He led her to his truck and helped her inside.

TJ fussed with her skirt and tried to hold back a grin. She could get used to this.

The hundred-year-old country church was a white-framed box with a spire and stained glass windows—a throwback to a time when life could be hard and people relied on their faith. As they walked toward the open front doors, TJ tugged on Garrett's arm. "Mallory said this is where your parents got married. And that all of you were christened here. Do you still attend? You and the rest of your family?"

"Uh, yeah. Mom and Dad do. James comes sometimes when Mallory nags him enough, and Cass attends when she's home. The rest of us have been ... a little lax."

Mallory sat halfway down on the right side of the

sanctuary and waved when she saw them.

TJ slipped into the pew next to her. She leaned over and whispered, "Where's James?"

"Working," Mallory whispered back, making a face.

The service wasn't much different from the churches TJ had attended growing up. Even the songs were familiar, old favorites like *A Mighty Fortress* and *What a Friend We Have in Jesus*. And then the closing hymn started. *Amazing Grace.* Her father's favorite. And the last song sung at his memorial service. Three years ago. Had it really been that long since she'd attended church?

Listening to the beautiful words that promised so much, TJ realized how much she'd missed church worship. This little bit of Americana made her yearn for something she hadn't felt for a long time. Like coming home.

Whoa! The errant thought left her head spinning. She hadn't been in Hastings Bluff all that long, and here she was already planting a garden. What was wrong with her?

Garrett, sitting on her other side, glanced down with a puzzled frown on his face. The service concluded then, forestalling any questions he might ask. At the door, Mallory introduced her to the pastor who shook hands and welcomed her.

Outside, Mallory's face lit up when she saw James leaning against his cruiser. He stood with both hands shoved deep in his pants pockets like he was afraid to touch her. "Hey, TJ.

Glad to see you were able to haul this guy out this morning. If anybody needs a good sermon, it's him. Sorry I couldn't get here in time for the service."

"Garrett Cameron, I haven't seen your face in forever," said a lady tugging three kids behind her, all under the age of ten. "Good to see you back in church. Say hi to your mama when she gets back."

"Glad you finally got yourself back in church, boy. Now, how 'bout working on them brothers of yours?" said an elderly gentleman in a plaid shirt and neatly pressed overalls.

TJ smiled at the affection the congregation had for the Camerons and grinned at Garrett's obvious discomfort.

After several more slaps on the back, the throng thinned out, leaving room for a gorgeous blonde to sidle up to Garrett. TJ's smile faltered when the woman slipped her arm around his waist.

"Garrett. Are you coming to the evening service? I'll save you a seat."

"Colleen, when did you get back to town?" Mallory took Colleen's arm and steered her to one side. "I thought you were visiting your boyfriend at college this weekend."

The relief on Garrett's face brought TJ's grin back. "Get a lot of that, do you?"

Instead of a smart comeback, the tough, gruff cowboy blushed. He took her arm and whisked her toward the parking lot. "C'mon. Let's go."

A tall woman with salt and pepper hair done up in a tight bun caught them before they'd gone a step. "Garrett Cameron. I can't remember the last time I saw you in church."

"Afternoon, ma'am." Garrett took her hand, holding it like a piece of delicate porcelain.

"Miz Tillberry." James tipped his hat.

"Why, hello, Sheriff. Now, where did Mallory get off to?"

"She's right over there, ma'am." He nodded to where Mallory stood with the blond.

"Ahhh, the intrepid Colleen." Mrs. Tillberry nodded, looking from Colleen to Garrett. "She and her sister have always fancied Cameron men. Looks like you owe that sister of yours."

When James laughed, the old woman turned to him. "I wouldn't be so amused if I were you, Sheriff. Colleen came to visit me in the hospital last week, right after you left. She had plenty of admiring comments to make about your … um, about you."

James blanched. His grin disappeared.

The elderly woman turned next to TJ. "Garrett, introduce me to the lovely young lady who enticed you back to church."

A hint of rosewater surrounded the older woman, stirring memories of Granny Flora McKendrick.

TJ accepted the thin hand extended to her. This was a formidable woman. Age hadn't slowed her mind one iota. Mrs. Tillberry could smooth the way for a stranger or make life in

Hastings Bluff decidedly uncomfortable. And the edict she'd delivered—that Garrett's return to the pious fold was inspired by TJ—screamed with hidden meaning.

From the corner of her eye, TJ saw Garrett run a finger under his shirt collar.

"Miz Tillberry, this is TJ McKendrick. She's ... uh ... visiting. TJ, this is Agnes Tillberry."

"May I call you TJ?" When TJ nodded, she went on. "And since Cate and Cody are out of town, you're here visiting ...?"

"Mallory," TJ and Garrett answered at the same time.

"Of course. And since Mallory's been staying with me since I got out of the hospital, you're at the Triple C?" Those sharp, bird-like eyes flitted from TJ to Garrett. "Did Wade or Jonas come with you this morning? No? Well, one can only pray."

TJ sneaked a peek at Garrett, noting that he looked as uncomfortable as she felt.

Mallory joined them then, turning back once to wave at Colleen. "Thank goodness, she finally took the hint. Hey, Miz Tillberry. You ready to go?"

"Actually, I'd like to invite your brother and ... friends for lunch. I put a nice pot roast in the oven before we left. And since my broken front porch step could use some attention from a good man or two, it seems like an opportune time to share Sunday dinner. Will the four of you join me? Mallory, dear, I can't wait to hear what you said to Colleen Weldon."

Mallory manufactured an air of innocence, going all wide-eyed. "Nothing that wasn't true. I happened to mention that Wade and Jonas admired her dancing at Sidewinders last week."

"You sicced Colleen on your own brothers?" Mrs. Tillberry burst out laughing.

"Mal, that's just wrong." Garrett grinned. "But you're right. I am grateful."

A short five-minute drive into town found them pulling up in front of a small white house in a tiny yard with a knee-high picket fence. Mallory drove Mrs. Tillberry. James followed in his patrol car with Garrett and TJ bringing up the rear.

The cozy little two-bedroom cottage was filled with mementos. TJ studied a framed picture of a much younger, almost giddy Agnes arm-in-arm with a good-looking boy. She guessed they had to be eighteen or twenty.

"That's my Elliott. We were married for forty-three years. The good Lord never saw fit to bless us with babes of our own, but He filled my life with children nonetheless. Did you know I taught Garrett and his siblings in fifth grade? Had them all again in high school when I took over as principal."

After a delicious lunch, James and Garrett went off to fix the broken porch step while TJ and Mallory helped in the kitchen. Mrs. Tillberry's tales of the Cameron brood's antics in school soon had all three of the women laughing hysterically. "I'm fairly certain Wade came up with the idea. That boy's always been too smart for his own good. And I have no doubt Garrett egged them on. Poor Jonas. He was the one caught making the anatomical improvements to the mascot statue. The Hastings Bluff Bulls were a devastating force when those three brothers played together on the football team, but … really. Basketballs? Once he finished detention, Jonas drove Garrett's truck for the remainder of the school year."

The conversation waned as they finished up in the kitchen. The older woman turned to TJ. "Tell me about you. What really brings you to a little known place like Hastings Bluff?"

TJ found herself sharing an abbreviated version of her trip to Honduras and how a friend introduced her to the Camerons and James. Under Mrs. Tillberry's careful probing, she told the older woman about the little girls from La Cruza and how they'd been sent to Atlanta for medical care and possible adoption. "I just wish I knew how they're doing."

"I can see you have a heart for the unfortunate, dear. And I'm not surprised you fret over the wellbeing of those precious children."

Mallory finished drying the last pot and put it away. "Why can't you call the Department of Family and Children's Services?"

"I doubt they'd give information about the children to a stranger."

Mrs. Tillberry placed the glass dome over the remaining pound cake. "When do your parents return, Mallory? Your

mother's literary agent has a friend who's an adoption lawyer. If you know the girls' names, she might be able to learn something."

"That's a great idea, Mrs. T. Mom's supposed to call tonight and let us know when they'll be home."

"Thank you." TJ took the older woman's arthritic hands in her own and squeezed gently.

The ride back to the ranch was quiet. When Garrett parked the truck and cut the engine, TJ released her seatbelt and reached for the door handle. She stopped when Garrett touched her arm.

"Wait. Let me have your cell phone."

She pulled the disposable Trackfone from her purse and handed it to him. "Why?"

"We got a mare about to deliver that I need to check on. I may not be back until late, but Wade's here." He punched in some numbers and handed the cell phone back to her. "I programmed the numbers for me and my brothers. Call one of us if you need anything. Okay?"

"Okay."

"I meant it when I said I don't want you going off anywhere alone."

"I understand. If I need anything or want to go somewhere, I'll call you or Wade or Jonas."

When she turned to get out, he caught her arm again. "TJ?"

Was that a twinkle in his eye?

"Wait. I'll get your door. Mama's rules." He got out and came around the front of the truck to open her door. Yep. Those ocean-blue eyes were definitely sparkling. After helping her down from the ridiculously high seat, he followed her inside.

TJ waited at the bottom of the stairs, knowing he wanted to say something more.

Garrett met her eyes and then looked away. "Tomorrow, if you're game, would you like to take one of the horses for a ride? I have to check on the far pasture. You could see some of the ranch. Maybe do some fishing." He fumbled with his hat.

"I haven't ridden in a long time."

He chuckled. "That's no problem. You can ride Buffy. That mare's about as docile as they come. You'll love her."

"Can we take a picnic lunch?" Was she actually considering this? What happened to polite and friendly but not too close?

He met her eyes then. "Sure. We can do that. We eat breakfast at six. Dress comfortable and wear your new boots."

Other than their initial encounter two years ago, she'd only known this man for a few days. Even so, something sizzled between them. This wasn't a good idea. She thought about declining his invitation ... for all of three seconds.

"Okay."

Chapter Twelve

TJ groaned and dragged a pillow over her head. There he went again, the maddening rooster. Every thirty seconds. Crowing relentlessly. She snuggled deeper under the covers.

The arrogant bird continued to trumpet the dawn like he was singlehandedly responsible for the sun rising. Boy, with a little flour and some buttermilk … a few spices …

Her eyes snapped open. Heart pounding, she rolled over and reached for the alarm clock. Why hadn't it gone off? Garrett was taking her riding today. And she had twelve minutes to get ready. Rats!

She threw the covers off and raced for the bathroom.

With two minutes to spare, TJ sat on the bottom stair step, tugging on her new boots. What was that heavenly smell? Coffee, biscuits, and—*oh yum*—bacon.

Following the delectable aroma to the kitchen, she found Garrett at the stove, stirring something in a cast iron frying pan. He turned, a slow smile lighting his face. "Morning. I wondered whether you'd make it. Breakfast in about five minutes."

"Wow, a man who cooks. Is there anything you can't do?"

He sprinkled in salt, added a few shakes of pepper, gave it a final stir, and poured the thick, white gravy into a bowl. "Nope."

TJ choked back a snort. The rooster had nothing on this guy, but you never insult the cook. Not if you wanted to eat. Her mouth watered. "Can I help?"

He nodded toward a stack of plates and a pile of silverware on the counter. "You can set the table. We usually eat breakfast in here."

"That's an awful lot of food. Are Wade and Jonas joining us?"

"We sure are, sweetheart," Jonas said behind her.

Wade appeared by him, both men sniffing like coon dogs on the hunt.

TJ bit her bottom lip to keep from laughing at the image that popped into her mind.

Jonas poured a steaming cup of coffee. "I nominate Garrett to do all the cooking while Roseanna's on vacation. Man, that smells good. Coffee, TJ?"

She accepted the mug he held out, added a splash of milk, took a sip … and choked. "This stuff is strong enough to take the enamel off your teeth." With a grimace, TJ reached for the milk again, ignoring their chuckles.

Garrett pulled a pan of biscuits from the oven and turned them out on a plate. "Jo, get the orange juice. And see if you can find the hot sauce." He handed TJ the bowl of gravy. "Set this on the table while I scramble up some eggs."

The men ate fast, taking seconds and leaving nothing, while TJ barely made a dent in hers. "How do you eat so much? And so fast?"

"Ranching is hard work, sweetheart." Jonas sopped up the gravy on his plate with a bite of biscuit.

"So, you do your own cooking?"

He crammed a last mouthful of egg in his mouth before getting up to rinse his dishes in the sink. "Mom and Roseanna—she's our housekeeper—handle most of the cooking. When they're both gone, we take turns. Of course, Garrett, here, is the only one of us who knows what he's doing. Me and Wade usually set out cereal in the morning and order pizza for supper."

"They'll be back next week." Garrett gave a pointed look at her plate. "You don't eat enough to keep a grasshopper alive." He snagged her bacon and ate it.

"Hey … I wanted that."

"Should've eaten it then. Let's get moving, cowgirl. Daylight's burning."

TJ turned to Wade. "Are you and Jonas coming with us?"

"No, darling." He winked at her. "We been told to stay away."

Garrett glared at his brothers. "You two can finish up the dishes. Let's go, TJ."

Wade called after them. "You coming back to the office

tomorrow, TJ? I really need your help finishing that financial statement for the Bar M contract."

"Sure thing, Wade."

Garrett handed her a pair of leather riding gloves. "Stuff these in your back pocket for now." He set her new cowgirl hat on her head and tugged on the leather neck cord. "We call this a stampede string—if your hat blows off, you won't lose it." He tipped the hat back until it hung down her back. "Let's go."

He threw a pair of bulging leather saddlebags over his shoulder and headed off toward the barn.

TJ followed, almost running to keep pace with his long strides. At the barn, he unlatched the gate to the corral and motioned her to go ahead of him.

"Much as I like all the stuff you and Mallory picked up shopping, I'm glad you wore the old jeans today. You'll be more comfortable in the saddle with a little give in your britches."

How did she respond to that? Heat crept up TJ's neck. At least he'd noticed.

An older cowboy waited at the rear of the barn, holding the reins of two saddled mounts. The big mahogany-colored horse danced around in circles, skittish. The smaller one, a buckskin, stood placidly swishing its long black tail.

"Morning, Rascal," Garrett said. "Thanks for getting the horses ready. This is TJ. She's visiting for the summer."

Rascal tipped his hat. "Morning, ma'am."

"TJ, this is Rascal Sutcliff, foreman of the Triple C since he and my dad started the place some forty-odd years ago."

"Nice to meet you, Mr. Sutcliff."

"My ninety-year-old pa is Mr. Sutcliff. Call me Rascal." He handed her the reins of the smaller horse. "This here's Buffy. She's Miss Cassidy's horse, but since Cassie hasn't bothered to visit in a while, you'll be doing us all a favor if you'd take Buffy out for a run. She's gettin' fat lazing around here all the time." He handed TJ several carrot pieces.

Buffy, a beautiful dun-colored quarter horse with black markings, tossed her mane when TJ approached. The mare whickered once and went for the carrots.

TJ stroked the velvet-soft muzzle. "We're going to do just fine, aren't we, Buffy?"

"I put the rifle in the sling," Rascal told Garrett. "Just in case you see that cougar that's been stalking the herd."

Garrett pocketed a box of ammunition. "That old cat been spotted near the far pasture?"

"Nah. But better safe than sorry, as your pa always says. You want a leg up, missy?"

TJ shook her head, set her left foot in the stirrup, and mounted. A second later she was in the saddle, but the stirrups dangled well below her feet. "Easy, girl." She patted the horse's neck and pulled in the slack on the reins.

"You're a short one. Seem to know what you're doing, though." Rascal adjusted the stirrup length on her left side.

"Been awhile. At least ten years. And never with a saddle like this."

"English, huh?" Rascal grunted as he adjusted the other stirrup.

"Yeah. My dad was stationed at Fort Knox. We had a little place out in the country with a neighbor who boarded horses. He taught me how to ride and let me help exercise them."

Rascal gave her a wink and tapped her leg. "How's that?"

She tested the fit. "Good."

"You ready?" Garrett asked.

She nodded. "Thanks, Rascal." Slipping her riding gloves on, TJ nudged the horse with her heel.

Garrett's mount wanted to frisk, not liking the slow pace, which made TJ grateful for Buffy's calm nature. "You know, old Devil Dog"—she gestured toward Garrett's horse—"seems a little boisterous this morning. Is he always this way?"

"Yeah, pretty much. Siggy likes to run. Don't suppose you want to go for a run?"

"Nope. Buffy and I are fine with walking. But you and old Hades there should go on and get the fidgets out."

"You sure?"

"Is it safe where we're going?"

"No place safer than the Triple C."

"What about the mountain lion?"

Garrett kept a tight rein, not letting the big quarter horse get away with anything. "Every once in a while a rogue cat turns up—one too old or too lazy to work for food. This one's been working the south pasture where the foothills come down to the range. Our path is north. You sure you're all right riding alone for a bit?"

She nodded and a grin spread across his face. The Garrett she'd come to know looked nothing like the carefree scamp sitting astride the giant horse beside her.

"Keep the river on your left and head for that rock outcropping that looks like an elephant."

TJ shaded her eyes and looked where he pointed. "An elephant? More like a giant's footstool."

"After Siggy works off some steam, I'll find you."

"Hmmm. You said that once before, cowboy." A lifetime ago.

"I meant it then. Same goes now. I'll always find you, TJ."

Uncomfortable with the unexpected intensity between them, she nudged Buffy into a reluctant trot. Before she could read more into his look than was there. "Have fun, boys."

"Put your hat on," he called after her. "It's gonna be hot today." He pulled the prancing Siggy around, and off they went, racing across the open range.

Man and horse merged into a single seamless entity, soon becoming a dot on the horizon. Moments later, she lost them in whorls of dust kicked up by Siggy's churning hooves. Garrett was every bit as high-spirited as the animal he rode. And

perhaps only half as tame.

TJ let out her breath. The distraction of Garrett Cameron couldn't have come at a more inopportune time. She had two goals right now—stay alive and testify at the trial.

She pushed thoughts of Garrett aside and concentrated on enjoying the ride. The terrain gradually changed, descending into a wide sweeping valley. Flat scrubland gave way to meadows filled with fragrant lavender. When Buffy ambled off to nose at the wildflowers dotting the land—white tricorn-shaped trillium, pink bitterroot, and wispy foxtail—TJ tugged gently on the reins and nudged her forward. A person could hyperventilate in air this clean and sweet.

A herd of horses grazed in the distance. Were they the elusive mustangs Mallory had spoken of? As TJ watched, several of the horses made their way down to the stream bisecting the valley. This must be where the Salmon River ran through the Triple C.

Foothills rose on the far side of the valley, growing into craggy silhouettes in the distance. TJ swayed with Buffy's easy gait. Except for the *clip-clop* of hooves and water chuckling over the rocks, she could almost imagine being in a watercolor painting. A deep, satisfying peace filled her. How easy it would be to fall in love with this land.

A pounding noise rose behind her. TJ glanced over her shoulder to see Garrett and Siggy thundering her way. Such raw power.

He reined in, slowing the big horse to a walk as he drew abreast. Siggy had worked up a lather and was blowing hard. He patted the big stallion's neck.

"Get it out of your system?" she asked.

"Yep. You miss us?"

Bemused by this teasing, fun-loving Garrett, TJ tilted her head and studied him. "Nope." She laughed when his face fell. "But I did fall under the spell of this place. It's beautiful." She waved her free arm to encompass the land.

Garrett's smile returned. "It is, isn't it? I didn't realize how much I loved this place until I came home last time. I can't imagine leaving it again."

They rode in comfortable silence for a long while, speaking only when Garrett pointed out a coyote slinking through hills across the river and a trio of bears foraging in the woods. He motioned her to stop when a small herd of elk emerged from the forested foothills to lap at the water's edge. Two hours into their ride, he pointed to a bend in the river where a weathered shed stood. "We'll stop there and give Siggy and Buffy a rest. Might be a surprise waiting for you, too."

TJ dismounted and looked around for something to loop Buffy's reins on. "Where do you tie the horses?"

"We don't. They might wander a bit, but they always come when called."

"I hope you're right, because I sure don't relish hiking

back to the ranch in new boots. Now, where's my surprise?"

Garrett pulled a small cardboard box from one of the saddlebags and handed it to her.

She opened it and peeked inside. Her nose wrinkled. "Worms?"

"Time for your first fishing lesson, angel."

Chapter Thirteen

He thought he had the little city girl figured out, and then she threw him another curve. There was something almost hedonistic about the way TJ enjoyed the outdoors—a real flower child.

She tumbled down the gentle knoll, squealing the whole way and then rolled around in the deep grass. She washed her face and hands in the stream and constructed a crown of posies for the horses. Siggy ate his, but Buffy still wore her coronet proudly.

Now she stood with her jeans rolled up to the knees, bare feet squishing in the mud at the river's edge. TJ gave a graceful flick and sent the fishing line arcing through the air to plop right smack in the middle of the river. She made casting look easy.

The bobber disappeared beneath the water only to pop up a second later. When the current caught it, she let the line play. Just a little—just like he showed her—and slowly reeled it in. For someone who'd never held a fishing pole before today, she caught on fast. Even wanted to bait her own hook. She might have hair like Allie's, but any similarity between the two women ended there.

Garrett snorted when TJ wrinkled her pert little nose and concentrated on baiting the hook the first time. He sank down on a grassy patch and leaned back on his elbows, a smile crooking his mouth. She'd been casting for the better part of an hour with nary a bite.

He hated dragging her away with nothing to show for her efforts, but the sun had shifted to the down side of day. They still had to get to the far pasture before heading home. He'd give her a few more minutes.

A shriek made him bolt to his feet.

"I got one. I got one!" TJ jumped around, tugging hard on the pole, not reeling in the line like she was supposed to.

He started toward her. "Use the reel, angel. You're gonna lose …"

Too late. A fish shot out of the water on a direct trajectory for TJ. She screamed, ducking at the last moment. The small brown trout hit the ground, stunned. But then it started thrashing.

TJ squealed, dropped the fishing pole, and jumped away. She tripped and landed on her bottom, scrabbling backward.

He couldn't help it. A gut-deep guffaw erupted.

"Stop laughing and help me. He's going to hurt himself." She hurried over to the flopping fish, unsure what to do. When it slimed her bare foot, she let out another screech and danced away. "Eeeew!"

Her antics set him off again. A spate of belly laughs left him gasping for breath with tears blurring his vision. When was the last time he'd seen something so funny?

Once he could draw a breath, Garrett wiped the tears away. The rod lay on the ground and TJ held the fishing line in her fingers, slowly hauling the flopping trout across the grass. Her eyes were narrowed in fierce determination, a look that almost stole what little sanity he had left.

"Stop laughing, you big … I mean … Garrett! Help me. What do I do?"

Garrett choked back spasms of laughter, moved to her side, picked up the pole, and reeled in the line until the fish dangled in mid-air. Grabbing the fishing line above the hook, he ran his other hand down the line over the fish's head. "Watch me. Ease your hand over the fish's head like this. Keep a firm grip and move down the body. You want those fins retracted, otherwise they'll rip your skin." He continued sliding his hand down over the fish's body until he had the little trout in a firm grip, spiky fins pinned. "Now, you try it."

Garrett felt a ridiculous surge of pride when she nudged her way under his arm and ran her small hand down the line. He made sure she wouldn't get finned before removing his hand. She felt good in his arms. A perfect fit.

"Ugh! He's slimy."

There went that cute little button nose again, squenching up like she smelled something bad. "Well done, Ms.

McKendrick. You caught your first fish."

TJ looked up at him with eyes filled with pride. But then the excitement dimmed. "What do we do with him?"

"You want to learn how to clean a fish?" Garrett pulled a pocketknife from his pocket.

"No! Uh … no. I mean, I …"

"It's okay. We don't have anything to keep it in anyway."

"So, we just leave him here? To die?"

Amusement bubbled up again. He'd never enjoyed fishing so much. "Nah. We let it go. Catch and release. Hold tight with that hand. Don't let it wiggle loose. Now, use your other hand and work the hook out."

She gave the hook a feeble twitch. "It's hurting him."

The laughter would strangle him if he had to choke it back much longer. "He's got a hook punched through his lip, angel. It'll only hurt for a minute. Go on. Give the poor thing some relief. You can do it."

She refocused her attention and carefully jiggled the hook free of the fish's mouth.

"Good girl. Now throw it back in the water."

Of course she wouldn't throw it. TJ walked back to bank and eased the traumatized fish into the shallow water. "There you go, little fella."

The little brown trout darted away.

TJ swished her hands in the water and looked over her shoulder at Garrett. Who knew such a simple pleasure like fishing would light up her face like the sun?

He squatted beside her and rinsed his hands, trying hard to keep a straight face. No luck. The laughter he'd been holding in burst forth again.

He stood and drew her upright, wrapped her in his arms, and lifting her high against his chest, swung around in circles. "I swear you're the most fun I've had in forever."

"Put me down, you crazy cowboy."

Her protest held too much delight. Her arms went around his neck. "You're making me dizzy."

The sound of her giggling was a thing of beauty that surely made the angels in heaven smile. He let her slide to her feet, but he didn't let go. She branded him with those fingers trailing down his chest. This little slip of a woman turned his brain to mush.

In the hidden recesses of his mind, a thought struggled to be heard, screaming "bad idea" and "too fast." Women wanted commitment, something he was allergic to. And yet, TJ pulled him like a flame drawing an unsuspecting moth.

She dropped her chin, hiding her eyes. Her body tensed in his arms as though sensing the change in him. Her laughter quieted.

"TJ?" A wealth of meaning lay in the question he made of her name.

She took a long quivery breath before looking up. Big blue eyes, the color of the heavens on a perfect sunny day,

shattered what defenses he had left. Her gaze seemed filled with guileless anticipation. "Yes," she answered, her voice a husky whisper.

A question? Or an answer? Did she want this, too?

One kiss—that's all—to see if she tasted as sweet as he imagined. Garrett lowered his head until his mouth hovered above hers. Warm, moist breath teased. When she didn't pull away, he kissed her.

The need for air made him pull back long moments later. Sanity returned bit by bit.

Garrett held her head with both his hands, the calloused pads of his thumbs stroking the silky softness of her cheeks while he committed every inch of her face to memory.

She clutched his wrists. Long, sooty lashes drooped against her cheeks. Her parted lips, plump and inviting, turned up at the corners.

Oh man, he was a goner.

Letting her go proved to be one of the hardest things he'd ever done, but he sure didn't want to scare her off by rushing. Garrett stepped back and let his hands fall to his side. "We'd best be moving along now. Still a ways to go before we reach the far pasture. Let's put the fishing poles back in the shed."

They rode the rest of the way in silence, conversation unnecessary. When the dilapidated barn came into view, TJ pointed. "It that where we're heading?"

"Yep."

"Thank goodness."

"What's the matter? You not enjoying the ride?"

The scowl TJ settled on him as she shifted in the saddle set his lips twitching again.

"Tell you what. Let me get the salt lick taken care of, and we'll have our picnic. Give your backside a rest. Deal?"

"Deal. I'm starving. How can I help?"

He stepped down out of the saddle. "Here, take this." He untied the blanket roll behind his saddle and handed it to her. "Spread it under the trees over there." He filched a paper sack from one of the saddlebags and tossed it to her. "And don't eat all the brownies. I'll be back in fifteen minutes."

"Wait—what's a salt lick?"

"Exactly that. A block of salt for the animals to lick. Kind of like Gatorade, only for horses. And not sweet or liquid. Helps replenish minerals and other nutrients when the summer heat hits."

"Don't you want some help?"

"Can you lug fifty pounds from the barn to the middle of the pasture?"

She thought about it for two seconds. "I'll set the food out."

"Smart girl. Be right back."

When Garrett returned, TJ lay on her belly, propped up on her elbows. She stared at an unwrapped sandwich on the blanket in front of her. "Peanut butter and jelly, Garrett?

Really? After the feast this morning, I expected a hearty campfire with meat and beans."

Dousing his head with water from the canteen, Garrett used his bandana to mop his face and neck. "Lots of protein in peanut butter and no refrigeration needed. The perfect food." He dropped to a seated position across from TJ, flexing his right shoulder in circles to ease the pinch under his shoulder blade. He inhaled two sandwiches and one of the brownies.

"What's wrong with your shoulder?"

"Nothing. Got a catch in my back. It'll ease in a bit."

Pushing to her knees, TJ crawled around behind him. "Well, maybe there's something I can help with after all."

He eyed her with suspicion. "What?"

"Bet you didn't know I worked my way through college as a massage therapist. I used to give chair massages in business offices. I'm pretty good."

Garrett's mind reeled from the images conjured by her words. "Uh, no need. I'm fine."

"Shut up, take your shirt off, and lie on your stomach."

Her touch started light, skimming over his back in ever widening swirls, warming his skin. She zoned in on the source of his discomfort, spreading heat as the pressure increased. When she hit the knot under his right shoulder blade, Garrett moaned. All the libidinous thoughts sailed away, lost in the agonizing hurt-so-good magic her hands wrought. Fifteen minutes later, he was a boneless mess, willing to crawl, beg, or stand on his head if she asked.

"Why don't you rest for a little? Keep that trapezoid loose before you climb back on that tornado you call a horse. I'll wander around."

He mumbled something unintelligible that was meant to be, "Don't go far." And then he drifted.

Sometime later—he had no idea how long—Garrett jerked awake with a feeling like butterflies tickling the back of his neck. A sensation he'd learned not to ignore.

The sun had dropped lower than he liked. Past time they started home. Had he really dozed off? "TJ?"

Climbing to his feet, he slipped his shirt on. She was nowhere in sight. "TJ," he called a little louder.

The horses grazed nearby, heads lowered and tails swishing. Insects buzzed. Birds flitted from tree to tree. Everything seemed tranquil—except for the insistent, crawling awareness that put him on full alert. Garrett whistled for Siggy. When the big quarter horse plodded to him, he pulled the rifle from the sling.

"TJ!" he yelled, this time cupping his hands around his mouth. He walked toward the river, looking upstream and down. "TJ!"

There were rapids not more than a half mile from here. Had she fallen in the river?

A small copse of trees rose behind the barn. Maybe she went exploring in the forest. Got lost or twisted her ankle. He could picture her lying on the ground, unable to walk. Or maybe she'd gone into the old barn. Up to the loft.

Worry wrapped him in a fog. And then a long scream rent the air, making his flesh crawl.

"TJ!"

When it came again, he recognized the sound. Not TJ. The cougar. The one they'd dubbed the Mountain Screamer. Garrett zeroed in on the sound, fixing the location. The rocks jutting out over the river—at the edge of the trees. A good thousand yards. Too far. His lungs convulsed in a rush of adrenalin as he set off at a dead run. "TJ!"

"Garrett!"

Relief flooded him. He slowed his pace as he neared the rocks, searching … scanning … there! She crouched near where the trees crept close to the water's edge.

The animal's screech came again, and Garrett's blood froze.

The cat sat perched on a limb, well within leaping distance of the outcropping below where TJ slowly backed away. The cougar's muzzle pulled back in a snarl, exposing lethal fangs. He was a big sucker. Had to be upward of two hundred pounds. Mangy fur and rail-like ribs gave testament of the aged cougar's inability to find prey. Until now. The cat's bulky muscles bunched. Tensed.

Garrett threw the rifle up against his shoulder, heart thundering like a herd of stampeding mustangs. One shot. He had one shot. His eye found the sight. The crosshairs locked on the mountain lion.

His aim led the cougar as the animal launched itself forward. Vicious hissing filled the air … and then cut off mid-cry. The rifle shot echoed in the silence. The mountain lion hit the rocks with a sickening thud, mere feet from where TJ cringed.

When he reached the rocks, TJ rushed into his arms, burrowing like she wanted to crawl inside his skin. She buried her face in his chest with harsh sobs wracking her body.

Corrosive bile filled Garrett's throat. His legs trembled. "TJ," he whispered, squeezing her like he'd never let go. "Shhh. It's okay." He stroked her hair with one hand, while the other tried to press her even closer. "I've got you, angel."

Her sobs slowed, changed to shudders. She put her palms against his chest and squirmed.

He couldn't let her go at first, not until she yanked her shirttail from her pants and used it to wipe her eyes and nose.

"What do you say we go home?"

She nodded.

He picked up the abandoned rifle, still holding her to his side with one arm, and led her to the horses. Anger, fierce and scorching, made his stomach clench. He'd fought it often enough, but the wrath wouldn't be contained this time. He'd fallen asleep. Asleep! A court-martial offense. And left her vulnerable. Defenseless.

Imperfect Wings

"Why'd you wander so far, TJ?"

She managed a snuffling answer. "I f-found a whole school of t-trout, just like the one I caught. They stayed together, moving as a group. I f-followed them downstream where they h-hid under the rock."

Fish? She'd tied his guts up like tangled yarn for a *school* of trout? He'd almost lost his ever-loving mind! Letting his breath out, he said through clenched teeth, "It's called a hover—a *hover* of trout. Not a school."

She must have sensed his rising anger. Or heard the barely contained fury in his voice. She moved away, wary.

Garrett struggled for control, not wanting to add to her fright. Cool under fire. That was him. The calm one his team looked to for assurance and reason in the worst of situations. He never let danger sway good judgment, never let fear influence his actions. But that shot …

Pure luck. Even with his training, to make a reaction hit on a moving target, with no time to line it up—impossible.

The fear he'd known in that moment unmanned him. "Let's go." He grabbed TJ's arm and hustled her along, making her skip to keep up. A second later, he gave a shrill whistle that brought both horses on the run.

"Let go!" TJ tried to wriggle out of his hold. "You're hurting me."

Garrett released her. She'd done nothing wrong. He was the one at fault. He'd failed to keep her safe.

Unable to look her in the eye, he growled over one shoulder. "Pack up. We're leaving."

They worked quickly to stow the picnic things in the saddlebags. When he offered his hands to boost her to the saddle, she squeaked at being tossed so high and had to scramble to keep from flying over the other side.

"What is your problem?"

Garrett ignored her.

He set a bruising pace on the return ride, one that allowed no opportunity for talk.

TJ McKendrick had breached his defenses. She'd bored deep into his well-protected heart and distracted him from the mission, from his responsibility. She'd almost died on his watch, a victim of a stinking mountain lion.

It couldn't happen again.

Imperfect Wings

Chapter Fourteen

The big red barn appeared in the distance and Garrett breathed a sigh of relief. Less than a mile now and the interminable ride would end. When they got back to the house, he would pass TJ off to one of his brothers. Find some much needed space and get a handle on his anger … figure out what to do about the dangerous fascination he had for her. His hands still shook from seeing the cougar spring, those lethal claws extended.

He shuddered, seeing the event unfold again … and reached the same conclusion. The odds were so far against making a kill shot at that distance, with no time to analyze wind gusts or trajectory and only a split-second to raise the rifle, point, and shoot. Had to be divine intervention. Nothing else made sense. Those few life-or-death seconds would give him nightmares for the rest of his life.

But something else rattled him. He glanced over at TJ and bam! Just looking at her made his heart lurch. She'd set her hooks in him, sure as sugar. And he hadn't seen it coming. The irony was she didn't know. When she did figure it out …

That thought left him spitless.

Garrett dismounted outside the corral and took her horse's reins. "I'll tend the horses. Go get cleaned up for supper."

TJ rolled her eyes before swinging a leg over the buckskin's rump to drop to the ground. "I rode Buffy. I'll take care of her." With her nose in the air, she snatched the leather straps out of his hand.

A calmer, saner part of him wanted to smile at her feistiness. None of what happened today was her fault, but a perverse demon rode him, fanning the unreasonable anger that had plagued him his whole life. Garrett covered the distance between them in three long strides and plucked Buffy's reins from TJ's hands. "I said I would deal with the horses, princess."

She tried to grab them back, but he raised them out of her reach.

"You have no right—"

"I own these horses. And the barn. I have every right."

TJ planted herself in his path, arms crossed over her chest and chin jutting out. She had that muley look women sometimes get.

"Buffy is my responsibility."

"Not this time."

Her hands went to her hips, a favorite stance when upset. Her frown deepened. "Why are you acting like this? Why do you want to spoil an almost perfect day? We had a great time. Deal with it."

Because women wanted more than a man wanted to give. TJ and Allie shared that trait. "Nothing special about it, except you almost got yourself killed. Now, go on up to the house like a good little girl."

Her face turned bright red, but then the fire in her eyes died out, replaced by hurt. Her lower lip quivered before she turned on her heel and walked away.

And didn't that make him feel ten feet tall? Watching her go almost killed him. Great. Where was Wade when you needed him? Or Jonas? Both of his brothers could sweet-talk a woman better than him. "TJ, wait."

She stopped but kept her back to him.

"Look, I'm sorry. I don't want to hurt your feelings."

She turned then and studied him. "I upset your carefully ordered little world, don't I?"

"What? No. I mean ... Look, I was supposed to protect you."

"I know better than to wander off like that, Garrett. The danger from the cougar was my fault. Yours lies in starting something you have no intention of finishing."

Hearing the truth of her words made him flinch. Allie had always tiptoed around his black moods. TJ didn't bat an eyelash. "We shared a friendly kiss. Don't make too much of it."

An unladylike snort made him flush. "I was there, remember? Friendly isn't exactly how I would describe the

way you stuck your tongue down my throat."

Stuck his tongue …? "My mistake. I never meant to put a fairytale in your head. It won't happen again."

She snorted again, louder this time.

"Look, I'm not in the market for happily-ever-after. Running a ranch takes sweat and blood and every ounce of a man's soul. And that's only because that's all there is to give. Sure I like a little female companionship now and then, but it doesn't mean I want a woman cluttering up my life."

"Cluttering up your life? You think that I …?"

Affronted didn't begin to describe the way TJ looked. Allie would've pouted. Maybe teased a little. She knew better than to poke a bear with a stick. Honest to Pete, he had no idea how to deal with *this* woman. "Honey, you're a little too young and way too soft for the likes of me. You deserve someone more—"

"That's it!" She stamped her foot. "I am *not* your *honey*. Don't call me *angel*. Or *darlin'*. And especially not *little girl*. You, Garrett Cameron"—she stormed up to him breathing fire and jabbed a finger in his chest—"are a coward. You're so afraid I might ask for more than you're willing to give. But worse, you're scared to death you might actually want to give it. Face it, cowboy. You need to see me as too young and too soft so the fact that you don't isn't very consoling."

He frowned and rubbed his chest where she'd poked him. When did the subject change from her safety to his dysfunctional love life? Goes to show a man can't trust simple attraction. And why did they have to talk in riddles? There wasn't a man on earth who could figure out what she said.

Behind him, the horses grew restless. He understood how they felt. "Let me get this straight. You're saying I see you as a woman, but I don't want to see you as a woman, and you don't like that?"

"Do you deny it?"

"Yes. Wait … no." The beginnings of a headache stirred. He yanked off his hat and hurled it to the floor. His voice rose, a sure sign he'd lost control of the situation. "I don't have a clue what you just said, and I sure don't know how to answer without digging myself in deeper."

"Both of you—get outta my barn. Now!"

The angry shout had Garrett and TJ whirling around to see Rascal Sutcliff stomp their way. He snatched both sets of reins from Garrett. "These horses have been worked hard. They deserve better than to stand around and listen to you two jawing all nice-nasty at each other." He left, pulling Buffy and Siggy after him.

After a long, drawn out silence TJ said, "Nice-nasty?"

Just like that, his anger disappeared. Garrett stifled a smile at her perplexed tone. "Means polite venom."

Time to retreat while the cease-fire held. Sometimes a man had to be smart enough to know when he couldn't win a battle. Garrett turned to walk away but stopped when she

tugged at his arm.

"Garrett? I really enjoyed our ride today. Fishing and seeing your land. Please don't ruin it for me. I don't understand what I did to make you so angry, but I'm truly sorry. Can we just forget about the kiss and the cougar and be friends?"

It took every bit of his control to keep from giving in to the sweet entreaty. Life had forced TJ to be tough, but she had a soft heart and a giving nature. She was always putting others ahead of herself. Even now, after he'd hurt her with his foolish actions and careless words, she wanted to make everything better.

And blast it. He didn't want to forget that kiss. No way friendship would be enough now. What he really wanted was to hide her away and keep her all to himself. But that wasn't an option. Neutralizing Castillo and the senator might be the only way to end this. That meant TJ had to testify. Until then, she needed someone with a clear head. One of them had to be strong enough to step away before he screwed up and got her killed.

"There's nothing to forget, TJ. You didn't do anything wrong. Now, get on up to the house and let me do my job."

Hurt filled her eyes a second time before she schooled her features.

Garrett felt bile rising up his throat. She hadn't worn that closed off look all day. Now he felt like he'd kicked a puppy.

She walked away, chin held high and boot heels thudding

on the soft earthen floor.

It was better this way. At least for now.

Jonas intercepted him with a hard shove when Garrett stepped into the corral. "Don't think Rascal wants your help."

Garrett looked over at their old foreman. Rascal had already stripped the saddles and blankets from the horses and had currycomb in hand. "You're probably right. What's got you riled up?"

"I swear, you hurt her again and I'll show you how a little brother grows up. TJ's not a one-night stand."

The anger Garrett had held in check all afternoon burst free. He got in Jonas's face. "I'm not the one trying to nail anything that wears a skirt. And I don't do one-nighters."

"Of course not. That'd be too much of a commitment, wouldn't it?"

Garrett shoved him then. "You're outta line."

Jonas stumbled, caught his balance, and came up swinging.

Garrett's head snapped back from the sucker punch, but he didn't go down. "You sure you want to do this, Jo?"

Wade appeared and stepped between them. "Whoa, boys. Much as I hate to interrupt a good fight, I doubt Mom wants to see your beautiful pusses all banged up."

"Mom and Dad are back?" Jonas asked, flexing his bruised fingers.

"Yep. Mallory picked them up from the airport about two

hours ago. You're lucky Dad went over to the big barn first thing to check on the foals. Otherwise, he'd be the one talking. Mom's in the kitchen, so you know what that means. Be at the dinner table on time, washed up, and wearing clean clothes. I figure that gives you about …" He glanced at his watch. "Oh…twenty minutes."

Garrett pointed a finger at Jonas. "We're not done, little brother."

Jonas glared back. "Yeah, we are. You remember what I said." He turned and loped off toward the house.

"Thought you had that anger stuff under control. What happened?"

Garrett slapped his dusty hat against his leg.

"Okay, how about Jonas's attitude. That have anything to do with TJ crying?"

Garrett looked away. She was crying? "Ask Mallory to warn TJ about Mom and Dad being home while I get cleaned up. She needs to know about the six o'clock dinner rule."

"Good idea."

"Wade, thanks, man. I owe you."

"Nah, it's TJ you owe. If you're playing her, you're gonna get your butt kicked—by me, Jonas, James, and Rascal. Probably Mallory and Dad, too. And then Mom will take a bullwhip to what's left."

Garrett opened his mouth, but his brother held up a palm. "TJ's safety comes first, and since you're the most capable man to look after her, she's your responsibility. Get your head in the game. Let's go. Clock's ticking."

Twenty minutes later, with his hair still damp from the shower, Garrett made it downstairs with seconds to spare. The other men had already moved into the dining room.

His father came over and slung an arm around his shoulder. "Place looks good, son. Real good. Makes me proud."

The words spread a balm over Garrett's wounded soul. Dad didn't give praise lightly. His old man had beaten the odds the old-fashioned way. Through hard work and determination, he'd built the Triple C Ranch from a few wild mustangs and a patch of scrubland nobody wanted into the multi-million dollar operation it was today. A legacy a son could be proud of.

The tension in his shoulders eased. His dad would step in if Garrett needed to focus his full attention on TJ. He wouldn't have to worry about neglecting the ranch.

At six o'clock sharp, his sister and mom came in carrying platters of food. There was no sign of TJ.

Mallory took the middle seat next to James on one side of the table. Garrett and his brothers sat on the other side while Cate took her usual place at the end opposite her husband. The seat between Mallory and their father, the one across from Garrett, remained empty.

Had he upset her that much?

After Cody said grace, Jonas reached for the platter of

grilled trout filets, one of their mother's special recipes
flavored with her secret marinade.

"Mom, tell us all about Spain," Wade encouraged. "And
don't skimp on the juicy parts, either. We know you didn't sign
books and look at horses every day."

His mom and dad took turns talking about their trip while
everyone ignored the elephant in the room—the clean plate and
empty chair. When the conversation finally flagged, his dad
cleared his throat.

"Well, I think we've avoided the subject of our absent
guest long enough. Now, who's gonna tell your momma and
me about this mysterious person? Why she's here but can't join
us for dinner?"

Everybody looked at Garrett.

Taking a deep breath he said, "Her name is TJ
McKendrick."

An unexpected voice interrupted him. "Hello, everyone."

TJ stood in the doorway dressed in snug jeans and a bright
yellow tee shirt, looking like a ray of sunshine.

"I'm sorry for being late to your table, Mrs. Cameron. No.
Please don't get up," she insisted when the men started to rise.
"I'm not hungry, but if you don't mind, I'd like to sit with you.
Perhaps I can answer Mr. Cameron's questions while you
finish supper?"

"Of course, dear. Have a seat." His mother's voice
remained neutral. She'd never been one for snap judgments.

The men ignored TJ's request to stay seated. They sat down again once she took the seat next to Mallory.

"My name is Trevian Jane McKendrick. Trevian is an old family name on my father's side, but it prompts a lot of questions. TJ is simpler."

Mallory squeezed one of TJ's hands.

"Two years ago, I went to Honduras. While there, I witnessed a murder. The man who died was an American Drug Enforcement agent. His murderer, also an American, worked for a U.S. senator. Garrett and James were part of the team that rescued me."

He'd always been reticent about his clandestine activities, but the look his parents turned on Garrett promised a more forthcoming response soon. Across the table, James squirmed.

"The killer was indicted and will stand trial soon. The man they were visiting in Honduras, a local drug dealer, avoided extradition and remains free, but he stands to lose a great deal of money—possibly his life—if I testify. Because of the threat he poses, I've been in hiding since I left Central America."

Forks stopped in mid-air, food forgotten, all eyes trained on TJ.

Garrett poured her a glass of water from the pitcher on the sideboard.

"Thank you," she said without looking at him.

An hour ago, the girl was a quivering mess of hurt and rejection. Now, she held her head high and faced an uncertain

future with conviction and determination. She might be impossibly soft, but TJ had an underlying core of iron.

A memory surfaced, a perfect recollection of her amazingly expressive blue eyes staring up from where she lay on the jungle floor. Vulnerable, outraged, scared to death, and yet courageous enough to fight off six grown men—and do some damage.

TJ would always do what had to be done, no matter the cost. That same conviction filled her eyes now. Life on an Idaho ranch wouldn't scare her one whit.

His heart skipped a beat with the realization that he'd never stood a chance against her.

"Ten days ago, Don Castillo's thugs found me, but Aaron, one of Garrett's former teammates who'd been assigned to watch over me, helped me get away. He sent me here. Said I'd be safe until the trial."

She scooted her chair back and stood. "I was frightened, with nowhere else to go, so I came here without giving any thought to the ramifications. I'm leaving tonight, but I thought you deserved an explanation first. Thank you for taking me in."

Garrett's chest tightened. He hadn't understood the burden TJ carried: guilt for the evil that followed her. Grief over the destruction of so many lives. It didn't matter that the load didn't belong to her. She claimed it. Shouldered it alone.

Mallory, James, Wade, and Jonas all rose with her, protesting her leaving. They quieted when she held up a hand.

"Mallory, thank you for being my friend. James, I need to get in touch with Aaron. He's the only one who knows the location of the trial." She offered a smile to the others. "Wade, I'm sorry I can't stay. Jonas, thank you for making me laugh again. And Mr. and Mrs. Cameron, I know you weren't consulted, but thank you for allowing me to stay in your lovely home."

Garrett's lungs shut down. She couldn't leave yet. She needed him to keep her safe.

When TJ looked across the table, she wouldn't meet his eyes, focusing instead somewhere between his chin and sternum. "Garrett, I never thanked you for saving my life—both in Honduras and again today."

Jonas was the first to break the stunned silence. "What do you mean he saved your life today?"

"You promised to help me with the Bar M reports," Wade whined. "I'll never meet the deadline without you."

"Miz Tillberry is expecting us for tea this week," Mallory added.

Even his mother had something to say. "Mallory's throwing Cody and me a welcome home party, but as usual she's dumped the planning in my lap. I hoped you'd help."

Garrett surged to his feet, knocking his chair over. "You're not going anywhere, angel. You're staying right here where I can keep an eye on you."

TJ stared at him like he'd grown a snout and oinked.

The others fell quiet.

His father, the only one still seated, patted his mouth with the napkin and slowly rose. "I think what this crazy family is trying to say, young lady, is please sit down. We'd like to discuss your options a bit more."

Chapter Fifteen

TJ slipped outside and let the night cloak her as she walked toward the barn. Lifting her face to the heavens, she welcomed the caress of the night's gentle breeze, her breaths deepening with each stride.

The storm from earlier in the day left a clean feeling in the air, lightly scented with sweet honeysuckle, mown hay, and that singular smell that lingered after a good rain. Near the barn, another unmistakable odor joined the mix. Horse manure.

She smothered a chuckle. Two years ago, the earthy aromas would have sent her running for an air-conditioned room with her nose pinched between her fingers. After a sojourn in the poorest village of Honduras, a stint in rural Mississippi, and now her stay on a horse ranch in Nowhere, Idaho, TJ had a new perspective. Manure was a fact of life here. Funny, how time and circumstances changed one's outlook.

The heavy barn door required an extra heave to muscle it open enough so she could squeeze inside. A quick visit with Buffy and the other horses, that's all she wanted. A few minutes alone. With no one hovering. That wasn't too much to

ask, was it? Cody wouldn't miss her. Garrett's father never stirred from his study in the evening. And the vague—"Cate, I think I'll go up to my room now"—she'd given his mother wasn't precisely lying. She *had* gone upstairs. And then right back down to creep out the kitchen door.

TJ didn't like tricking Mr. and Mrs. Cameron, but the opportunity proved too golden to pass up. For the first time in two weeks, since Garrett imposed house arrest to keep her hidden, all of her self-appointed watchdogs missed dinner. With luck, she'd return before anyone missed her.

Two emergency bulbs cast a weak glow inside the barn. In the last stall, Buffy moved restlessly.

"Hey, girl." TJ offered the apple chunks. "I'm sorry I haven't been out to see you in a while, but Garrett's got me under lock and key. I had to sneak out tonight like a thief."

Apple gone, Buffy whickered and tossed her head.

"You feeling cooped up, too? Eat, sleep, putter around the house, eat some more, sleep some more." She added a mocking twang. "'Stay away from the windows in case someone wants to take a potshot at you, darlin'. And don't be calling nobody.' Aaaggh! I'm not the one supposed to be in prison."

TJ found a soft-bristle brush and joined Buffy inside the stall. She loved currying the horse's satiny flanks. With a pat on Buffy's side, she added, "No offense, girl, but you're developing some serious girth here. If this is what confinement does to you, I'm staging a jail break."

Buffy shifted her weight, bumping TJ against the stall wall.

"I can take a hint." She smiled and resumed the long brush strokes. The horse's dun colored coat gleamed in the dim light.

"How about you and me blow this place? Ride off into the sunset." A silent moment passed while TJ considered the idea. "We'd have to ride really far and fast because you-know-who will go nuts when he finds us gone." She paused again and shook her head. "Nah. Wouldn't work. He'd track us down and drag us back, and then there'd be a price to pay. Still, it might be worth it to shake things up a little. Shake *him* up."

A man cleared his throat behind her.

"Aaaeeee!" TJ whirled, wielding the brush like a weapon. She ducked under the horse's head, putting Buffy between her and the intruder. Soft bristles wouldn't inflict much damage, but the wooden handle might hurt him.

The shadows coalesced. A man stepped forward, his hands held wide at his sides.

"Garrett! You scared me!" Her heart slowed a fraction. He hadn't made a sound. The man moved like a ghost. "What are you doing here?"

Startled as she was, all the trembling her arms and legs were doing couldn't be attributed solely to fright. Why did every one of her brain cells hum whenever he came near?

"I think the better question is what are *you* doing here? I thought we agreed you'd stay in the house, out of sight, unless

one of us went with you. How'd you get by Wade?"

Resentment gave her voice an edge. "Did you draw straws and Wade got the short one?" She turned her back on Garrett and resumed her work on the horse. "I don't need a babysitter."

He chuckled, a soft, seductive little laugh. "We're not your sitters, and you're sure not a baby. I thought you understood."

"You didn't think it necessary when I first arrived," she said over her shoulder. "We went out to eat. And to church. I went shopping with Mallory. There's no way Don Castillo could track me here, but you want me locked up anyway. I can't even look out the window because someone might see me."

He chuckled but then grew serious. "I made a mistake. Is that what you want to hear? It was arrogant and stupid, but I never considered you might not be safe here."

"What changed your mind?" TJ kept her focus on Buffy. Every time she looked in his eyes, she caved to whatever he wanted.

"James showed me some pictures the night after we … uh … argued … when you said you were leaving. He took them the first day you arrived. Your face was black and blue."

The harsh rasp of his voice made her risk a glance.

"I guess I've been out of action too long. My heart tells me you're safe here because it's my home. I know it like the back of my hand and can't imagine how a stranger could infiltrate the Triple C. The first lesson I learned in the service is that evil is alive and well and thrives in the world. Lesson two was evil doesn't follow the same rules we do. If someone wants to hurt you bad enough, and I believe Castillo is desperate, nowhere is completely safe. Not backwoods Mississippi. Not even here in Idaho surrounded by the toughest, meanest men alive. I won't let him have another crack at you."

His steely voice and deadly expression made TJ shiver. Garrett personified warrior with an indomitable will and all the confidence in the world. More important, he held to a fierce code of honor. She felt safe with Garrett.

But she was only a responsibility to him. He didn't want anything more. Not even to be friends. Could she get through a few more weeks of being close enough to touch him but also close enough to see his indifference? Did she have a choice?

Her chin dropped. "You're smothering me."

"Look at me, TJ."

Buffy shifted in the stall. The horse made a good diversion, but Garrett wouldn't be ignored much longer. TJ turned around and felt the full impact of his stare. Those eyes of his, the color of a fathomless ocean in the daytime, had darkened in the gloom.

He opened Buffy's gate and beckoned her out. "You didn't answer. How'd you slip away from my brother?"

"Wade's not here," she mumbled. With a last pat for the

horse, TJ closed the stall gate behind her.

"Where is he?"

She sighed. "We finished the Bar M contract this afternoon. He went into town. Wanted to make sure the packet got out today."

"And probably stopped off at Sidewinder's afterwards. I'll break his head this time. Why'd you come out here alone, TJ? Why didn't Dad come with you?"

"Your dad doesn't know I'm gone. I needed some fresh air. A little alone time."

"Alone time? You've been working in Mom's office by yourself for two solid weeks."

She snorted. "Obviously, you have no idea how many people pass through that front door every day. There is no way a person could be alone in your house."

For a writer, the interior room seemed perfect. Cate claimed she could shut the door and get lost in one of her story worlds.

"You can shut the door."

TJ forced back a shudder as dark memories rose unbidden. They'd been growing with each day she remained tucked inside the house. Why'd he have to go there now? A fantasy might be ideal for a writer, but she needed the solid touch of reality. And space. A lot more room than the small office offered.

"What about your bedroom," he persisted. "No one would intrude there, except maybe Mallory."

His attempt to lighten the mood fell short. Instead, another shudder built like a wave and the ugly past washed over her. She didn't want him to see her like this. Not now. She turned to leave, stumbled, and grabbed blindly for the rails of Buffy's stall.

"TJ?" His hands steadied her.

She shrugged away from him, unable to halt the bitter memories. *"You are such a bad child. Why do you force me to punish you?"* Mother had a beautiful voice. When she sang, the birds quieted to listen. But when six-year-old TJ pushed her beyond reason, the sweetness disappeared. *"You'll stay in your room until you've learned your lesson."* Lessons that could take days, with no food or water. And the shame of relieving herself in a corner of the room. Or when she was really bad, locked in the closet. That small, dark place. To this day she still left her bedroom door ajar at night.

Dr. Horton's explanation, overheard when father insisted her mother seek treatment, remained engraved in TJ's mind. The words, even after all the years, came with perfect recall. *"The patient's grasp on reality is fragile. With her spouse—her emotional support structure—absent for long periods of time, the ordeal of parenting an overactive child is daunting. The discipline she employs might be unorthodox, but it works for her. She would never inflict physical harm on her child."*

Tamping down a rush of nausea, she shoved the past away. Age might have provided an adult perspective, but in her

child's heart the burden of guilt lingered. Down deep she knew she'd provoked her mother's need for drugs, an addiction that consumed the vivacious woman. And of course TJ had been driving when the terrible accident occurred.

"TJ? Talk to me, baby. What is it?"

Garrett's voice startled her from the unwelcome reverie, his deep baritone drawing her back to the present. She took a shuddering breath and tried to slow her racing heart. His eyes held questions she didn't want to answer.

"Nothing," she murmured. His pity would destroy her.

"You went away for a moment."

"I don't know what you're talking about. I'm going back to the house now."

He caught her arm when she would have walked away. "Wait. Much as I want to know what's bothering you, I won't press it right now. But you will tell me one day. Right now, there's something else we need to discuss."

With a pointed look at the hand clutching her arm, she arched an eyebrow and glared at him. His grip loosened, and she pulled free.

Garrett's features took on a hard cast. "James called. It seems Kyle—you remember Kyle? His new deputy?"

How could she forget Kyle? He'd looked so familiar. Like she'd know someone who looked like he belonged on a modeling runway. Kyle had shadowed Mallory and her when they'd gone shopping. A lifetime ago. "Yes."

"He reported some unusual traffic yesterday. A black sedan rolled into town with two men in suits and sunglasses. That in itself isn't unusual. We do have an occasional businessman come through."

TJ's heart picked up speed again. "You think …?"

"I don't know what to think yet, but I can tell you what I feel—the same thing that's got James and Kyle in a dither has the skin on my neck crawling. It wasn't just one black car. There were four. Came in from different directions, driving through town nice and slow. Eight men, all muscle. They didn't stay long, and there's been no sign of them since." His eyes bore into hers. "They stopped at a few places to ask questions. And show your picture."

"I have to get out of here! I have to leave. Now. Tonight. Before they find me here!" She turned to rush back to the house, mumbling a prayer under her breath. "Oh, please, Lord. Don't let more innocent people get hurt because of me."

Garrett caught her before she managed two steps. He whirled her around to face him with a gentle shake. "Calm down, angel. Breathe. Nothing's going to happen tonight. If these city boys were sent by the don, we'll find out soon enough. Right now, they don't know for sure that you're here. That uncertainty will make them hesitant to do anything."

Could she believe him? Did she dare?

"Just to be sure, I've relocated a dozen of the ranch hands over to the house. They're bunking down in the other side of

the barn and taking turns patrolling around the house. They're armed, TJ. And more than willing to put a bullet in anybody who sticks their nose where it doesn't belong. But you have to help us." He gave her another little shake for emphasis. "You have to stay inside, out of sight."

"How could they find me again?"

Garrett let her go and leaned against one of the upright support beams. "I've been wondering about that myself. Fowler convinced the Attorney General's office that a breach had occurred inside Homeland, so they gave jurisdiction over you back to the Bureau of International Intelligence. Both Aaron and Fowler are back with the BII now. That puts them out of both Senator Farleigh's and Don Castillo's reach."

"You spoke to Agent Fowler?"

He nodded. "The only way I can figure how they found you here is through the task force sent to La Cruza. If Farleigh dug deep enough, he'd find the names of the men on the team. Aaron blew his cover when he spirited you from Mississippi. It would be logical to track down the rest of the team. With four of us clustered here ... well, we might as well put up a sign."

"Four?"

He took his hat off and ran his hands through his hair, making it stand up in wild disarray. "Yeah, four. The only other connection is the orphans, but they've been out of the picture since you forced them on my helicopter back in that burned out clearing."

She clapped a hand over her mouth.

"TJ? The girls are out of the picture, aren't they?"

"Maybe."

That had him pushing away from the post. "Maybe? What do you mean? Have you been in touch with them?"

"No ... but Sally Hasper has."

Garrett muttered something under his breath that sounded suspiciously like a curse. He scrubbed at his hair again and took a deep breath. "Sally who?"

"Sally Hasper. An adoption attorney in New York. She called on my behalf."

"And how is it that Miz Hasper came to call about the girls for you?"

"It was after Sunday dinner with Mrs. Tillberry. While we cleaned the kitchen, she started talking about all the mission trips she's gone on over the years. I found myself telling her a little about Honduras." At the thunderous look on his face, she quickly added, "The sanitized version. I know better than to reveal anything about the case. I told her about the girls and how they'd been sent to the States."

"Go on."

"I ... I wanted to know they were okay. When Mrs. Tillberry mentioned your mother had a friend who had a friend—an adoption lawyer—it seemed like a good idea to get her to call. We were pretty sure the orphanage wouldn't give information to just anyone. But I can't imagine how they could link her to me. Anyway, Sally called yesterday. All the girls went to Atlanta and all but Gaby are in foster homes now." She looked at him, unable to hide the despair she felt. "I led Don Rafael here, didn't I?"

She didn't see him move, but suddenly Garrett had his arms around her. His heart beat in a slow, steady rhythm beneath her cheek. Like a lullaby, a melody promising everything would be okay. And she believed it. For now, she would let him carry the load.

"Garrett?"

"Hmmm?" He stroked her hair.

"What do we do about your mother's party tomorrow night?"

His groan filled the barn.

Chapter Sixteen

Garrett opened the front door and shook hands with the Jamesons. "Millie, George, glad you could come to Mom's party. C'mon in. They're in the family room."

He scanned the folks already gathered. Good friends and neighbors he'd grown up around. People his dad trusted. So why did the crawling sensation on the back of his neck persist? Not the heart-pounding one that screamed danger, but an edgy awareness nonetheless.

Why? Because TJ didn't need to be flaunted at a stupid party in front of half the town.

He glanced at his watch again. She should've been down by now where he could keep his eyes on her. If Mom hadn't stuck him manning the front door, he'd go drag her out of her room.

One hand felt for the IWB holster clipped on his belt. The discreet inside-the-waistband pancake pouch was hardly noticeable, not that it mattered. People saw what they expected to see and the black leather gun holster hidden under his western vest looked a lot like a cell phone. The P238 subcompact pistol had been a last minute addition—thanks to

the uneasiness that made his antenna twitch. Something didn't feel right tonight.

Two names remained on the list—Harmon and Louise Vincent. Allie's parents. The last people he wanted to see. Maybe they wouldn't show.

Not with elections coming up in the fall. Councilman Vincent wouldn't miss an opportunity to finagle a contribution or two from the landowners gathered here tonight. And Mrs. Vincent wouldn't miss a chance to rip another pound of flesh from Garrett's hide. She blamed him for Allie leaving.

Deputy Kyle Abbott opened the front door and stepped inside. "The Vincents are here. Rascal closed the gate after them." He removed his hat. "Sheriff wants me inside now."

Garrett grinned. Saved from Louise Vincent and her barbed tongue. "Great. You can wait here and let them in." He clapped Kyle on the shoulder and fled. He could watch for TJ from the dining room.

"Garrett?"

His mother hooked her arm through his.

"I want you to meet Shea Townsend. She teaches third grade over in Challis but is helping her uncle at Starlight Catering this summer. You remember Wilbur Townsend? Shea, this is my oldest son, Garrett."

The new caterer looked more like a student than a teacher, with her long blond ringlets and baby face. Another of Mom's protégées, no doubt. Well, if they wanted a guinea pig to sample the food, he was their man. He dipped his head. "Miss Townsend."

Her eyes dropped and long dark lashes fanned out over pretty pink cheeks. This one was a beauty … and bound to catch Jonas's roving eye. He liked the shy ones. Mom better keep little Miss Shea out of his brother's crosshairs.

"Shea's introducing some new recipes tonight. Here, try these." She shoved a little plate into his hands.

Garrett plucked a puffy half-moon pastry from the saucer and crammed it in his mouth. The meat stuffing had a mildly spicy flavor and a touch of heat. "Wow. What is this?" he mumbled while sucking in air around the hot mouthful.

"Beef empanada."

Shea's brown eyes sparkled when he popped what looked like a ball of pale yellow cheese in his mouth. A tart sweetness burst on his tongue. The little cheese ball had a lemony raspberry center. "Mmmm."

"Those are Gouda Bites." Her lips twitched.

Not shy, more like sly. Shea Townsend knew how good her food tasted. She had to also know every man here tonight would be eating out of her hand. He chomped down on a bacon-wrapped crunchy something.

"Garrett!" Kyle waved at him from across the room. And then Garrett saw why. Behind him, Harmon Vincent advanced through the guests, shaking hands along the way, a politician on campaign. Louise, on the other hand, seemed to be scanning the crowd. Searching …

Should he get it over with? Louise wouldn't rest until she'd cornered him. The crazy woman still harbored hopes of him and Allie getting back together and seemed intent on making his life miserable until they did. He crammed the last morsel in his mouth and planned his escape. He sure didn't want a confrontation in front of TJ. Why'd Mom have to invite them anyway?

Garrett had always suspected his mother could read minds, and she proved it with her next words. "They're our friends, son. Have been since before you were born," she chided. "And don't cock that eyebrow at me, Garrett Jackson Cameron. It's bad enough your father does." She took pity on him then and reached for his empty plate. "Go on before Louise spots you. The food will hold them here for a while."

"Thanks, Mom." Here he was a grown man and his mother could still reduce him to a guilty boy of ten. "Excuse me, ladies. It appears I'm needed elsewhere." He leaned down and kissed his mother's cheek before turning to the other lady. "Miss Townsend, a pleasure." Garrett slouched, trying not to tower over the other people as he crept away.

The circuitous route back to the front entry took a few minutes. He arrived in the foyer as James sent Kyle out the front door.

The deputy paused at the door, "Someone's in Cate's office waiting for you." He ran down the front steps and disappeared.

Garrett turned to James. "Where you sending Kyle?"

"One of your hands spotted some fancy tread marks out on one of the field roads," James said. "The kind you don't much find around these parts. I put Kyle on it."

Knowing Kyle's unique tracking ability, Garrett had no doubt the deputy would discover if the unknown vehicle remained in the area. Nodding toward his mother's office he asked, "Know who's in there?"

James shook his head. "Nope, but Rascal let them through. Think I'll do another circuit of the doors and windows. Catch you later."

Garrett glanced at his watch and then up the stairs again. He'd give TJ five more minutes. He turned aside to his mother's office.

In the dimly lit room, a woman stood by the desk with her back to the door. The lamp light burnished the familiar mass of wavy hair hanging down her back. Confused, Garrett took a step toward her. "TJ?"

The slim black dress she wore made her look almost thin. Had to be a trick of the light. "What are you doing in here, angel?"

She spun around … and his brain cells fried.

"Hello, Garrett."

The nasal lilt rolled over him, knocking him off kilter. "Allie?"

The last time he'd seen the woman who claimed she carried—and lost—his baby, she'd stood on the steps of a Greyhound bus, bound for anywhere that would take her away from Idaho.

She leaned her hips against the desk, beautiful as always. A little older, a little harder, but still a walking-talking temptation on two legs. Any man would find her hard to resist. Any man but him.

Lately, a short, curvy tomboy with a sassy mouth and a big heart claimed his attention. How could he have mistaken Allie for TJ? Other than their hair, the two women had nothing in common.

Before Garrett could regain his wits, Allie closed the distance between them and curled her hands around his neck. "I've missed you, Garrett. Lean down here and give me a proper welcome."

With his mind sputtering like an engine firing on one sparkplug, he let her pull his head down. Warm breath teased his lips.

What am I doing?

His hands spanned Allie's tiny waist and set her away at the same time a soft gasp sounded behind him.

Garrett whirled around.

TJ stood on the bottom stair, her wounded expression requiring no words. She'd witnessed the whole, sorry encounter. Three thoughts struck him concurrently. He'd hurt her again. He'd shattered the tenuous trust she'd given him. And what in the world had happened to her gorgeous hair?

"TJ?" He took a step forward, one hand reaching out to her. "You cut your hair?"

The hurt expression she wore disappeared, replaced by icy indifference. He hated that mask, hated that she felt the need to hide from him.

"You should have no trouble telling us apart now. Not that it matters."

Allie tugged at his arm. Garrett glanced back and shook her off, but when he turned to TJ again, she had disappeared into the crowd.

"TJ, wait."

"What's with the little mouse? Things must be pretty bad if you're trolling the high school."

He wanted to go after TJ, chase her down, and make it right between them, but reason won out. First, he had to deal with Allie once and for all. And it might be easier to talk to TJ once the little fireball had calmed down.

Why had she cut her hair? He loved the way the sun brought out the whiskey colored tints. He remembered the silky texture of it running through his fingers when he kissed her.

He pictured her standing on the stair step again, the pixie cut framing a heart-shaped face. Without the distraction of the glorious mass of hair, her skin glowed. But it was her big, too-blue eyes that captured him.

With a last look in the direction where TJ disappeared, he confronted the woman he once considered marrying. "Why are you here?"

Allie reached up to caress his cheek. "Aren't you glad to see me? Here I've come all the way from—"

He stepped out of her reach. "Cut the act and answer me. Why'd you come back?"

Her lower lip pooched out in a delectable pout. Sulky mouth, woebegone expression, the only thing missing was a martyred accusation. "You never cared that I waited all those years while you flitted from one exotic locale to another."

Nothing had changed. Allie had always been about I, me, my. She made the nasty hellholes he'd risked his life in sound like a tropical vacation. Without meaning to, he asked the one question that had any meaning for him. "There never was a baby, was there?"

Something flickered in her expression—guilt? Regret? Her gaze slid away.

"Why, Allie? After we fooled around for all those years, why'd you claim to be pregnant only to hightail it out of here the minute I came home?"

Her brown eyes turned dark as motor oil. An ugly flush mottled her neck. "Six years, Garrett. Six hideously long years I waited in this ghost town, hoping you'd finally man up." Her laugh held no humor. "You never intended to marry me, did you? You were using me all along."

"You used me, too. And no, I didn't want to get married. But I would have. For the baby."

A bleak look touched her face long enough for Garrett to see the impact of his words—that he would tie the knot for a nameless, faceless baby, but not for her. Why did women attach emotion to everything? A simple kiss set them dreaming about china patterns.

"You were my ticket out," she snapped. "I wanted to live in San Diego or New York, anyplace but here. But no, you came back with your tail tucked between your legs. Left a glamorous career to work like a hired hand for your daddy. If I'd wanted a dirt rancher, Garrett, I could've had my pick at any time."

Glamorous career? Was she kidding?

Like she'd flipped a switch, Allie turned sweet as blueberries in August, all wide-eyed innocence with no hint of the poison underneath. "I saw the magazine interview about Cate and her new book. They took several nice shots of you and the family. The place looks good, Garrett. You look good."

She tapped his chest with a long, red-lacquered fingernail. "The article said you'd taken over the ranch. I figured life might not be so bad here now. And we were always good together." She inched closer. "Weren't we?"

Garrett recoiled. "You wouldn't last a month on a ranch." He'd said something similar to TJ recently. The difference being TJ could handle the hardships. Allie wouldn't even try.

The temptress retreated. "You've changed, Garrett, and not for the better. You're mean like your granddaddy."

The tainted words held a hateful undertone. Why had he never seen the real Allie before? "And you haven't changed at all."

She sniffed, nose lifting high. "To answer your question, no. There was no baby. Not that you cared." She laughed. "I'd never let a baby ruin my figure, not even for you."

He backed up a step then, torn by a curious mix of loss and relief.

"You know that little girl can't handle a man like you. You'll wind up breaking the little mouse."

"Goodbye, Allie."

"You want me to leave?" She laughed. "Then go find my daddy and tell him he'll have to take me home." Allie brushed past him, heading for the party.

Garrett stared after her for a long time, trying to decide if it would be worth the trouble of throwing her and her parents out.

"Well that sounded a mite unpleasant." Aaron stepped out of the shadows by the stairs.

Surprised by his old teammate's unexpected appearance, Garrett snorted. "You have no idea. When did you get in, Farmboy? We didn't expect you for another month. More important, how did you get in? James has this place locked down tighter than old man Tucker's still."

"Farmboy, huh?" The older man chuckled. "Haven't heard that in a while. Got in about an hour ago. Took a room at the Prairie Rose Motel and then booked it over here. Didn't know about the party. Danged fool at the gate almost blew my head off before I could convince him to call someone."

The front door opened and James stepped inside, laughing at Aaron's last words. "Rascal wanted to hogtie and hold him 'til after the party. Said he needed to be interrogated."

"That old coot's dangerous." Aaron stepped around Garrett and peered into Cate's office. "We need to talk. Can we use this room?"

"What's going on?" The uneasy feeling plaguing Garrett for most of the day cranked up a notch when Aaron closed the door behind them.

Aaron sat in the desk chair. "Robert Bannon, the judge assigned to Krieger's trial, had a stroke last week. Edith Franks is replacing him."

Garrett folded his arms across his chest. "And that brings you here four weeks early because …?"

"Judge Franks plays by the book. In other words, hardnosed and perfect for us."

James leaned against a wall. "So?"

"So, Bannon keeled over before he could rule on Krieger's latest motion to delay." Aaron's lips twitched. "Everyone assumed it a done deal that would put the trial off until the end of August, but Judge Franks threw it out. That means TJ goes

to trial in a week. Quigley, the prosecutor, wants her in Washington no later than Friday."

"Friday? That's only five days away!" Garrett's mind reeled. The thought of her walking out of his life again left an ache in his chest.

"She'll get her life back," Aaron said.

"Five days to move her, what ... twenty-five hundred miles?" James, ever the pragmatist, was already working on the logistics. "They'll pull out all the stops which means no airplanes, trains, or buses. Have to move her by car."

"There's something else you need to know," Aaron continued. "Three months ago, Castillo sent two of his boys to Atlanta to nose around. The La Cruza orphans went to an orphanage there, and all but one of them found foster homes."

Garrett lifted one eyebrow. "How do you know all this?"

"Fowler's been watching the don since he arrived stateside a year ago. Seems Castillo and the senator have gotten pretty thick. Anyway, Gabriela Carliez, the little girl who's still at the orphanage, got snatched two days ago. And Castillo's goons have left Atlanta. We have to assume he has her.

Gaby. He recalled the tough little girl and how she'd been sick at leaving TJ behind when he flew the girls to safety. Gaby sat beside him in the co-pilot's seat, shedding silent tears while acting as mother hen to the younger girls. "TJ can't know about Gaby. She'd do anything to get her back, and Castillo probably knows it."

James frowned and paced the room. "We have to get her out of here tonight."

Aaron fixed him with a stare. "Why?"

"A bunch of strangers drove through town yesterday. They made inquiries, but never at the same place, and then they disappeared as quietly as they arrived. There's been no sign of them since."

Aaron looked thoughtful. "Black sedans? Out of state plates? Muscle in suits?"

James gave a quick nod after each question.

"How'd they find her here? Nobody knows about this place. Not even Fowler." Aaron lurched to his feet and paced.

Garrett sighed. "TJ got my mom's lawyer friend to call and find out what she could about the girls. Odds are the don had the orphanage telephones tapped, traced the call to the lawyer, and then hijacked her records from the phone company. That would explain the reconnaissance drive-by yesterday. Rafael Castillo can't know for sure TJ is here, but Hastings Bluff fits the classic hideaway—small, remote, and odd enough that city boys in shiny black cars stick out like a herd of goats in church."

"You're right. She goes tonight," Aaron agreed. "Where is TJ anyway?"

Garrett opened the door, knowing the time had come to bare his soul. He'd run out of time. "I'll go get her."

Before he reached the dining room, the disquiet that had

pricked at him most of the day kicked into high gear. Cold sweat beaded on his brow. Behind him, James's radio warbled.

"Evers."

Kyle's voice crackled over the speaker. "TJ's out back," he screamed. "Get her inside now! We got snipers in the woods!"

Garrett pulled his Sig P238 in one smooth motion, holding it in both hands with the barrel pointed at the floor. He hurried toward the back of the house, jostling old friends out of the way.

James followed close on his tail with his Glock in hand.

Aaron leaned down, retrieved a Beretta from his ankle holster, and followed.

Garrett reached the halfway point through the dining room when one of the French doors on the far side shattered. The guests on that side of the room screamed and turned to flee, showered by flying glass. Shrieks of pain filled the air. A chair overturned. Dishes crashed to the floor.

"Go on. Find TJ." Aaron called from behind him.

Garrett didn't hesitate. "TJ!"

Chapter Seventeen

TJ pushed through the throng of people in the dining room. "Excuse me. I need to get through, please." Had Cate invited the whole town?

"Hold your horses, missy," an older woman said. "You'll get your turn. Cate won't let us starve."

The man ahead of her took a step back, squashing her between him and another man. An elbow jabbed into her ribs. Warm flesh brushed against the bare skin of her shoulder, sending shivers crawling across her flesh. Chin high, TJ wormed ahead another step. She needed a place to hide out for a few minutes. Alone. Until her nerves were under control.

Who was she kidding? Her nerves were fine, but her heart might not recover. Somehow, in the span of a few days, Garrett Cameron had become very important to her. Everything she did or thought revolved around him, like cutting her hair because he mentioned it might be too easily recognizable by Castillo's men. Wearing the slinky black dress tonight because she needed him to see her as a woman.

Instead, he'd stared in horror at her chopped hair, never glancing at her outfit.

TJ laughed, a short bitter sound that edged perilously close to being a sob. Why would he notice? He had his hands full of Allie.

TJ flinched when a rough hand touched her arm.

"Excuse me, miss. An elderly gentleman wearing leather suspenders squeezed behind her, heading for the buffet spread.

Beads of sweat broke out on her forehead as she realized her predicament. The mélange of odors filling the room stole her breath—spicy meat, sugary desserts, heavy colognes, cloying perfumes ... and bodies. Too many people. Too close. She wiped clammy hands on her skirt and pushed by another man blocking her way. "Please, I have to get out!"

He turned. Heavy eyebrows liberally peppered with gray arched high as light gray eyes peered at her. A lifelong cowboy by the looks of him. His face was deeply tanned and weathered, giving evidence of many years under the hot sun.

"I'm so sorry, sir. I need to get out." Could he hear the desperation in her voice?

"Okay, little lady. Stay close and I'll clear the way."

She followed on his boot heels, one hand all but clutching his shirt.

Her guide veered to one side and put a steadying hand on her shoulder. "Can't get out this way. Best you wait in this corner 'til the crowd thins. I'll fetch you some water."

Scooting as far back into the corner as she could, TJ closed her eyes. As soon as she did, though, the image of

Garrett kissing Allie returned. Why hadn't someone told her Garrett's ex looked like a super model? Or that she would be here tonight? So foolish. Had TJ really thought a man like Garrett would be interested in her?"

Someone bumped her. "Hey. TJ, right? Mind if I hide out here with you?"

Blinking furiously to stem her tears, she looked at the man who'd sidled up. His eyes, green as a spring lawn, twinkled with amusement. She knew those eyes. From where?

"Do I know you?"

White teeth flashed and his smile escalated to a cheeky grin. "Derek Naughton, at your service, ma'am. I'm one of James's deputies."

He'd broken his nose at some point, not that a little crookedness detracted from his good looks.

"What?" he asked. "Do I have spinach in my teeth?"

Random images zipped through her mind. "I do know you."

His smile never faltered. "I'm flattered that a gorgeous thing like you would think so."

Bits and pieces of the past came together. The jungle. Night slipping into dawn. "You were in Honduras." One of six shadow warriors with camouflage-painted faces. Black uniforms. Each man carrying an arsenal.

"You were part of the team that pulled me out. You're Romeo ... wait ..."

Kyle Abbot's face swam into focus. Kyle? "No. Kyle is Romeo. You're ... Iceman." Why hadn't she realized it before now? Her eyes went to his crooked nose. "Did I do that?"

"Nope." He reached down and rubbed his leg. "I'm the one you kicked."

TJ looked around. "Are the others here, too?"

"Some. Not all."

"Why?"

He gave her an odd look. "Why are we here? To finish the job. Nail the bad guy. Rescue the damsel in distress. Save the day." He shrugged. "Pick one. It's who we are. What we do."

"But this mission ended two years ago."

"Maybe. Maybe not." He held out a glass of water and nodded toward someone across the room. "Duffy asked me to bring you this."

Duffy. The stranger who plowed a way through the crowd for her. The old man met her eyes and tipped his own glass in salute.

TJ wagged her fingers in acknowledgement and downed half the ice water. "Thanks. Is he part of the team, too?

"Duffy? Nah. He owns the next ranch over. You want something stronger?"

"No, thank you."

"Want to tell me why we're hiding in the corner?"

Too perceptive by far. "I kind of freaked in the middle of all that." She pointed at the snarl of people jockeying for a place at the buffet table. "Short people don't fare well in crowds. And tight places make me uncomfortable. What's your excuse?"

"Keeping an eye on you." His gaze ran down to her toes and back up again. "Nice dress."

She blushed and crossed her arms over her chest. Figured that *he* would notice. And she sure didn't need another too-good-looking-for-his-own-good cowboy prowling around. Then again, maybe that was exactly what she needed? A little hair of the dog, so to speak.

A barricade of people stood between her and any sanctuary she might find. The kitchen swarmed with the caterer's staff. And she couldn't go outside with the threat of Don Rafael's men lurking. Maybe she could squirm her way to the laundry room. She could handle a small room for a little while, couldn't she? It would be quieter. "Maybe I'll take something stronger after all."

"Sure thing. What would you like?" He smiled again, a gut-punching, steal your breath grin. That much virility ought to be outlawed. Except he did nothing for her. No tingle, no thrill, and certainly no breathlessness. Why couldn't she like Derek instead? "One of those pink fruity things looks good."

"Okay. Stay put. I'll be right back." Moments later, the crowd hid him from sight.

TJ didn't hesitate. "Excuse me. Excuse me. Sorry." She stayed close to the wall and pushed her way past those hanging on the fringe.

Across the room, Cate and Mallory squealed in harmony and flung their arms around another woman.

TJ caught sight of the new arrival's face—Mallory's clone, Cassidy. It looked like the absentee twin had finally come home.

Jonas and Wade magically appeared by Cassidy's side and took turns folding their sister into bear hugs. They finally relinquished her to Cody, who swung his daughter in a tight circle. Mallory was there as well, but more reticent than the others. Garrett was nowhere to be seen, but TJ had an idea where he might be.

The catty thought brought the hurt clawing back up.

Someone else crowded in behind Cassidy. Well, well— Derek Naughton—the deputy who'd been flirting with her only moments ago. The intent look he wore now had Miss Cassidy blushing and looking anywhere but at him. Interesting.

Someone tapped TJ's shoulder. She jumped. And then her mouth dropped.

Allie Vincent towered over her by at least six inches, but looked like she weighed a good twenty pounds less. Tall and willowy versus short and dumpy. How could Garrett possibly mistake them?

TJ fingered her short curls and poured all the disdain she could muster into a glare. "What?"

"I think we need to have a little talk."

Allie's voice surprised TJ as much as her words. High pitched with a nasally tone. Not at all what a sultry siren should sound like. "I don't think so."

"I can say my piece right out here, in front of everybody, if that's how you want to play."

TJ stiffened.

"Yeah, that's what I thought. Let's step out on the back porch." Allie disappeared through the kitchen doorway.

All the hurt, disappointment, and anger boiled up. Garrett might reduce her to tears, but Allie held no power over her. TJ followed the prodigal fiancée, more than ready to erase the sneer from her too perfect face.

Outside, Allie had descended the steps to the brick patio.

TJ remained near the door, mindful of Garrett's insistence to stay inside. Were Castillo's men lurking nearby? Two minutes. She'd let Allie say what she had to say and then scoot back in. "Well?"

Allie turned, her long hair cascading over one shoulder. "Aren't you a little young to be panting after a man Garrett's age? You do know we're engaged?"

"You ditched him. Or did he dump you? I get mixed up on the finer points." She faked a yawn.

"Water under the bridge. He asked me to come back."

A fist squeezed TJ's heart.

Allie crossed the patio to the brick knee-wall, gliding in the moonlight. "I'm back now, so you'll have to leave." She

perched on the bricks, head tilted back, every move a pose.

"I don't think so." TJ was tired of running.

Ping.

"Ow!" Allie jerked, clapping a hand to her arm.

TJ straightened up, instantly alert. What ...?

Another ping, off the metal grill this time.

"Get down!" she yelled at Allie and launched herself at the other woman. The impact took them both to the ground.

Allie clawed and shoved in her struggle to get up. "Get off me."

TJ wound her hand in the other woman's long hair, grabbed her uninjured arm, and slammed her back down on the ground. One advantage she had over Miss Beauty Queen—TJ knew how to fight. "Stay down. Someone's shooting at us." She growled.

"Whaaat?" All the struggle went out of Allie but not the outrage. "You're crazy. Let me go, or I'll scream."

Ping. Ping. Ping-ping. Brick exploded. Masonry shards rained down on them. One of the dining room windows shattered.

Allie screamed and buried her face in the grass.

"Hush, Allie. We're safe for now. Help's on the way."

The floodlights came on and banished the night. A barrage of automatic weapons fire burst from the side of the house. TJ thought her heart might burst. What had she been thinking to come out here?

The kitchen screen door slammed open and banged against the wall.

"TJ!" Garrett roared.

Heavy footsteps, running. Another voice barking orders.

Allie whimpered, her body trembling so hard, she could have been a dog shaking off water after a flea dip.

"Shhh, Allie. It's okay. Help is here."

He said he would always come and TJ believed him.

The next second Garrett hunkered over the two women, his big body shielding them. A host of ticked-off cowboys swarmed after him to set up a defensive perimeter.

From his crouched position, Garrett asked, "Are you hurt?"

Allie blubbered, clutching at her arm. "They shot me!"

TJ rolled up on her side and wriggled out from Garrett's confining weight. "You're safe now, Allie. Garrett's here." To Garrett she said, "Check her left arm. I think she caught a bullet."

Garrett pulled Allie's hand from her injury. "Just a scratch. Probably won't even need a stitch." He yanked a handkerchief from his pocket anyway and wound it around her arm.

He turned to TJ, one large hand roaming down her arm. "TJ, are you hurt?"

She shook her head and tried to shrug his hand off, but Garrett pulled her into his chest.

"You're gonna be the death of me yet, woman."

Hope flared in TJ's heart ... and died in that same instant. If she wanted to survive this night, survive *him*, she had to get control of this crazy weakness of hers for Garrett Cameron. He didn't want her. The man and his super-sized ego simply couldn't deal with failure. He'd sworn to protect her. That's all. She couldn't read more into it. Wouldn't fall for the concerned hero bit again.

"I'm fine." TJ struggled in his arms. "You need to take care of Allie."

His arms wouldn't let her go. "Both of you stay put until James tells us it's clear."

Garrett's warm breath tickled her cheek, and she relaxed, taking what she could of the moment.

James barked out orders. "Form a shield. Three around each woman. Get them inside. Now!"

Hands gripped her arms and pulled her upright into a cocoon of large bodies. At the door she managed a peek back. Allie, hysterical now, had Garrett in a stranglehold, her good arm wrapped around his neck and both legs locked around his waist.

TJ closed her eyes and let her burly escorts manhandle her inside. Seeing Allie draped over Garrett like a long-legged leech might be humorous, but it didn't diminish the hurt from his rejection. How long before her heart stopped chasing the fairytale?

"Stop it, Allie. You aren't dying." Garrett sounded more annoyed than concerned. "Would someone pull her off me so I can breathe?"

Jonas, one of the guys hauling TJ through the kitchen door, mumbled under his breath. "'Bout time." His retort initiated a chorus of laughs.

"Take them to Cate's office," James directed. "Derek, clear a path. Get Cassie."

Coos and whispers trailed after them as they hurried through the house. Her three man-barriers deposited TJ like a priceless treasure on Cate's desk chair.

Cassidy materialized carrying a first aid kit. She knelt in front of TJ and smiled. "Hi, TJ, I'm Cassie, the other sister." She pushed TJ's skirt up and clucked at the bloody knees revealed. "We need to clean these up. It might sting a bit so bear with me." She dabbed at the scrapes on TJ's knees with a gauze pad.

"Allie's the one who's hurt." TJ nodded at the doorway where Garrett lugged the weeping, clinging woman into the room.

"What are you up to this time, girl? I thought I taught you better."

The gravelly southern drawl brought TJ's eyes up in a rush. "Aaron!" She jumped up, almost knocking Cassie over as she threw herself at her old friend. "I missed you so much."

He pulled her into a hug, one big hand gently smoothing

her short hair. "The new do looks good. Sexy. Like a naughty little pixie."

His soft chuckle calmed her frazzled nerves. Aaron had always accepted her, warts and everything. Plain Jane. No fuss. No frills. No expectations. The thought brought the ache back on a shuddering breath.

"Hush, now. I got you." Aaron's arms tightened around her.

The floodgates opened, and TJ cried like a lost child.

"TJ?" Garrett's voice, full of concern reached her ears. He tried to turn her around, to pull her into his arms. "Don't cry, angel. I can't stand it when you cry."

She burrowed deeper into Aaron's chest. "Take me away from here, Aaron."

Chapter Eighteen

Garrett backed away, reeling from the lash of TJ's words. He'd finally succeeded in pushing her away. But now … he didn't want her to leave.

Aaron glared at him over her head.

Behind him, Allie wailed. "Where's Garrett. I need Garrett."

TJ stiffened. At least she'd stopped crying, unlike Allie. Bawling women made him uncomfortable, but TJ's tears ripped his guts apart.

"That does it," he pronounced. "TJ goes. Tonight. While it's still dark."

He turned away from the disbelieving look on her face, as her tears welled again. "Mom, would you get Allie and Mr. and Mrs. Vincent settled in the guest rooms? It'll be safer if they remain here until James and his men neutralize the threat."

Mallory joined forces with her mother and hustled Allie and her parents away.

With the Vincents gone, blessed silence returned, Garrett turned to James. "Get an update from Kyle. Find out how many tangos are still out there and where. We need to move TJ before they regroup."

James was already punching numbers into his cell as he stepped from the room.

"Dad, would you, Jonas, and Wade see our guests out? They'll be safe once they get away from here."

The three Cameron men hurried off.

Now came the hard part, dealing with TJ. Clamping down on his nerves—you never went into battle with less than one hundred percent confidence—Garrett pulled her from Aaron's embrace. "Sit down, TJ. We have to talk."

To his surprise, she didn't protest.

He pulled her around so he could kneel facing her. This close he caught her unique scent, a clean, flowery fragrance that brought memories of spring. The lamplight gave her a halo, making his fingers itch to plow through the short curls. "Why'd you go outside, angel? You knew the danger."

He ran one finger down her bare arm and smiled as goose bumps pebbled her skin. Her soft snuffles pulled at his heart. "TJ?"

She wouldn't look up. "Allie found me in the dining room. I didn't want a scene at Cate's party. The porch seemed the best place for privacy. I thought we'd be okay for a few minutes."

"How'd the two of you wind up on the ground?"

At last, those stunning eyes tipped up, full of anger and hurt. His fierce little angel was back and now she wanted to roast him. And, oh man, did he want to be charred.

"She said you asked her to come back. That I'd have to clear out."

Garrett choked. "What?"

"I politely declined to leave. I mean, you have to finish your *mission*. We can't have someone else step in to *protect* me since it's your *responsibility*."

She skewered him with his own words. Garrett closed his gaping mouth, trying hard to hold back a grin. He could deal with her anger but would have to tread carefully through the minefield of hurts and misunderstandings, not to mention his own stupidity. "I've had zero contact with Allie since she left Hastings Bluff all those years ago. Her arrival tonight took me by complete surprise—which is why you saw her kissing me and *not* the other way around. Of course, you ran off before you saw me push her away. Now, one more time, why'd you leave the porch?"

The defensive fury she couldn't hide turned to … guilt?

He loved her expressive face. Loved knowing she'd never be able to hide her feelings from him. Temptation won out and Garrett let his fingers sift through her hair. So soft. His hand cupped the back of her head, not letting her look away.

"Oh, for Pete's sake. Allie caught a bullet. She had no idea what was happening and sure wasn't going to listen to anything I said." Her eyes heated to about a thousand degrees. "They were shooting at her, Garrett. At her. Not me. I knocked her

down. I mean, what would you have done?"

Of course she would try to protect Allie. TJ always put everyone else first. Life with his idealistic, naive little pixie would be a constant challenge, but so worth the bother. He choked on the thought and quickly covered it with a cough. Might as well snap a collar around his neck and hand her the leash.

He nodded. "I'd have done exactly what you did."

That shut her up for a moment, but then she leaned in, whispering so only he could hear. "They think she's me, Garrett."

"I know. Allie and her parents will have to stay at the Triple C for a while, where we can protect them."

TJ's animation drained away, replaced by the cold mask.

He wasn't having any more of that. "TJ, look at me."

When her eyes met his again, Garrett went on. "Hear me. Allie will be safe here with Dad, Wade, Jonas, and the hands looking out for her. I'm taking you outta here. Tonight. Before Castillo's men can regroup."

She blinked, thawing a little.

James came back in. "Got an update."

Cody, Jonas, and Wade wandered back in when James started talking.

"The guys followed the tread marks into the woods behind the house. Found the sniper in a deer stand and a half-dozen tangos hovering nearby. That's when Kyle realized TJ was outside and called. They took three out and captured two. The other one got away. They're on the way back with the prisoners."

Garrett nodded. "We need a plan to get TJ away before they regroup and trap her here. A delay is as good as a kill if it keeps her from testifying. Can't let that happen."

He turned to TJ. "Go change into jeans and boots, angel. And grab your scat bag. You can get the rest of your stuff after the trial. Tonight, we travel light."

"C'mon. I'll help you." Cassidy took her hand and hustled her up the stairs.

After the two women disappeared, Aaron asked the question on everyone's mind. "All right, Cowboy, spit it out. What's your plan?"

Garrett considered where to start. So many moving parts were still coming together in his head. "Aaron, Castillo's goons know you now. They'll have a tail on you 'til doomsday. TJ can't go with you."

Aaron nodded.

"James, you and your deputies are needed here. Since TJ cut her hair, they seem to think Allie is the target. I need you to help my family keep the Vincents safe." Garrett made direct, probing eye contact with the former members of his team. These men would hang with him to the bitter end if he asked it of them. Probably even if he didn't. Add his family into the mix, and he liked the odds.

James nodded, but a muscle ticked in his jaw. Derek leaned against the wall in stony silence, his arms folded across his chest. None of them wanted to be left out of the action.

Garrett wouldn't like being left out either had their roles been reversed. "We have to assume they know our vehicles and have lookouts posted. It's what I'd do."

Jonas asked, "So how do you get her out?"

"We sneak her out to the barn, then she and I will take two of the horses—probably not Buffy. That old horse has gone to fat. Maybe Shoofly. Anyway, we'll slip out the back once the moon starts to wane. Head toward Mustang Valley and ford the river at the bend then follow the ridgeline to Morning Glory Peak."

He turned to his father and brothers. "You remember that old trapper's shack where we used to stay over on roundups?"

They nodded.

"A four-wheel drive can make it up there." He turned to Aaron. "We need transportation Castillo can't identify. Dad can give you the coordinates to the shack. Use your secure phone and call Fowler. Have him send a fully stocked vehicle there by noon tomorrow."

"Noon's cutting it a mite close, don't you think?" Jonas said. "That's a tough ride in daylight. At night, it'll be tricky. You sure TJ can make it?"

Garrett answered without hesitation. "I have no doubts about TJ's abilities. She spent a night alone in a savage jungle with an army on her tail. She ran mile after mile, keeping pace with my team over some pretty rugged terrain. She got thrown off a cliff and swam through the ocean, not to mention surviving two years of hell on her own while the legal eagles dilly-dallied. TJ can handle anything we throw at her. She might be a little on the short side, but the girl's got a heart like a lion."

"Why you?" Wade asked. "Why not me or Jonas. We're less likely to be missed."

"Because she's mine to protect."

Garrett might've gotten his grandpa's anger, but his brothers inherited the same steely eyes. Wade's stare could plumb the depths of an innocent man's soul and leave him confessing to sins never committed, but Garrett remained steadfast, unflinching.

Wade finally looked away, his lips twitching. "Good enough. You can turn the horses loose in the valley below the cabin. We'll collect them once things quiet down here."

"What then?" Aaron asked.

"We'll take a circuitous route and head for D.C. Castillo pays for muscle and obedience, not brains. His thugs won't catch on right away that Allie's not TJ. Especially if Aaron hangs around. James, you'll need to call in some IOUs. A show of force should deter any more attacks and bolster the assumption that TJ is still here."

"So I'm a decoy?" Aaron chuckled.

"Yeah, but you're also our primary—our *only* point of contact. I need you to coordinate activities and give us a few diversions while we make our run."

"And give my men time to comb every inch of the area, maybe pick up a few more prisoners." James rubbed his hands together.

"I got a spare satellite phone in my car. You can take it," Aaron offered.

"Thanks. Can't take much with us on horseback, but a sat phone will be welcome. Be sure the getaway truck is stocked with plenty of firepower."

His mom squeezed into the office then. "The Vincents have settled in for the night. The guests are all gone, and the caterers are about ready to leave."

Derek Naughton walked to the door and spoke to James. "No need to assign rotations. I'll stay out here for the next few days."

Garrett's protective instincts stirred. Derek—the Iceman—had come by the name honestly. Cold and dangerous, with green eyes like a big, jungle cat. And now the predator stalked new prey—Cassie, by the way his eyes kept going back to her. Garrett decided he'd have a chat with his old teammate about boundaries. From the way little sis's cheeks had colored at Derek's intentions, it needed to be soon.

Aaron left shaking his head. "I'll go get my bag of tricks from the car."

The others scattered quickly, each one to his assigned job, until only Garrett and his father remained.

"You know, son, you might be thirty-four years old and a grown man, one I'm real proud of, but I think you're in need of a little fatherly advice." He pointed to a chair. "Sit for a minute."

Garrett sat.

"You got feelings for that little girl?"

After a long few seconds, Garrett dipped his head once. "Yes, sir. I do."

"She got feelings for you?"

The constriction is his chest eased a little as he considered his father's question. Garrett nodded.

"Then explain to me what's got her so upset, because it's plain as Fred Myner's mongrel coon dog that you're not high on her list right now. What makes you think she'll ride off into the hills with you, alone and without a fight?"

Because he'd tie her to his saddle if he had to. Garrett searched for a way to explain, but nothing came out.

"It don't really matter how you got to this point. I figure you'll beat yourself up enough without anybody's help, but what I want to know is your intentions."

How could he explain it to his father when he didn't understand himself? Like how TJ tore his guts up. Made him forget everything but her. How the thought of her in danger made him sick with fear. Or how he'd wanted to rip Aaron's head off for holding her. How could he explain why he'd tried to keep her at a distance?

The words started slow but grew easier. "She's more than a curvy handful and a pretty face. TJ's strong. And tough. But soft and kind, too. She's always looking out for others. The girl drives me crazy with the way she keeps stepping into trouble."

"Sounds like she might be the one."

The one. His dad always claimed each man had a special woman somewhere. You only had to be patient until the good Lord sent her your way. Might be something to that.

Garrett leaned forward, elbows on his knees. "I've never felt like this before, Dad. When that cat almost got her, I blamed TJ for making me weak. I might've pushed her away one too many times."

"Allie jump you when she came in tonight?"

Garrett nodded.

"TJ see it?"

"Yeah."

His father didn't say anymore for a long time, and then he started laughing.

Garrett waited while his father regained his composure. Dad never shied away from giving hard advice when it was needed. He'd never betray a confidence and sure wouldn't make fun of someone else's troubles.

"I'm not laughing at you, son. I'm laughing because Cameron men have a way of making life difficult for themselves and everyone around them. I can personally attest to that. When you find yourself in a hole, it's best to stop digging. Unfortunately, by the time you figure that out, you're usually in way over your head."

"I know."

"The first thing is be honest with yourself. Admit you fell for that little gal."

He could do that. "I fell hard."

"Good judgment comes from living and a lot of that comes from bad choices, so don't let your fling with Allie flavor the rest of your life. Chalk it up to experience."

"How do I make it right with TJ?"

"You can't undo what's been done, but you can fix it going forward. And you don't make it right. You make it better. Tell me what you think you should do?"

"Apologize for what I said. For hurting her feelings."

"Whoa. Hold up, boy. Did you mean those things you said?"

Garrett shook his head.

"Then tell her you're sorry because you were wrong, not that her feelings were hurt. Tell her you're a fool for letting your past with Allie affect your now with TJ. If she's the one—tell her straight out. And make the commitment."

"You mean … get married?" Garrett paled.

His father snorted. "Commitment don't mean you have to get hitched tomorrow. That would be a disaster. You two got a spark going, but you barely know each other. Commitment means you're willing to spend the time and effort to get to know her. Learn to trust and be trusted, without letting anyone else muddy the water. Figure out if you want to spend the rest of your life with her, and vice versa. And then you grovel. A lot. Women like that."

"But she doesn't want anything to do with me."

"If you want her, you'll find a way to break down her barriers. You're the one who helped put them up."

"You know I have to stay with her through the trial? Until she's really safe."

"Don't worry none about the ranch. I'm not so old I can't still handle things here." He got up and pulled Garrett into a hug. "All things come to pass according to God's will, and He don't need your help to make it so. You'll learn that lesson one day, too. Good luck, son."

Garrett sat alone in the room after his father left. Maybe— with a whole lot of begging and a lot more help from the good Lord—he could work his way back into TJ's good graces.

Chapter Nineteen

Garrett went still. Funny how he could sense the moment TJ entered a room. What was this crazy link between them that set every nerve of his tingling when she came near?

He looked around and, sure enough, she stood in the doorway of the family room. The clothes she'd put on swallowed her. Baggy jeans and a too big black shirt—so that's where his old shirt went. It might be his favorite, but man, he liked the idea of her wearing his stuff.

"What's all this?" She dropped her backpack on the floor and gestured at the disarray.

"We're getting you outta here while James and his men have the attackers on the run." He held a hand out. "C'mere. Wade's bringing the truck up from the barn so we can load it up with the party stuff like we're hauling it back to the barn. We'll hide you in one of the boxes and slip you in with the tables and chairs."

She looked unconvinced.

"Nobody outside the house will know you're gone."

Those eyes he adored looked turbulent. One minute TJ held his gaze, the next she turned away.

He caught her arm and pulled her around to face him. "Look at me, TJ. What's going on inside your head?"

TJ tensed as though she might bolt. "Why are you doing this, Garrett?"

"Doing what, angel?"

"You want me; you don't want me. You pull me close and push me away. I can't do this anymore."

The pain in her voice cut him to the quick. Garrett settled an arm around her shoulders and pulled into his side. "It's okay, baby. I know I've been a fool, but I'm not running from what's between us anymore. And I'd die before I let anyone hurt you again."

"I don't think I can hide in a box. I don't like small places."

Garrett whispered soft little words of comfort. She'd been skittish like this the night before, out in the barn. But her withdrawal didn't start until he'd suggested she close the office door for privacy. What was it she said?

I needed to get away. That's all. Get some fresh air.

What had happened to make her this way? She'd only revealed bits and pieces about her life before Honduras. There was so much he still needed to learn.

You're smothering me.

She wouldn't even shut her bedroom door all the way at night. "You're afraid of the dark, aren't you? Afraid of being closed in."

Her head jerked up.

"It's okay, TJ. I'm not being judgmental. Everybody has fears." He kept his tone soft, not letting her pull away. "Why are you afraid?"

The slightest side-to-side motion of her head confirmed his suspicions. "It happened a long time ago. I'm over it now. It's just that sometimes …"

Whatever had happened in her past, she sure as heck wasn't over it. If it was the last thing he did, she'd tell him the rest of her story. One day.

A fierce need to punish whoever had reduced her to this quivering, fearful mess filled Garrett's veins.

TJ whimpered.

His arms relaxed, but he kept her close. No time for Plan B—even if they had one. How could he get her to do this? They had a small window of opportunity, which might make the difference in her getting safely away. And making the trial.

"It's okay. I'm here. We'll find another way."

She looked up at him. "There's no other way, is there?"

When he didn't answer, she leaned into him and laid her face against his chest. The top of her head barely reached his shoulder. A perfect fit. "If I let you put me in the box, you have to promise to stay close and talk to me. I need to hear your voice."

Pride surged through him. TJ refused to stay broken. A fighter to the end.

"Truck's ready," Jonas reported from the front door.

Garrett picked up one of the padded quilts they used for packing. "No box. We'll use this instead." He wrapped it around her like a mummy.

"It's be a quick, bumpy ride—three minutes, tops. I won't leave you, TJ."

"You promise?"

Her muffled plea made him groan. "Cross my heart. Every step. Quiet now. Listen for my voice." He picked her up like a rolled carpet and carried her out the front door to the truck. After laying her gently on the floor, he sat beside her. "Okay, let's roll."

Moments later, the truck pulled inside the barn. Garrett stripped the blanket away. "You okay, angel?"

TJ's eyes found his right away, her expression filled with relief … and maybe a little trust.

Garrett swept her into his arms. "You're so brave, baby. I've got you now. I got you." He sat on a nearby bale of hay and rocked, holding her on his lap. His rough fingers trailed up and down her arms. Such soft skin.

Behind them, Jonas cleared his throat. "Er … don't mean to rush you, but the night's wasting."

Wade squatted beside Garrett and TJ. "We got cloud cover, but I don't know how long it'll last. If you're really gonna do this, now's the time." He touched TJ's arm. "You okay?"

"Yeah. I am." She slid off Garrett's lap. "Okay, cowboys, what's next on this rodeo?"

Garrett tried hard to suppress his grin. He felt like he could bench press a buffalo. "We ride. Just you and me."

Rascal waited with the horses by the rear door of the barn. "Hey TJ, come meet Shoofly. She's your ride tonight."

"I want Buffy."

Garrett looked at his brothers and then at Rascal. Their expressions showed the same bewilderment he felt.

Rascal answered her. "Buffy can't go the distance, honey. I doubt she can make it across the river, much less get up those hills. C'mon, now. Shoofly's a real lady."

When Garrett tried again to push TJ forward, she sidestepped him.

"Why don't you want to ride Shoofly?"

She looked from the horse to Garrett and back again. "She's too big."

Garrett took TJ by the arm and marched her to where Shoofly stood waiting. "I've seen you drop three grown men to their knees, one after the other. Men trained in combat and armed to the teeth. You're the bravest person I know. I think you can handle a horse that thinks she's a pet."

Rascal slapped a piece of carrot in her hand. "TJ, meet Shoofly."

Shoofly tossed her head and closed the distance between them. With a soft whicker, the big roan nuzzled TJ's palm and daintily plucked the carrot away.

TJ stroked the horse's muzzle. "Are you sure she won't throw me?"

"I'm sure," Rascal said.

Jonas secured her pack to the backside of Shoofly's saddle, while Garrett withdrew a Sig P238 from his pocket and handed it to her. "I know you got that little peashooter in your backpack, but I thought you might like something a little more substantial for this ride."

TJ looked at Garrett. "You're giving me your gun?"

"Naw. Got you one just like mine. Easier if we don't have to worry about what bullets to use. Mine's right here." He patted the gun at his waist.

Wade handed Garrett a sack and saddlebags. "Left side has clothes and shaving gear. Right side is filled with ammo. Mom filled the sack with food."

Rascal nodded toward Shoofly and told TJ, "That little bag hanging off the horn has two days' worth of oats." He bent down and cupped his hands. "C'mon girl. Let me give you a leg up."

Garrett mounted, tightened the reins on a dancing Siggy, and patted the horse's sleek neck. "We're not gonna run tonight, boy. Not unless we have to."

The horse calmed.

"One more thing," Jonas ran back to the cart and returned carrying two jackets. "Summer nights can get chilly in the hills." He threw a heavy denim jacket to Garrett and held out the other for TJ to slip on.

"You each got cash in the right breast pocket, courtesy of Dad," Wade explained.

TJ leaned down to kiss Jonas on the cheek and then Wade. "Thank you." Even Rascal came over to get a quick peck.

Garrett stretched his hand out to Jonas. "No hard feelings, little brother."

His youngest brother took his hand and pulled him into an embrace. "None whatsoever. You take good care of TJ, you hear? And yourself. I don't expect to carry your workload and mine for long."

Wade stepped over and took Garrett's hand when Jonas walked away. "Vaya con Dios, Gare. Bring her back soon as you can."

Garrett gave him a sharp nod.

Then came Rascal's turn.

"Took a while, but you finally wised up. Might be hope for the next generation after all. I like that little filly. A lot."

After a quick handshake, Garrett mounted and guided Siggy to TJ's side. "You ready to do this?" When she nodded, he gave her instructions. "They'll turn the lights off and head back to the house. We'll wait a few more minutes to get our night vision and then set out through the corral. Rascal left the gate open for us. Stay close. And keep to a walk. Movement draws attention, so slower is better. We'll head down the same path we took on our ride, only this time we stay on the grass."

Rascal flipped the lights out and opened the rear door just enough for a single horse to slip through.

A moment later, TJ touched Garrett's arm.

He took her hand. They had a long, hard night ahead of them, and an even longer morning. Who knew when he'd have another chance to enjoy her touch?

A thick layer of clouds obscured the moon when they left the barn. Luck was on their side, but he'd sure feel better once they got across the river.

Garrett calculated they'd gone about five miles when his neck began to tingle. The bend should be coming in sight soon, but would it be in time? He fixed TJ's position. She followed a half a length behind on his right flank. "TJ, come closer. Move over to my left side, closer to the river."

To her credit, she obeyed. Did she feel what he did? Jonas laughingly called it his super-powered radar, but James claimed it was soldier's intuition. Whatever, Garrett had learned long ago to pay attention. Something or someone stalked them in the night.

Garrett's eyes widened to expand his peripheral vision. His ears strained for the slightest out of place sound. The itchy sensation intensified.

"Garrett?" TJ whispered.

She'd pulled up beside him now. At least he was between her and whatever tracked them.

"Do you hear that?"

A soft whine, barely audible. No wonder he hadn't picked it up sooner.

"We're gonna cross the river here." Potholes and loose rock dotted the down slope, with little gullies and washouts where the storm runoff fed the river. "Give me your reins, TJ. I don't want us gettin separated. You hold tight to that horn, and don't let go for nothing. Understand?"

"Yes." She gave him the reins.

The whining sound grew louder, closer. An electric motor. Garrett figured he had only minutes to get them across the river and find cover. "C'mon, Siggy. Let's go for a swim, boy." He dug his heels into the horse's sides. Shoofly's reins jerked tight, and then the mare was running with them. "Hang onto that saddle horn!"

Five more steps and they hit the river.

The horses jerked up and down as they tried to run in the fast flowing water. The jarring motions smoothed out once they reached the deeper parts. Water rose to the saddle as the horses settled into a swimming pace. Beside him, TJ gasped.

"Steady, angel. It's deeper here than I'd like, but we'll get there. Siggy and Shoofly are strong in the water. They'll buck a bit coming out on the other side, so keep a tight grip."

"Okay."

They scrambled out of the water on the other side before their stalker reached the river. One vehicle, no lights. Which meant they had night vision capability. Not good.

Garrett double wrapped Shoofly's wet reins around his fist and kicked Siggy into a trot. They'd have to chance the uneven ground. He had to get TJ behind cover.

A shot rang out, whistling off to their right, making both Garrett and TJ flinch. "Stay low. We're almost to the trees." He pushed Siggy to go faster.

As they reached the tree line and slipped into a stand of big Ponderosa pines, Shoofly screamed and bucked. The gentle roan's front legs clawed at the air.

TJ tried to hold on, but she was no eight-second bronc rider. One foot came free of a stirrup. Her body slipped sideways, and she went airborne.

Garrett's heart stopped when TJ hit the ground. She rolled down the hill they'd just climbed and plowed into a big rock outcropping.

He was off Siggy and half-sliding, half-running down the hill calling her name. "Talk to me, TJ!" he whispered when he reached her side.

TJ didn't move.

Chapter Twenty

Sticks and loose shale jabbed as she slid down the slope. Half way down a boulder roughly the size of a small pony interrupted her tumble. TJ slammed into it and her wits scattered into a million little beads like mercury in a broken thermometer.

"TJ!"

Garrett's voice penetrated, allowing her mind to clear.

"TJ!"

Louder now. Closer.

She lay semi-prone on the ground, dazed and more than a little afraid to move. Worse, her lungs wouldn't work.

"Talk to me, TJ!"

His voice, deep and strong, calmed the rising panic. The weight in her chest eased and sweet, blessed air filled her lungs. That's when she noticed the fist hammering inside her skull.

Work-roughened hands touched her cheek. "Angel? Talk to me."

She opened her eyes. Garrett hovered above her like a shadow. Behind him, the clouds continued to roil across the sky, playing hide and seek with the moon and stars.

"Garrett?" Did that croaking voice belong to her?

"Tell me where you hurt, baby."

"E-everywhere. What happened?" Even as she asked, memory rushed back—the horses plunging into the river. Their mad scramble uphill. Shoofly screaming, crazy, bucking.

"You took a spill." His hands squeezed her thighs and knees before moving down to her ankles.

TJ closed her eyes again and took a mental inventory. Her head felt like John Phillips Sousa himself led a marching band through her skull. Other than that, everything seemed to be somewhat functional. She raised a hand to explore the throbbing behind her ear and found a Texas-sized lump forming. She squirmed.

"Easy now. Let's make sure nothing's broken before you move."

Her hand clenched around a fistful of Garrett's shirt. "Get me off this rock. It's digging into my side."

He chuckled softly. "You must be okay given the way you're wiggling around." Instead of helping her up though, Garrett worked his arms under her body and lifted her away from the jagged rock.

TJ gritted her teeth as he settled her on a relatively flat, grassy patch.

"Better?"

"Yeah. Better."

She'd distracted Garrett enough. With the shooter still out there, he needed to focus on the threat. "Is he still there? The shooter? Is Shoofly hurt?" Her throat tightened. Even the animals weren't safe around her.

"He's still out there and Shoofly's fine. Now lie still and let me see how badly you're hurt." Garrett's hands continue to roam, searching for injuries.

"Shouldn't we get out of here?"

"Not yet. Our pesky friend is using some kind of night scope. Since he can't get across the river, he'll wait for us to make a move."

"So, we wait him out?"

Ignoring her question, he countered, "Besides the knot on your head and the bruises you'll likely have in the morning, what else hurts?"

"Nothing a handful of ibuprofen won't fix."

The clouds parted for a few seconds and the moonlight revealed his face set in hard lines. A terrible resolve raged in his midnight eyes.

"I want you to stay put while I go take care of some business. Don't sit up. Don't move an inch."

She caught his arm before he turned away. "Garrett, please don't."

"You'll be okay, angel. I wouldn't leave if I didn't think you'd be safe." When she didn't release him, he leaned down and brushed his lips across her forehead.

"Don't kill him."

Garrett held her gaze for a long ten-count before he slipped away to blend with the night.

Fury seethed inside him like a living thing. The fool had signed his death warrant with the potshot at TJ. *Don't kill him?* The moment he had the fool in his crosshairs—pfft! Done. Erased. No more threat.

Garrett scrambled up the slope in a zigzag pattern, moving fast. A shot rang out, plowing into the grass twenty feet to his left—*not even close, jerk wad*—and then he reached the trees. The shooter obviously had an older version of night vision goggles, the kind that used ambient light to reveal images in an eerie green glow. The distance between where their attacker hid on the other side of the river and where Garrett now stood stretched the limits of the device's effectiveness. The creep had fired blindly, drawn by movement. That or he was a really bad shot.

In the clearing where the horses waited, Garrett hurried to Siggy's side and searched through the saddlebags. He extracted the satellite phone, tucked a wireless Bluetooth earpiece in his ear, and punched in some numbers.

Aaron's gruff voice answered on the second ring. "You in trouble already?"

Garrett pulled his trusty M14 rifle from the sling attached to Siggy's saddle. "Yeah. Picked up a tail. Dude's driving something with an electric motor. Didn't hear him 'til he was on top of us."

He rummaged in the saddlebag again and removed the ELCAN Specter thermal infrared scope from its protective pouch and attached it to the scope mounts on the rifle, familiar actions he'd performed a thousand times before. "He took a shot at us when we crossed the river."

"Anybody hurt?" Aaron's voice sounded anxious through the earpiece.

"Shoofly's limping but still on her feet. TJ got thrown." Garrett dropped to his belly and low-crawled to a clear spot that let him see the river and far bank. With the rifle set against his shoulder, he looked through the scope, adjusted the focus, and let years of training and instinct take over. He formed a mental grid of the area and started a sweeping search.

"TJ all right?"

"She banged her head, but seems okay otherwise."

"You take care of the shooter?"

"Looking for a heat signature as we speak." He moved the scope in small increments. Back and forth ... up and down ... and stopped. "Gotcha. Target is standing in the open like he's the only one with hot toys."

Aaron chuckled.

Garrett continued to scan, using the powerful lens to

search for others. "I think he's alone. Looks like he took Mom's golf cart. Sucker better hope she don't get her hands on him."

"Cate plays golf?"

"Nah. She uses it to run around the ranch. Mostly over to the big barn in foaling season when Dad practically lives there. She won't be happy when she finds out he boosted her little giddyap."

Satisfied he had only one gunman to contend with, Garrett checked the wind currents and settled on his target.

TJ's pleading voice filled his ears.

Pfft-pfft. Two shots, a split-second apart. The first one hit the shooter's gun, a solid strike to the trigger guard. Be a long time before the scumbag used that hand. The second bullet slammed into his lower leg. He wouldn't be dancing much either.

Their would-be attacker dropped his rifle with a scream that shattered the night. He toppled over, writhing on the ground.

Pfft-pfft. The next two shots took out the front tires of Garrett's mom's cart. Sucker wouldn't be shooting at them anymore tonight or running away.

"Cowboy? Talk me to me, son."

"Threat neutralized but still breathing. I suspect he'll sing like a choirboy now. Tell Jonas we crossed the river a quarter mile short of the bend. Bring the horse trailer for Shoofly. He'll probably be able to coax her back across the river, but I doubt she'll make it back home under her own power."

"You need a replacement mount?"

"Nah. It'll take too long, and we've already wasted more time than we can afford. We'll ride double."

"Hold on a sec."

Garrett heard muffled voices on the other end of the line and then Aaron came back. "Cody says we can be there in twenty minutes, half-hour tops."

"I'm not willing to risk that our amigo down there hasn't called one of his compadres for help, so be careful on your way out. I'll touch base after we reach the rendezvous point. Oh yeah, you'll have to tow Mom's golf cart back. Just don't tell her it was me that shot her tires out." He pressed the off button on Aaron's chuckle and dropped the phone into his jacket pocket.

Garrett turned his attention to Shoofly next. "Easy, girl. Easy." The traumatized animal shivered continually but let him approach. Using a pocket flashlight, he inspected the wound she'd taken.

"Know what it feels like, girl. But you'll survive to brag about it." The gash was deep, running from the horse's tail across her flank. Garrett followed the wound, faltering when he encountered the ragged notch on the left lip of the saddle. Another inch to the right and—

He left the what-if thought for another time. Taking a

length of rope from Shoofly's saddle bags, he fashioned a long tether for the horse and tied it to a tree. With a final pat, Garrett gathered TJ's backpack, her saddlebags, and feed bag, and added them to Siggy's load. Pulling his big stallion's reins, he led him down the hill. Time to get TJ and move out.

"Garrett?" Her voice was husky, a little sultry, and laced with fear.

He should've eliminated the target when he had the chance. Well, he wouldn't make that mistake again. These men were roaches. Always returning. Multiplying. The only way to get rid of them … pinch off their head.

"I'm here, angel. Let's get you up on Siggy and get moving."

"Is Shoofly …?"

"Shoofly's gonna be fine. She has a pretty good gash on her flank, so Jo's coming to get her. You'll ride with me now."

"I heard shots."

"Yeah, well, that guy won't be bothering us no more. And before you ask—no, I'll didn't kill him. I already regret it, so don't bother asking again." He knelt at her side. "You sure you're okay?"

"I'm good. As long as I don't have to jump off a cliff." She let him pull her to her feet.

Garrett frowned. TJ had to be one of the strongest, most pig-headed people he knew, but by allowing him to take over—without argument—she was either rattled or hurt worse than she let on. Probably both.

"Five more steps this way." He kept an arm around her waist until she reached Siggy's side, and then he put her hands on the horse's mane. "Grab his hair and hold on."

To Siggy's credit, the big roan stood quiet when TJ slumped against him. Garrett mounted, slipped his left foot out of the stirrup, and reach down for TJ. "Give me your hand, angel. Now put your right foot in the stirrup."

She reached up and took his hand but missed the stirrup.

"Try again. Foot in the stirrup."

This time she managed to find the tread. He caught her under her armpits and lifted. When she settled sideways on the saddle in front of him, he patted her right leg. "Swing your leg over now. Good job. Now lean back and rest against me, baby. We got a long ride ahead."

Imperfect Wings

Chapter Twenty-One

The rocking motion slowed and came to a stop. TJ stirred, opening her eyes to a pale gray dawn. She blinked twice … and then settled back against Garrett's chest.

His chuckle hummed through her body.

"Morning, angel. Rise and shine."

She groaned.

He stepped out of the saddle then, leaving her skin cold where his body had warmed her. Had she really slept through the wee hours of the morning? Astride a horse and leaning against Garrett? No wonder everything hurt.

"C'mon, lazy bones. Siggy needs a break. He's worked hard, and we need to stretch." He reached up and plucked her off the big horse, holding her steady until she got both feet under her.

TJ took a tentative step and almost cried when her achy muscles and rusty joints protested. A tiny woodpecker rapped inside of her head. Better than last night but still not great. "I feel a hundred and fifty years old," she moaned.

"Take it slow. You'll loosen up in a bit. The … uh …

facilities are that way." He pointed off to the left. "Don't go far."

TJ looked where he indicated and saw only trees—and more trees. With a heavy sigh, she started for the *ladies room.*

When she returned, Garrett had spread a tarp on the ground. Several plastic-wrapped sandwiches, some apples, and a canteen of water were piled in the middle. He stood some distance away, near a plateau that looked out over a valley.

TJ walked to his side.

"I love it out here." Garrett draped an arm around her shoulders and pointed. "Look across the way. You'll see the sun rise any minute now."

They waited in silence broken only by the waking birds and rustling leaves. A babbling brook meandered downhill to disappear in the morning mist. No cars, no radios, no voices.

The gray dawn deepened to a soft blue as licks of fire gilded the mountains on the far side of the valley. She held her breath, awaiting the moment the sun popped into view.

"Breathe, angel."

He pulled her into his side, and she snuggled in, sharing his body heat. Time seemed to stand still as they watched until the mist burned away. A wonderland emerged. The stream reappeared far down in the valley, a silver ribbon sparkling in the sunlight. Four deer—two mamas and two Bambi-spotted babies—crept from the woods, noses lifted high as they searched for danger. Squirrels scampered through the trees.

"This must be the way God intended life." She couldn't find the words to describe the untouched beauty lying before her.

"I know what you mean. I've been all over the world, but this place ..." Garrett swept one arm wide. "I think it's about as close to Heaven on earth as we'll get."

She filled her lungs with the rarified air. Peace reigned here, uncorrupted by the world.

Siggy whinnied, breaking the idyllic moment.

"Let's grab something to eat. We got a long way to go yet."

Hours later, with the sun approaching its zenith, Garrett patted the arm she'd wrapped around his waist.

TJ straightened up from where she'd dozed against his broad back and rubbed at the drool spot on his shirt. The steep descent made it difficult to sit up straight ... which explained why he insisted she ride behind this morning. He'd given her his chest to lean against as they climbed and now his back for the downward slant. Always the gentleman. Always looking out for her.

"I can see the line shack through the trees. Another fifteen minutes tops and we'll be there."

They'd spoken little on the journey, mostly because their positions made it difficult to converse. She'd also slept for most of the ride.

TJ leaned to one side and caught a glimpse of a

ramshackle cabin tucked into the hill below. Sunlight glinted on the chrome bumper of a truck.

Their little trip through paradise had come to an end. "I'm coming back here one day. After I'm done with Castillo and Farleigh and all the ugliness in my life."

"You don't know how much that pleases me, angel."

TJ hadn't meant to say the words aloud. He already knew too many of her vulnerabilities, but it was past time to fix the brokenness within her. How else could she embrace a future, be it with Garrett, with someone else, or alone?

He raised an arm and waved toward the cabin.

A man she hadn't noticed returned the wave. "Yo, Cowboy. You're late." The man's voice carried on the thin mountain air.

"Dingo, that you?" Garrett yelled.

"Who is that man?"

"Dingo's an old teammate. Don't worry, angel. We can trust him" Garrett nudged Siggy to a canter.

The man jogged over to the horse's side.

Garrett pulled back on the reins and leaned down to shake hands.

"Is this little kitten glued to your back the same wildcat we pulled out of Honduras?"

TJ bristled at his words. Garrett had called him Dingo— another member of his team? She stuck her hand out. "Hi. I'm TJ. Are you the one I kicked in the leg or the head?"

Garrett laughed.

Color rose up the man's neck. "I'm the one you clubbed upside the head with your gun. Hopefully, you won't see fit to repeat the lesson." His grin seemed a little forced.

"Hop down, TJ." Garrett gripped her arm and bore most of her weight as she swung her leg over the horse's rump and slid down. Her breath hitched when another set of hands spanned her waist and helped her to the ground.

She moved away.

"Did your parents name you after the Australian wild dog, or do you have a civilized name?"

His smile faltered, but the happy-go-lucky grin soon reasserted itself. "My mom christened me Dorton Orris Gurden the third."

TJ winced. "Ouch."

"My initials are D-O-G, but since we already had a Dawg on the team, Cowboy here came up with Dingo. It stuck."

Garrett dismounted and turned toward the cabin. "What'd you bring us?"

TJ lagged behind as Garrett led Siggy toward the cabin.

Dingo matched him step for step. "F-250, super hemi, communications console with wireless, GPS, and a new radar gizmo." Dingo pointed to the truck bed. "Back here you got rifles, pistols, ammo, grenades, and the latest in night scopes … almost anything you can imagine."

"I don't know. I can imagine a lot." Garrett took the keys

from Dingo, unlocked the toolbox, and let out a low whistle.

The truck stood too high for her to see what the box contained, but apparently Garrett approved. He closed the lid with a nod and relocked it.

Dingo opened the driver's door and then the rear passenger door. "There's food and water for a week. Tank is three-quarters full. Plenty of gas to put some distance behind us."

TJ's eyes snapped up. What do you mean—us?"

Dingo looked from TJ to Garrett, his confusion plain. "I'm going with you."

"Nah-uh. That's not the plan. We'll drop you off in the first town we come to."

Ignoring TJ, Dingo confronted Garrett. "That right, man? She calling the shots here?"

When Garrett didn't say anything, Dingo went on. "Aw, c'mon, Cowboy. Be smart about this. You been up all night riding a horse and she"—he jerked a thumb at TJ—"looks like she'll pass out any minute. How far you think you'll get? At least let me drive for a few hours while you catch some shuteye."

Garrett nodded.

The argument made sense, but she bristled anyway. Garrett trusted him, but could she close her eyes with Dingo along?

"Fine. But I'm cleaning up first." Grabbing her pack, TJ

went inside the cabin.

Ten minutes later, feeling somewhat better after using bottled water to wash off most of the grime, TJ stepped outside and found Dingo in the driver's seat, the engine running. Garrett stood near the tree line stroking Siggy. When he removed the halter and smacked the stallion on the rump. Siggy bolted.

She walked to Garrett's side. "Will he be okay until they can get him?"

"Yeah. He'll be fine. You ready to roll?" Exhaustion shadowed his eyes.

It took an hour to get down the mountain. Dingo drove while Garrett filled him in on the details of the attack and their escape. When they reached the valley floor, Dingo stopped and looked at Garrett. "Okay, boss. Where're we heading?"

"Left."

Imperfect Wings

Chapter Twenty-Two

They traveled through a heavily forested area, jouncing on the rutted hardpan that seemed barely wide enough for one vehicle. She didn't know what they'd do if they met an oncoming vehicle. "How much longer?"

"Not long now."

Garrett had been saying the same thing for the past two hours. The man really needed to work on his communication skills.

A short time later and the dirt road ended abruptly.

"Turn right."

He'd fed Dingo turn-by-turn directions since they set out. Like he could only be trusted so far.

TJ watched Dingo's expression in the rearview mirror and had to choke off a laugh when he rolled his eyes. They could be aiming for the North Pole for all he knew. For all she knew as well.

Four small highway signs were planted at the side of the road, one after the other—Speed Limit 55—Challis, Idaho. Population 1,072—U.S. Route 93—and thankfully, a sign pointing to I-15.

Garrett tipped his hat down over his eyes, and dropped his chin to his chest. "Take the interstate up ahead and shoot south to Ogden, Utah. From there, we'll take I-80 over to Cheyenne. Wake me up if you run into any trouble."

That was more than he'd said since leaving the cabin.

TJ couldn't sleep, occupying her time instead by creating a list of what all she'd have to do once the trial ended. Like finding a job. Getting access to her bank account. And buying more clothes that actually fit.

Dingo grabbed his phone and thumb-typed a short message. He'd been texting with someone for the last hour. When he caught her watching him, he flushed. "Girlfriend troubles," was all he said as he set the cell in the console cup holder.

Twilight darkened the sky and the lights of Ogden appeared on the horizon. Dingo flipped the turn signal on and took the exit. "Don't think there's much between here and Cheyenne. We need to gas up." He pulled into a mini mart, parked by a pump, and got out of the truck, taking a credit card from his wallet.

When he leaned in to grab his phone, TJ warned him, "No credit cards."

He froze in mid-motion, "No worries, sweetheart. I'd have to go inside to pre-pay with cash, and you know we're supposed to keep a low profile. Pay at the pump is quicker." He turned the full force of his smile on her.

"Cash only, Dingo."

"What? You think Castillo will trace *my* credit card?" He laughed. "They don't know I'm involved."

"Let's wake Garrett and ask him."

Dingo hesitated and glanced at the sleeping cowboy in the passenger seat. When he looked at her again, his smile slipped into a darker emotion. "Whatever." He jammed the credit card back into his wallet, and turned with a huff, slamming the truck door.

TJ glared after him.

Then she looked at Garrett who still slouched in the front passenger seat. He couldn't be comfortable. She wasn't even sure how he managed to breathe with his head angled like that.

TJ reached over and rescued his black Stetson from where it had fallen on his lap.

"You don't like him much."

Startled, she looked at Garrett's face.

His eyes remained closed.

"I thought you were asleep," she said.

"I was."

"Are you hungry? There are sandwiches in the cooler— and not one peanut butter." How did she respond when she had no idea why Dingo irked her?

"No. Answer my question."

"You didn't ask a question."

Garrett's chest rose on a deep breath. He pushed upright

and stretched his neck before shifting sideways to face her.

"Why don't you like Dingo?"

Okay, she wouldn't deny it. "I don't know. He's been a soldier for how long? Shouldn't he know his away around all this covert stuff? And yet he wanted to use a credit card for the gas. Someone with his background should know credit cards can be tracked."

"It's more than that, TJ. Back on the mountain, when you first saw him, you drew up stiff as a priest's collar. Went all snippy. Why?"

"I'm not snippy."

His "I told you so" smirk made her want to snarl.

"Exactly. Polite and prissy with a little ice princess going on, but I'm the only one who provokes your snippy side. Until now. What's up with the attitude toward Dingo?"

Persistent, aggravating man. With no ready answer, she told him the truth. "I don't really know. There's something about him that rubs me the wrong way. He makes the hair on the back of my neck stand up. Haven't you ever run into somebody you just don't like?"

"He's a good man."

"I'm sure you think so."

A soft chime broke the standoff.

"Another text message? Really? That has to be at least a dozen now". She gestured at the cell phone Dingo had left in the cup holder on the door. "I don't think his focus is where it needs to be. He's been texting with his girlfriend for the past two hours. She'll probably freak if he doesn't respond right back."

Garrett lifted one eyebrow. "Girlfriend?"

"Yeah, girlfriend. You know, female companion. Sweetheart. A date. Dingo and his girlfriend are fighting."

Garrett scowled but said nothing more.

Okay, he didn't appreciate her sarcasm. "Sorry. I get crabby when I'm tired."

"Last I heard he was married with a two-year-old daughter and a baby on the way."

"And you said he was a good man." She really didn't like Dingo now. "I didn't see a ring on his finger … or any sign of one."

"Not unusual. Men in our profession don't wear rings. It's not safe given all the equipment we handle. They also reveal a weakness."

She mulled that over for a moment, understanding the need to protect their families. "So you think he's fooling around?"

"Maybe. Maybe not."

"And what is that supposed to mean?" Now that she thought about it, Dingo didn't act like a typical bachelor. At least not the ones she knew, like Derek and Kyle, Wade and Jonas, and even Garrett to some extent. Unattached guys were mostly players, always on the prowl, looking for an easy

hookup. Not Dingo. The only vibe she got from him was … resentment.

She didn't like him because he didn't like her? Oh mercy, exhaustion had numbed too many gray cells.

Rubbing her temples didn't clear her head or help the nagging headache she hadn't been able to shake. Okay. Deal with what she knew. The simple truth—Dingo set her teeth on edge. She didn't like him. Didn't trust him. And couldn't put her finger on why. "Maybe he's divorced." Her knee jabbed the back of Garrett's seat when she tried to stretch her legs. "Sorry."

"No apology necessary. Thanks for not making me take a turn back there. I'm not sure I'd be able to walk if I did."

TJ giggled at the image his words invoked.

"What's so funny?"

"You. You're like, what—seven feet tall? If you could squeeze back here, we'd need the Jaws of Life to get you out again."

"Har-har. And I'm six-five."

Only six-five. Good thing she was short. Neither of these men would like being crammed back here.

Her smile slid away. Did Fowler expect her to make the whole trip back here?

The text chime dinged again.

Garrett reached across the seat for the phone and looked at the display. A second later he let out a roar.

"What? What is it?"

He held the phone up so she could read the text notification with part of the message visible on the main screen: *HAVE YOU ON GPS. RENDEZVOUS CHEYE...* The message tag read RC.

Rafael Castillo. He'd found her again. TJ's insides turned to ice. "Garrett?"

"Dingo was part of my team. I trusted him." The dark blue eyes she found so mesmerizing had blackened with rage. "And he put a bug on the truck."

"The keys are in the ignition. Let's leave him and go." She started to climb over the console, but Garrett's outstretched arm barred her way.

"No. Let me think a minute."

"We don't have time, Garrett. He'll be back any minute. Let's leave, find the device, and remove it." Her voice rose on each word. She felt the old familiar panic rising.

"Finding a bug on a truck this size...he wouldn't make that easy.

"How do you know?" Her heart bounced around in her chest like a bronco.

"Because it's what I'd do." Garrett took her hand. "I need you calm, TJ. Will you trust me?"

Did she have a choice? "He's coming."

"TJ?"

She took a second to clamp down on the fear. "Okay. I

trust you."

"Good. When he gets in, ask him to pull up to the curb. You need to use the ladies' room. Once he parks …"

"Won't he think it odd that I didn't go while he was paying for the gas?"

His mouth twitched. "Men understand that ladies don't always do things the way we would. Now as I was saying, once he parks I'll open my door so you can get out. That's when you mention his text alert went off. Can you do that?"

"That's all?"

He nodded.

"Okay, but I still think we should leave his sorry butt here and get out of town."

"If we leave him, he'll call Castillo from a pay phone. They'll find us before we can ditch the truck. As long as they don't know we're onto them, we have the advantage."

Dingo sauntered across the pavement toward them and pulled the hose from the pump. After filling the gas tank, he climbed back inside. "I can't believe the line in there this time of night. Everybody's gone lottery crazy. You guys ready for the next leg?" He yawned. "I'm probably gonna need a break once we get to Cheyenne." The big Ford rumbled.

"Uh … Dingo?"

"Yeah, TJ?"

"Would you pull over to the curb first? I think maybe I should … um …"

"Why didn't you—" He sighed. "Never mind. No problem. Ladies' room is inside on the left. Take your time." He parked at the end of the row in front of the store.

Garrett got out and opened her door.

TJ's feet hit the pavement. She turned to look back inside. "Thanks. I won't be long. By the way, your cell went off again while you were in the store."

Dingo snatched up his phone from the cup holder and punched in his security code.

The next instant, Garrett lunged back inside and slugged him. Dingo's head cracked against the driver's side window, his body slumped against the door.

TJ jammed her fist in her mouth to keep from screaming. It happened so quickly. Over before she could blink.

Garrett raced around the front of the truck. "TJ, get over here now. I need your help."

She hurried after him. Thank goodness there weren't any other cars nearby.

He eased the driver's door open and slipped one hand inside to keep Dingo from spilling out. "Open the back door."

She yanked the door open.

Garrett hauled Dingo's boneless body from the cab. "Get in the front and find his cell phone before it locks. Go to Settings and then General. Find the Passcode Lock and turn it off. I want to know what Dingo and Mr. Castillo have been talking about all afternoon."

TJ scrambled out of the way as Garrett heaved Dingo's limp frame onto the backseat, head first and belly down. She climbed up in the cab, located Dingo's iPhone on the floor, and ran through the menu settings. "Done. Now what?"

"Go around to the other side. In the back, under the seat. Get the rope."

She located the coil of rope and handed it over and watched in fascination as Garrett deftly bound Dingo's wrists and elbows behind his back.

"Find something for a gag."

A search through the bags unearthed nothing suitable. Stumped for a moment, TJ grabbed her backpack and pulled out a sock. "Will this do?"

Garrett's grin would've made Satan proud. "Perfect. Stuff it in his mouth. All of it."

With Dingo face down on the seat, TJ had to wedge herself in the small leg space and jimmy his mouth open. "Okay."

"Grab his arms now. Pull when I lift him. Let's get him all the way inside so I can tie his ankles and close the door."

On her knees in the backseat, she tugged when Garrett hefted the deadweight inside. She almost swallowed her tongue when Garrett pulled a lethal-looking knife from a sheath strapped under his pants leg and lopped off a length of rope. He wound the cord between the unconscious man's teeth to secure the gag before tying it off and addressing his legs.

With a satisfied nod, Garrett checked the knots again. "Okay, he's not going anywhere. Your turn to drive, angel."

TJ adjusted the driver's seat forward as far as it would go and pulled out of the gas station. She turned east per their original plan while Garrett fiddled with the fancy radar gadget. After a few minutes of thumbing through the manual, he punched a few buttons, twisted a couple of knobs, and a map appeared on the screen. "Head east on I-80."

"But...isn't that where Castillo's men are waiting for us?"

"They need to believe we're still on course. Don't worry, we're not going to Cheyenne."

Garrett spent the next few minutes reading the text messages on Dingo's phone, breaking the silence now and then with a muttered oath. "The texts from Castillo started four days ago. He wanted Dingo to finagle his way into Fowler's inner circle and get assigned to your case. Aaron offered them the perfect opportunity when he called Fowler for help last night. Dingo got the assignment to deliver the truck. Their text messages haven't let up since."

"Fowler? Do you think he ...?"

"I don't know. I'm not sure who to trust right now, but we need help."

"I trust Aaron. He's kept watch over me for two years. Call him."

Garrett nodded and picked up the satellite phone.

"Aaron, we got a real stinker of a situation here. Were you

aware Dingo delivered the new wheels?" He tapped TJ's arm and pointed toward the road sign. I-80 East. To Cheyenne.

She nodded and flipped on the turn signal.

"I didn't think so. Surprised me, too. Didn't think he was still active. We lost touch after Honduras. He claims Fowler instructed him to stay with us. No, I didn't like it either."

TJ tapped Garrett's arm. "Tell him about the text messages and the GPS."

He held up a hand while he listened. "Well, here's the sticky part. Dingo's been getting text message from Castillo all afternoon. We found out when he went inside to pay for gas."

Garrett held the phone away from his ear as Aaron's irate curses filled the air.

"Calm down. There's a bigger problem. They have a GPS tracker on us. Somewhere on the road near Cheyenne. No, Dingo's hogtied in the back seat." Garrett chuckled, a really evil-sounding laugh that held no humor. "I'm looking for a nice, quiet spot where we can have a private conversation."

TJ set the cruise control and listened to Garrett explain his plan to Aaron. An hour later, he pointed at the road sign ahead. "Rock Springs. Exit there."

Dingo had remained quiet during the drive, but now his muffled rants filled the truck as he bucked and kicked.

TJ left the interstate and came to a stop at the end of the exit ramp.

"Left. About four miles."

"Are you sure? It looks like nothing but desert out here."

"Exactly."

Another twenty minutes and Garrett pointed ahead. "There. Turn down that road."

"That's not a road. It's a pair of ruts."

"We'll be fine. Do as I say."

She bristled at his tone but turned where he indicated.

The truck's headlights punched a hole in the shadowy landscape. Her line of vision penetrated no more than a dozen yards ahead. "How far?" Their speed topped out at fifteen miles per hour as she navigated across the desert floor, dodging dry arroyos. Any faster and they'd flip for sure.

"A little more."

Dingo had fallen off the seat when they turned onto the rutted path. His groans and oomphs punctuated the silence as they bumped over the dusty plain.

Finally, Garrett spoke. "Here is good. Cut the headlights and stay put. Leave the engine running. I'll only be a minute."

Garrett yanked open the back door. With one hand fisted in Dingo's shirt and the other gripping his belt, Garrett propelled his prisoner through the sagebrush. Trussed like a turkey with barely enough slack between his feet for a shuffle step, Dingo hobbled along as fast as he could.

TJ opened her door. She had no doubts about Garrett's honor, but he was also a soldier. One who'd done his duty, unpleasant as it may be. Would he kill Dingo? In cold blood?

Leaving the motor running, she grabbed a flashlight and hurried after the two men.

Overhead, stars twinkled in the sky like fireflies on a summer's night, providing the only other source of light. When she reached the two men, the gag was gone from Dingo's mouth.

"What's the going price for betrayal? The team bled for you, man. We were brothers. What's Castillo got on you?" Garrett shoved Dingo, making him fall to his knees.

"Not Castillo." Dingo spat, his voice raspy. "Farleigh. He's been behind the whole thing from the start. He smoothed the way for Castillo's takeover in La Cruza. His contacts set up the pipeline from Honduras to North Carolina. His money funded the first deal … while he stayed in the background. It was the Senator who gave Castillo our intel. We wasted a whole year while they played us. But if Krieger goes down, he'll take Farleigh with him.

"That doesn't explain now. What's he got on you, Gurden?"

"He has my pregnant wife and baby girl."

Garrett reeled from the words. "Why didn't you go to Fowler? Or me … or any of the team. You know what we can do. We can get them back."

Dingo's voice cracked. The once proud and confident warrior dropped his head. "All those hostages we rescued in Iraq and Afghanistan, Honduras, and Columbia—they were strangers. You can't understand, but it's different—intolerable—when it's your own loved ones. I had zero time to decide. He had a gun to Gina's head."

"You know he'll kill you. Kill Gina and Missy, too."

"I don't care about me but if my family has a chance—any chance—I had to take it."

Night temperatures in the desert varied dramatically from the daytime readings. Even so, TJ couldn't attribute the chill in her bones to the barren land. This cold went deeper.

"Where'd you stick the tracking device on the truck?"

"I swear, Cowboy, I didn't know there was a bug until that last text."

"Fowler?"

Dingo shrugged. "Don't think so, but I don't know."

Half an hour later, armed with all the information Dingo could provide, they left him in the desert. In the dark. Bound hand and foot. Garrett had refused Dingo's offer to essentially get himself killed in a mission to take the senator down. With a little bit of luck and a whole lot of God's mercy, though, Aaron would get someone out to the desert to collect the wretched traitor by midday. Before the heat made rescue unnecessary.

"Garrett, when Dingo doesn't respond to text messages, Castillo will think he's been neutralized. And move the timeline up. What do we do?"

He pointed at the onscreen map. "Follow the driving directions to Denver International Airport."

Imperfect Wings

Chapter Twenty-Three

Denver International lit up the Colorado night like a Hollywood movie grand opening. The terminal's strange architectural facade looked more like a futuristic encampment of billowy, white circus tents more than an airport.

"Turn there."

TJ glanced at the sign that read Economy Parking. "You sure?"

The location of the airport, situated northeast of Denver's city limits, could work against them if Castillo's men showed up. There would be no blending into the city's traffic. No hiding in built up areas. Late as it was, traffic would be sparse with nothing but a long toll road and mile after mile of empty interstate.

"No, TJ. I'm making this up as I go. If you have a better idea, then by all means, let's hear it. Otherwise, you need to shut up and follow …"

Garrett's mouth clamped shut. A muscle twitched in his jaw as he turned to stare out the passenger window.

Shut up and follow orders? Like one of his men? TJ swallowed the knot in her throat and struggled to hold back the

quick tears. And that only made her angry. When had she become such a crybaby? And how could this maddening cowboy with his asinine, superior male arrogance provoke such a knee-jerk response?

She trusted him—wanted to trust him. But apparently he didn't trust her with even a simple explanation. Like why he would take them into this dead-end trap knowing Castillo's men had to be close. She deserved an explanation. A hint or something.

With a deep sigh and an angry swipe at her eyes, TJ choked off a blistering retort. No need to throw gasoline on the tension between them.

"You're right." She hated that her voice deepened as she struggled to keep her emotions in check. "You're the experienced one here. I won't second guess you anymore."

Flipping the right turn signal, TJ let the truck's speed drop before merging onto Peña Boulevard. From there, more signs led them to the long-term parking lot entrance and the ticket dispenser.

"Give me the ticket stub." His stern voice held a chill that made her shiver. "Head toward the far end of the lot."

She bristled at the command. Yes, sir, General, sir. By the way, sir, why are we making it easy for them to corner us like rats?

The words screamed for release, but TJ clamped her teeth together. She would trust him, if it killed her ... and it might.

As they neared the rear of the parking lot, he pointed toward the next to last aisle. "Cut the lights and turn down this row. Stop here."

Her hands trembled as she tapped the brakes and brought the vehicle to a halt.

Garrett reached up and disconnected the front and rear ceiling lights. When the truck rolled to a halt, he jumped out and disappeared from sight. A moment later, four soft raps reverberated from the rear of the truck followed by a sound like breaking glass. If he'd broken the taillights, they wouldn't be going very far in this vehicle.

"Pull up next to that SUV at the end of the row," he said climbing back inside. "Get close like you're gonna park right beside it."

TJ maneuvered the truck next to the light blue Honda Pilot.

"We need the ticket stub to get out with our new ride. Aaron will send someone to collect this truck. They'll pay the lost ticket fee."

Surprised, TJ gaped at him. He'd given an explanation. Wow. Was that an attempt to meet her halfway?

"We have more vehicle options at the airport than the city. A vehicle from long term parking won't be missed right away, and there are fewer people to get in the way of a stray bullet at this time of night. The guys tracking us by GPS will waste time looking for the truck—time we'll spend putting miles between

us and them." Garrett gave her a quick look but then returned to searching for whatever it was he wanted.

TJ remained quiet, unwilling to break the unexpected truce.

"Pull up some more. Okay, that's good. Leave the engine running and come help me." He slipped out and eased his door closed. "We'll stash our gear between these parked cars for now," he told her over the top of the truck. "You get the stuff out of the backseat while I unload the cargo box."

He didn't provide many details, but at least he seemed to be making an effort to include her.

Working fast, it took them less than five minutes to unload and stash the weapons and supplies between the last two cars in the row.

"What kind of vehicle are we looking for?"

"We aren't. You're staying here with the gear."

TJ grabbed his arm when he turned to go. "You're leaving me here?"

His large hand covered hers and squeezed. "I'm not leaving you, angel. I can do this faster without you. You'll be safe here once I move the truck. Trust me, okay?" His hand lifted to her face, the knuckles scraping across one cheek in a rough caress. "I won't be long."

Every fiber of her being wanted to scream, "No!" Wanted to latch onto him and not let go. She forced a nod instead. "Okay. But you better be quick."

"Just call me Speedy." Garrett chuckled and leaned down to brush her lips with his. "Stay down below car level, stay frosty, and keep your six-shooter handy."

She stared at him in confusion. "What?"

"Sorry. Army talk. Stay frosty—cold, emotionless, alert." His soft chuckle faded away just like he did. A moment later the soft rumble announced the truck's departure, and then the night fell silent.

TJ flipped off the safety on the P238 Garrett had given her. She ejected the magazine and pulled back the slide to check the chamber. Satisfied, she slapped the clip home and thumbed the safety on again before tucking the gun in the waistband holster. She nudged the single wooden crate with a foot, trying to slide it closer to the Honda. It barely moved. The way Garrett's muscles had bulged when he lifted the locked box from the truck bed, it must contain some really heavy munitions. Another, harder shove moved it a few inches. Good enough. She settled down on the hard seat and leaned against the car.

From her perch on the crate, TJ took inventory of all the gear they'd removed from the truck—the two saddle bags, her scat bag, his duffle, the cooler of sandwiches and drinks, a case of water, a weird looking rifle, two shoulder holsters with handguns, and eight large canvas sacks filled with Kevlar vests, boxes of ammunition for the handguns and rifle, some things that looked like night vision scopes, communications

equipment that she had no idea how to operate, and who knew what else. She untied the heaviest of the sacks to reveal a long, flat, wooden box. Beyond curious, TJ opened the lid and looked inside—and almost dropped it.

Grenades? Were they going to war?

With nothing else to fill the time, TJ tried to relax and do what she did best—worry. Garrett said he wouldn't be long, but how long was long? Ten minutes? Twenty? An hour? A quick glance at her wristwatch showed only five minutes since he left. Her head thumped against the side of the car.

Okay, time to scope out the area. See where her best chances lay if the worst happened. TJ rose to a semi-squat and peered over the hood of the Camry next to the Honda. She turned in a slow circle, gauging likely escape routes. From this vantage, it looked like one way in and one way out. A prison, surrounded by a twelve-foot high chain-linked fence with concertina wire at the top, security cameras, and probably motion sensors. Not good.

She hated the helplessness of waiting almost as much as she hated the dark. At least the parking lot provided uniform lighting. The big metal halide lights covered the enormous acreage, but fell short in reaching the extreme perimeters.

The low rumble of a vehicle in the distance caught her attention? Garrett? Had he found their replacement already? TJ rose a little higher, anxious to find the source of the noise. There. Near the entrance.

The vehicle, a dark colored sedan, crept down the wide middle entrance row. It inched along, seemingly in no hurry. Too slow. As though the driver searched for more than an available parking space. Garrett knew exactly where he'd left her. He wouldn't waste time like this car did.

She had a bad feeling.

As she watched, the sedan's headlights winked out. Smaller lights flashed from the sides of the car, methodically playing over each parked vehicle. It had to be them.

Mind racing with fear and uncertainty, TJ discarded option after option. Did Garrett see the new threat? How could she warn him? If they spotted the pile of equipment—and from the way they conducted the methodical search they would—her cover would be blown.

Don't panic. Remember what Garrett said. She was safe here. He would come for her. Trust him.

Decision made, TJ returned to the equipment and started shoving the bags and sacks underneath the nearest cars. She had to sit on the ground and use her legs to move the big wooden box, but with one final thrust, and not a moment too soon, the heavy crate slipped out of sight under the rear of the Honda.

The slow-moving sedan inched closer to where she knelt. TJ held her breath and rose in freeze-frame increments to peek. Only two cars away. Should she slink away now? Put more distance between them? Yes.

TJ scrambled backward, taking care to make as little noise as possible while keeping watch on the sedan's progress. She withdrew the pistol from its holster, thumb sliding toward the safety.

Two massive arms came around her. One trapped the gun between them, while the other hand covered her mouth and pulled her back against what felt like a concrete wall.

"Shhh, it's me."

TJ's bones melted like warm butter. Garrett's whispers soothed the paralyzing fear.

"Breathe, angel."

She took a shuddering breath and opened her mouth to warn him, but he covered her mouth again.

Pressing his lips against her ear he whispered. "Good job hiding the gear. Now, I want you to duck-walk to the row behind us as quietly as you can. When the sedan passes, scoot down two more cars and then over to the row they just left. Stay low. Move fast but with stealth. Once they're far enough away, go to Section R, Row 6, near the middle. Here." He put a key in her hand and closed her fingers around it. "Look for a silver Toyota Tundra. It's the only one on that row. Get in quick and wait inside the truck. When you see my signal, crank her up and get over here fast to help me reload our gear."

"What signal?"

His low laugh made the hair on her arms stand up. "You'll know when you see it. Go on now. You can do this."

"What about you?" she asked over her shoulder, but he'd already disappeared. The relief she'd felt at his return vanished.

TJ worked her way through the rows of parked cars, always aware of the sedan's position, the low rumble of the car's engine the only sound breaking the silence of the night. Garrett's words looped through her mind. Stay low. Move fast. Use stealth. Watch for his signal.

She choked back a snort. A shadow made more noise than Garrett. And he wanted her to be stealthy?

Section R lay two-thirds of the way across the sizable parking lot. Following a zigzag path up and down the rows of cars, she checked the location of the prowling sedan before bending low to run across the open lanes. She reached Row 8 near the rear of the lot. Two more to go. This might work yet.

A light wavered. Two rows over. Someone walking with a flashlight. Did they drop a man at the entrance? Split up to cover more ground? Was there more than one?

She eased the gun from the waist holster and flicked the safety off. Could she kill a living, breathing man?

Conviction had her teeth clenching. Yeah, she could.

TJ sank to a crouch, as the searcher's silhouette moved away. From her position near the end of Row 8, the overhead lights illuminated the man as he moved to the next row. The fool walked brazenly down the middle of the aisles. She waited with a slow count to fifty: one-Mississippi, two-Mississippi …

No more lights bobbed in semi-darkness. No more

movement among the cars. Think, TJ.

Three silhouettes in the car. Two in the front and one in the back. The sedan would seat four comfortably, but more than that—especially if the passengers were all men—would make for a very close fit. Could it really be that easy? Was the man she'd seen with the flashlight the only one on this side?

Holding her breath, she hunkered down and hurried across the open lane where she dropped to the ground between an older model van and a Hyundai. She strained to hear sounds of pursuit over the thumping of her heart.

Crickets chirped in the brush outside the fence perimeter. One more peek showed the bobbing flashlight still moving away.

With a final dash, TJ reached Row 6 and found the silver truck, right where Garrett said it would be, backed into the parking space.

She tried the door, found it unlocked, and climbed in fast, pulling the door closed as quietly as possible and shaking with relief. The elation of reaching her goal unseen disappeared with the realization that Garrett didn't know about the man on foot. Should she warn him? No. He said wait for his signal.

An explosion ripped through the quiet night.

TJ screamed and almost strangled herself with the seatbelt when she wrenched around to look behind her. That was no signal. It was an all out declaration of war.

A flick of her wrist and the silver truck leapt from the

parking spot, clipping the rear bumper of the car parked beside it. Grit spewed. She hit thirty crossing the wide middle row that led to the exit. Not far now. Where was he?

Movement drew her eye to the left. Flashlight Man raced between the parked cars, angling toward the raging inferno that was all that remained of the sedan. He spied her at the same time she saw him. He slid to a stop behind a car, leaned across the hood, and leveled his handgun her way.

Ping!

She felt the bullet hit the truck. He'd fired at her! She had to find Garrett and get out of here.

TJ forced her eyes back to the road just in time to correct her course before the truck took out the chain-link fence on the right ... and spotted Garrett.

He peered over the top of the Honda Pilot where they'd dropped their gear. He had a funny looking rifle wedged against his shoulder. One little recoil and he slung the weapon over his shoulder.

What...?

She threw a quick glance back at the flashlight man and saw him jerk upright and clutch at his chest and drop out of sight.

He shot him. Oh dear Lord, Garrett shot Flashlight Man!

When she looked for Garrett again, he'd dragged the heavy wooden box from beneath the car. He paused to wave her forward.

She jumped on the brakes, sending the rear of the truck skidding sideways. The Tundra came to a halt right beside the Honda.

"Leave it running and come help me. Quick!"

Slamming the gearshift into park, she hopped down from the cab.

"Grab everything and throw it in. We'll sort it later." He heaved the heavy wooden box over the side and let it drop with a clang.

TJ sprinted to the pile of gear and snatched up the saddlebags, her scat bag, and his duffle and threw them into the backseat before returning for the cooler. They had everything reloaded in little more than a minute.

"I'll drive. Get in." Tossing the last sack in the back, Garrett slid behind the wheel and floored it. He pulled the parking ticket from his shirt pocket with a wad of cash. "Here, hold this. Count out what we need when I tell you."

The truck skidded to a stop at the auto-pay kiosk. "Six dollars. Give me a ten." He fed the money into the cash slot. The machine whirred and spit out a receipt. Sirens blared in the distance.

Garrett drove away in the opposite direction.

Chapter Twenty-Four

TJ gathered the baggy jeans and oversized football shirt from the bathroom floor—clothing they'd purchased from the thrift store in Wichita five days ago. "A disguise," he'd insisted. "We need to blend in when we reach D.C."

Blend in. Right. No problem for her. She looked like a scrawny teenage boy in this getup. Garrett on the other hand, wearing a skin-tight tee shirt, jeans that seemed molded to his long legs, and army boots, looked like the ultimate bad boy. With his physique, the man drew the eye of every female under eighty.

Donning her last pair of clean undies, TJ stepped into the pants and pulled the Redskins jersey over her head. Yanking the grungy baseball cap down, she dared a last quick peek at the cracked mirror. Much as she hated to admit it, Garrett was right. A young punk stared back. With a sigh, she tossed her few toiletries in the backpack. If they stuck to the schedule, she'd enjoy a long, hot bath tonight.

Outside the bathroom, two rumpled beds waited, their disarray adding to the seediness of the small motel room. Not using credit cards limited their lodging options, but at least

they'd both gotten some much needed sack time—in a real bed. They'd taken turns last night, one sleeping while the other kept watch. Now, after a few hours rest on the lumpy mattress and a lukewarm shower that didn't encourage lingering, TJ felt remarkably refreshed. It sure beat riding in a truck 24/7.

Only a few more days and the craziness would be over.

TJ sat on the side of the bed to pull on her sneakers and thought about Garrett. Such a contrast of light and dark. The ruthless machine she'd seen in action back in Denver didn't jive with the sweet cowboy who sang along with George Strait and Willie Nelson all the way through Oklahoma. The man who'd brooded behind dark sunglasses, studying her for hours while she drove across Tennessee. And now, waiting for her outside to give her some much needed alone time.

After sweeping the room one more time for any missed items, she tied her shoes, grabbed the backpack, and walked outside.

Garrett sat behind the wheel of the shiny, midnight blue Suburban, a step up from the truck they'd lifted in Denver. He smiled and held out a Styrofoam cup in invitation.

TJ zeroed in on his mouth as he lifted his own cup for a sip. So unfair. The man had a smile that could curl a woman's toes or drop a grown man to his knees with a frown. A man's man in a man's world. And for today, he was still all hers.

She walked toward the vehicle, unable to hold back a grin, climbed inside, and tossed the pack in the backseat. "Where to,

Ace?"

He lifted that one quirky eyebrow. "On the home stretch now, Slick. No more detours. Good-bye, Charlotte. Hello, D.C." He handed her the second cup of coffee when she settled.

"Mmmm." Nothing like fresh brewed coffee. She took a noisy sip. "How long will it take?"

"Six hours, but we got plenty of time. We'll head north and cut over to I-95. It's a straight shot from there. Aaron's expecting us around four."

"Aaron's there? Then everything's okay at the ranch?"

"Talked to him while you showered. Castillo's men left not long after we met up with Dingo." He chuckled. "That's a good thing since Allie and her parents wore out their welcome. Aaron said Dad threatened to stuff Allie and her mother in a sack and drown them."

Yeah, she could see that happening. "So everybody's okay? What about Shoofly? And Siggy?"

"Wade and Jonas got Siggy back home on Tuesday. Shoofly didn't need stitches. She's enjoying all the attention and eating like a—"

"Horse?" TJ finished for him with a laugh. "What else did Aaron say?"

"Fowler says the jury's been picked, and Dan Quigley, the U.S. Attorney who's prosecuting the case, expects to finish all the preliminary stuff today." Garrett followed the sign pointing toward Greensboro. "If all goes like he thinks, you'll be on the stand first thing Monday morning. Quigley's driving him nuts, calling every hour. He won't rest 'til you're in the safe house. He plans to spend Saturday and Sunday prepping you to take the stand."

TJ choked, the hot coffee burning her mouth. "Monday? So fast?"

"Fast? It's been two years, TJ."

"I mean … I didn't think …"

"Hey, think of it this way. Three more days and you get your life back. And I'll be right by your side the whole way."

"Won't Castillo have people watching the prosecutor's office?"

"Fowler's talking video conference. Said he'd give us details tomorrow. Once we reach the safe house, you won't leave again until the trial."

"Will Aaron be there? Who else?"

"I wanted to surprise you, but yeah, Aaron will be there. He insisted on heading up your security. Derek and Kyle came, too. Fowler has a whole unit assigned to protect you."

Her eyebrows shot sky high.

"Rest easy, angel." He patted her hand. "They're all men Aaron knows. And I've worked with a few of them. We'll keep you safe."

Should she point out that he'd also known and worked with Dingo?

Their conversation died down, falling into an easy silence that still amazed her after five days in the truck. She finished her coffee, fiddled with the radio, straightened the stuff in her backpack, and finally turned to face him again.

"Garrett?"

"Yeah?"

"Why'd we have to swap vehicles again? Don't get me wrong, this is much nicer, but ... will the owner of the Tundra get his truck back? I mean, grand theft might throw a monkey wrench in our schedule. How much trouble did we cause the truck owner and his family?"

"The truck was reported stolen yesterday. While it's unlikely the cops would look for it sixteen hundred miles away, it's too late in the game to take the risk."

At her gasp, Garrett chuckled. "Don't worry. Aaron had the Tundra picked up. It'll get serviced, get any dings fixed and whatever maintenance is needed, and then detailed so it looks brand new. In a few days, the Denver police will find it conveniently parked back in the airport parking lot. A week or so after that, the owner will receive an anonymous thank you note in the mail, along with a little monetary show of appreciation."

"Money? That's good. How much?"

"I dunno. Couple of hundred, I'd guess. Enough to say thanks, but not so much it'll draw unwanted attention."

"What about Dingo? And his family? What will happen to

him?"

His good humor faded. "Dingo's in custody. Fowler's working on getting his wife and kid back. I'm sure we'll get an update tonight."

"You have a lot of faith in Agent Fowler, don't you?"

"No, but I trust Aaron. He's the one with faith in Fowler."

North of Richmond, they stopped for a late lunch. The restaurant had four giant flat-screen televisions, three tuned to sports channels and the fourth to a local news station.

TJ studied the menu, not really hungry. The closer they got to their destination, the more unsettled her stomach became. Now, with justice dangling within reach, all she wanted to do was curl up in a corner somewhere and hide.

After the waitress took their order, Garrett asked, "What's got you so knotted up, angel?"

"It's all wrong. All this happened because of me."

"TJ, don't …"

"It's true. I didn't go to La Cruza for benevolent reasons. Not to help the orphanage. Not to see my father's work. I was angry that he chose them over me. When the government wouldn't do anything about his murder, I made it my mission to force their hand. I wanted proof, something too big for them to ignore. Anything that would put Castillo behind bars. Well, I got my evidence, but look at the cost. How many others have died because of me? People I don't know about?"

"Look, TJ. There's a reason he's called El Carnicero—

The Butcher. He torched La Cruza. How many more villages would he have destroyed if you hadn't drawn his attention? You didn't start this reign of terror, but you can finish it."

"The end shouldn't justify the means."

He clasped her hands in his bigger ones. His expression grew hard. "Sometimes it does."

The waitress interrupted to serve their food then, forcing Garrett to pull his hands away. As soon as she left, Garrett reached across to snag TJ's fingers again.

"Look, I haven't been to church in a while, but that doesn't mean I didn't get a good grounding in the scriptures growing up. I remember one Bible verse in particular because it pulled me through some rough times. 'God causes all things to work together for good to those who love Him, to those who are called according to His purpose.' TJ, you're an instrument of justice. You're only responsible for your own actions, not Castillo's."

TJ contemplated Garrett's words while nibbling at her salad. She pushed the half-eaten food away.

Garrett looked up, a question in his eyes.

Emotion made her voice quaver, but she staved off the tears. "I might not be responsible for his actions, but I'm the reason he razed La Cruza. If I'm an instrument of justice, then I'm a broken one. I shouldn't hate him so much."

"Tell me something. When you set out to spy on Castillo, did you intend for him to kill those villagers?"

"No!"

"If you'd known the consequences, would you have gone searching for your proof?"

She shook her head.

"Exactly. You're only fault is not knowing of the evil that haunts this world. As for hating Castillo, well, we all have broken wings. We make mistakes every day, yet we continue our struggle to fly. The alternative is give up and let the winds take you where they will. I won't let you do that. Now, wipe your nose and get those imperfect wings flapping. We still got some flying to do today."

TJ used one of the paper napkins to blow her nose. How could she resist this man when he made it clear he would see her through this mess? Garrett might be hardened by his years of combat, but his heart was soft enough to want to soothe her fears. She stacked her fork and knife on the plate and pushed them away.

The television behind Garrett broadcast the local news. An Amber alert flashed across the screen, warning of a child's abduction. With the volume muted, TJ squinted and tried to follow the captions about the ten-year-old missing girl. A photo of a pretty little Latino girl with long, straight black hair and somber dark eyes flashed on the screen. The caption scrolled across the screen—Gabriela Carliez, ten years old, last seen yesterday.

It couldn't be! TJ's runaway heart thudded painfully.

"TJ? Baby, what's wrong?"

"He has Gaby!" The words came out in a harsh whisper.

Garrett turned to look behind him just as another photo flashed up on the screen—this one of TJ.

The world went into a crazy spin and for a moment she thought her stomach might reject everything she'd eaten. The noisy restaurant faded away, replaced by a loud rushing sound.

"TJ!" Garrett's sharp bark broke through. And then he was by her side, forcing her head down between her legs. "Slow breaths." His hand rubbed circles up and down her spine.

She was vaguely aware of him dropping some bills on the table, and then he pulled her to her feet. With one arm around her shoulders and the other hand pressing her face against his chest, he guided her out of the restaurant.

Imperfect Wings

Chapter Twenty-Five

Garrett glanced away from the road to look at TJ's profile again. She hadn't uttered a peep since leaving the restaurant almost an hour ago. He'd expected tears or anger, some kind of reaction, but she just sat there.

Her body language smacked of defeat—slumped posture, fixed stare, with no attempt to shift positions. He knew this behavior. Battle-hardened soldiers who thought they'd seen everything sometimes shut down like this. Everyone had a limit. Had she reached hers?

She'd fallen into a nightmare in Honduras, one that had her running for her life while the government moved at the speed of mud in bringing Krieger to trial. But this, to get so close to the end only to have Castillo snatch one of her little orphan girls ... Those girls meant so much to her.

TJ might know on a conscious level she held no responsibility for Castillo's actions, but the human heart seldom listened to reason. Head knowledge couldn't eradicate soul-deep wounds. Only time could do that ... and never completely.

The past couldn't be undone, but he could help her carry

the burden from now on. Reaching over the console to tug one of her hands from her lap, he intertwined their fingers and infused as much confidence as possible into his voice. "Fowler will get her back."

Garrett knew all too well how self-blame clung like a shadow. Faces from his own past remained constant companions, their names a chanted litany like a memory button stuck on repeat. Team members he'd lost in places the devil wouldn't even go. They all understood the risks going in. Each one knew a routine patrol could go belly-up without warning. Even so, at the end of the day, it was his responsibility as their team leader to bring them home.

But on his last mission, five of their number—soldiers he'd shared meals with, slept next to, men he'd trusted with his life and who'd trusted him with theirs—made the return journey back to the States in flag-draped boxes. Five scars he would carry for the rest of his life.

Yeah, he understood how guilt worked.

"Baby, you're staggering under a load that's way too heavy and not yours to carry."

TJ wriggled her fingers, trying to tug loose.

For a moment, disappointment got the better of him. Garrett tightened his grip. He wanted to savor the feel of her soft skin against his calloused palm. He liked holding her hand. But when she continued to pull, he let go.

"Your hands are too big, cowboy. My fingers are going

numb." She pulled her splayed fingers free and flexed them a few times before tucking her hand in his. "There. That's better."

Garrett grinned. Thank goodness his brothers weren't here to see him beaming like a fool. Those two would taunt him without mercy.

"I'm okay, Garrett. I won't break."

Her voice warmed him. She might protest her fragility, but her small hand felt like a fine-boned bird in his, one he could crush with a squeeze. It scared him how much he wanted to take care of this woman.

She turned sideways in the seat to face him, one leg curled under. "I hate that he took Gaby. It's killing me inside, but I can't let him win. He and Farleigh have to be stopped and apparently Krieger is the only way to do it. I have to trust that Fowler will get Gaby back, and I realize she can't be my focus right now. My job is to make the jury see what happened that awful day."

A single tear shimmered before it spilled over and dribbled down her cheek. She brushed it away.

Garrett thought his heart might burst. The petite warrior he'd first seen in the jungles of Central America was back. TJ McKendrick might be a little bitty thing, but she had an enormous spirit. "I always knew you were strong, even when you didn't want to be, but now ..." He whistled softly. "You take my breath away, woman."

She looked away, her cheeks turning a delightful pink.

"I meant it. About Fowler getting Gaby back. He has resources you can't begin to imagine. If anyone can find her, it's him."

She nodded but didn't raise her eyes. "I believe you, Garrett. And I trust you."

He lifted her hand and kissed her palm. "Thank you. I know trust comes hard for you, and I treasure the gift. But there's something else messing with your head today. How about we get all your worries out on the table right now and deal with them?"

Her response took a long time coming, but at least she didn't pull away. Garrett let her move at her own speed.

"Everything in me screams with hatred for Don Castillo, and yet feeling that way seems wrong, like I'm no better than him. I mean, aren't we supposed to forgive our enemies? My own mother blamed me for ruining her life and couldn't forgive me. How can I forgive a sadistic killer?"

Her anguish surprised Garrett. Why did women have to think everything to death? He'd never felt a need to forgive those he'd fought against. A good, healthy fear—sure. But not anger or hatred. Strong emotion skewed your judgment. It had no place in war, not if you wanted to come out alive and in one piece.

"TJ, listen to me. I know you've been alone for a long time with no one but yourself to rely on. Whatever went on with your mother—you were only a child."

"You don't understand."

"Okay, put it this way—do you blame Gaby for what's happened? I mean, that little girl didn't have to take you out to Castillo's encampment. All the tragedy that followed might have been avoided if she'd said no."

TJ's eyes went wide, her voice rose with indignation. "No, it wasn't like that. Gaby did what I asked her to do. She didn't know ..."

Garrett waited as comprehension dawned in those gorgeous blue eyes. He lifted her hand and kissed her palm again. "Forgiving someone else seems a little meaningless if you can't forgive yourself."

"Oh ..." The single word came out in a strangled whisper.

Garrett gripped the steering wheel. He wanted to shout. Her head knew a child held no responsibility for what happened in childhood. Maybe now she could believe it for herself.

Something shifted inside him as he watched her with surreptitious glances. Some indefinable something clicked into place. Light flooded the dark corner of his soul he kept locked up tight. This little dab of a woman, with all her insecurities and fierce determination, stirred feelings he'd thought long buried. Made him think the dreams he'd abandoned might yet be possible.

Could any woman handle the reality of his true nature?

How he'd almost killed a kid with his bare hands in high school because his rage got away from him. The thought of revealing the ugliness of his soul made him sweat. Scared him worse than any firefight.

"Hey, you all right?" She squeezed his hand this time.

"Yeah, I am. In fact, I'm better than I've been in a long time."

As the afternoon wore on, traffic on the interstate picked up, mostly coming from the Capitol. Garrett took the exit for Fort Belvoir and stopped at a gas station to refuel. After waiting outside the door while TJ visited the ladies room, he moved the Suburban over to the area by the air pressure pump. "I need to call Aaron." He pressed the speaker button so TJ could listen.

Aaron's brusque, no-nonsense voice answered on the first ring.

"You close?"

"Yeah, about ten miles south of 495. We heading toward Alexandria?"

"Yep. Cross the Potomac and stay on the Beltway. Turn south on Branch Avenue. You'll know where to go from there." He disconnected before Garrett could say anything more.

TJ stared, confusion written on her face. "Well, can we be a little more mysterious? I wanted to ask about Gaby. And I don't have any more clean underwear. I'll need a washer and dryer, and I don't have anything suitable to wear to court because I will not wear this awful, gross jersey again. And talk about court, when do I meet with the prosecutor? I'm sure he has to be concerned about what I'll say. I don't know what to expect, what time to be where. What did Aaron mean we'll know where to go from there? Call him back."

Garrett pursed his lips, trying to contain his amusement. TJ could talk a mile a minute when she got rattled. "Whoa, baby. Take a breath. I can't keep up. First off, I'm sure Aaron's got his reasons for going all need-to-know on us. He's a cautious old bird. Probably worried about the signal getting hacked or something. I'm sure we'll have the rest of your answers before much longer."

Once they got back on the highway, he kept a wary eye on the traffic around them. They merged right and took the turn to I-495, turning onto Branch Avenue not long after.

"Um, Garrett?"

"Yeah?"

TJ stared out her side window. "See that green Honda Accord a few cars back? I think it might be following us."

"Yeah."

"Yeah?"

"Yeah."

"Okay, what are we gonna do about it?"

"Nothing."

She gaped at him. "What if it's one of Castillo's men?"

"It's not."

She punched his arm. "You are such a failure at communication. Talk to me."

"Ow! That hurt." He rubbed his arm.

"It did not hurt. Your hide is thicker than a buffalo. Now stop doing your Aaron imitation and explain what's going on."

"Okay. See the silver Acura trailing a couple of cars back of the Honda?"

She scrunched over to study the outside rearview mirror. "I see it."

"And the black Crown Vic up ahead?"

"Are they Aaron's men?"

"Yep. They picked us up right after we crossed the river."

"So that's what he meant. And why you're not worried."

"I always worry, angel, especially where your safety is concerned, but I believe we're in good hands now. You can relax."

A moment later, the silver Acura pulled out into the left lane to hang behind their bumper. With one car in front, one behind, and the third in the way of anyone who wanted to pass, their escort had the suburban boxed in. Garrett let out a relieved sigh. He wouldn't entrust TJ's safety to anyone else, but it felt awfully good to have help.

He followed the Ford Crown Victoria down Branch Avenue and through the built-up area around Brandywine before their little caravan turned off on a two-lane side road.

The Acura slowed and fell in behind the Honda. Three blocks more and their caravan turned down another side street where the urban area gave way to a rougher section of town. The forties-era, buildings disappeared after a few miles. Fifteen minutes more, they turned right at a big brick marquee that said Capitol Industrial Park. A line of vehicles streamed out of the complex. Quitting time on Friday.

Acres of buildings filled the park. Signs pointed to a commercial trucking facility, a major foreign auto parts provider, several small production plants, a large office supply depot, a furniture distributor, and a multitude of other warehouses. Their route took them through several more turns, until they finally stopped in front of a huge abandoned warehouse. The two-story rectangular structure looked big enough to house a dozen football fields. Add the single story wing fronting the building and the whole thing could easily surpass a hundred thousand square feet.

The car in the lead parked at the curb. The driver got out and walked toward them.

Garrett pulled up behind and rolled down his window.

"Cowboy, how you doing, man? I ain't seen you in a coon's age."

"Madman? Is that you? What's it been ... six years? Seven?" Garrett thrust his hand out the window and shook the other man's hand. "Last time had to be ..."

"Yeah, Afghanistan. Rough assignment, that one. I heard

you quit the teams and yet, here you are, still getting into trouble and needing me to pull your bacon out of the fire." Madman leaned down with one beefy forearm resting on the driver's door and looked over at TJ. "That her?"

"Yeah. That the safe house?"

Madman snickered. "Not what you expected? Farmboy's inside. Pull up to the gate so the security camera can get a good look at your vehicle. He'll buzz you in."

"What about them?" Garrett nodded toward the other two cars. "They inside team or out?"

"Outside. Whitaker's driving the Honda. The other one is Snyder. We also got Keller, Rubenstein, and Feller on day patrol around the perimeter. The six of us been working for Fowler, must be three years now. They're good men. I'll see you inside." Madman turned on his heel and returned to his car.

Garrett wheeled the Suburban into the drive and up to where a gate blocked the way.

TJ looked around. "I don't see a camera."

He smiled. "You're not supposed to." He pointed off to her right. "See that fifth section of fence there…the little bubble shape on top of the post?"

"Mmm-hmmm." She nodded, though from the way her eyes kept moving she probably hadn't spotted it yet.

"That's the camera. There's another one on this side." He pointed off to the left.

"You mean that little black cap-thing? How can it see

anything from that distance?"

He laughed outright this time. "I told you before. Fowler has all the hot toys. I suspect he's using Fly Specs."

"Fly whats?"

"Fly Specs…like insect eyes. The official name is Omni Optics. It's fairly new technology developed for long-range observation. It's a smart device. Looks like a golf ball, only the dimples are convex lenses that can zoom in on a target from multiple angles and provide a three-dimensional image.

"Wouldn't a guard at the gate be just as effective?"

He shook his head. Civilian naiveté both appalled and amused him. "Not even. Besides visual imaging, this little beauty does facial recognition like what the TSA does in airports. Scans for illicit content, too."

"You mean like guns?"

"Guns, RPGs, ammunition, even explosives. Pretty nifty, huh?"

TJ stared at him with a blank look.

He winked. "I probably ought to warn you, not only can they see the freckles on your nose, they can hear that little snort you make when you laugh."

"I do not snort! And what is this, Big Brother or something?

Garrett laughed again. "You could say that. There'll be a secure room inside where the video and audio surveillance feeds are monitored round the clock. They know if anyone approaches within a half mile. Knowing Aaron, there's a second feed, probably to Fowler's office."

The entry gate rolled to the left. Garrett drove toward the double doors at the front of the offices.

"Farmboy? Aaron? Is he the leader?"

"He is on this mission."

"And Madman is someone you used to work with?"

Another nod. "Raymond Askew. Good man. One of the best."

"Do I want to know how he came by the nickname?"

Garrett chuckled. "Probably not."

Chapter Twenty-Six

"This is the safe house?" TJ leaned over to peer out Garrett's window at the abandoned building.

"Looks that way."

Instead of a homey split level ranch in a middleclass neighborhood with kids and barking dogs, or maybe a snug condo in a high rise with a Starbucks down the street, they sat in front of some kind of discarded industrial building.

"What part of *house* did I miss?"

"Aaron's gone to a lot of trouble here. You really think he'd stick you someplace that's not safe?" Garrett made a tsking sound as he parked the Suburban in the front row of the empty parking lot.

Where were the other vehicles?

The warehouse, a two story metal rectangle with corrugated siding, sat in the middle of the property, its roofline sporting a number of mechanical units. A single-story wing that looked like offices fronted the building. Weeds offered the only greenery on the vast property, forcing their way through cracks in the pavement.

TJ's shoulders slumped. No hot bath tonight. Or clean

Imperfect Wings

clothes.

"A safe house is a broad term. In the simplest concept, it's meant to be a refuge where a person can hide for a short time. It might be a barn or a sewer, a penthouse or tree house." Garrett cut the ignition and turned to face her. "The more unlikely, the better. If you find it unthinkable, so will the enemy. I'm sorry."

"For what? It's not your fault."

"For not anticipating your expectations. Movies and novels put out a lot of misinformation. Civilians have no idea how this stuff really works. There's nothing glamorous about what spies or soldiers do. The truth is, it's dirty, dangerous work. Lonely, too. Did I mention uncomfortable?"

Well, didn't this little confession leave her feeling like a spoiled brat? She tried to dredge up a smile. "I had hopes of a hot bath and a bed with clean sheets. A washing machine would be nice."

"Don't know about the bath, but I'm pretty sure we can get you a hot shower and clean sheets." Garrett opened his door and stepped out.

Aaron came jogging across the pavement and yanked her door open. "'Bout time you two got here. C'mere, girl." He pulled TJ into a big hug, released her, and shook hands with Garrett. After a quick glance around, he motioned them toward the building. "Let's get inside."

When TJ turned to grab her stuff, Aaron caught her arm.

302

"Leave it." He whistled, pointed at the Suburban and then at the building, and tugged her toward the front entrance. "Some of the guys will bring everything in." He led the way into the maw of the abandoned building. "C'mon into the family room. I'll get you current on what's happening."

With a quick look at Garrett, TJ lifted her eyebrows, and mouthed, "Family room?"

He shrugged.

They entered what might have once been a small reception area. Two long hallways branched off to either side. Aaron turned right, stopping halfway down the hall at a door with a horizontal bar. When TJ and Garrett caught up, he pushed the heavy metal door open and entered the warehouse section.

Feeling a bit like Jonah when the whale swallowed him, TJ walked into the belly of the beast. A few steps beyond the threshold, she stopped, eyes going wide.

A meager wash of daylight leaked through exterior windows at the far reaches of the warehouse, barely penetrating the interior. A few incandescent lights strung about helped but did little to dispel the overwhelming gloom.

TJ blinked as objects took shape. Tall columns rose from the concrete floor only to disappear high overhead. Crates, tables, and odds and ends were stacked nearby, and ... trucks? So that's where they'd stashed the vehicles.

To the right, a blurred section of wall materialized. Painted a matte gray, the wall appeared insubstantial.

TJ shivered. Memories clawed their way up from the past, reminding her of time spent locked in her bedroom. Sometimes in the darkness of the tiny closet. Yet, somehow, this industrial cavern seemed so much worse for its size. A void without boundaries. Where she might never find a way out.

Garrett's warm hand kneaded her shoulder, pulling her back from the edge of panic. How well he read her.

Her gaze roamed upward, studying the wall. On second thought, partition might better describe the structure since it didn't come close to reaching the top of the double-story building. A few patches of soft yellow light glowed above the ceiling-less wall.

"Your design?" Garrett said to Aaron. His deep baritone echoed through the warehouse.

"Oh, there's more. Come along."

He led the way toward a door in the wall and opened it with a flourish. "The family room."

An interior wall created a narrow corridor, with a doorway that led into a small room. TJ's mouth dropped. They'd created a living space, complete with walls and separate rooms … and light.

Her jaw fell even more when she entered the family room. A plush wine-colored sofa dominated, with two leather recliners flanking it—all facing one of the biggest flat screen televisions she'd ever seen. Thick Berber carpet covered the floor. A simple swag chandelier was suspended overhead.

"Make yourself at home." Aaron motioned toward the sofa. "The others will be along shortly."

Garrett took TJ's hand and drew her with him to the sofa. A freestanding furnace filled one corner of the room, electric flames dancing in the faux hearth. The appliance emitted a surprising amount of heat. TJ rubbed her arms, noticing the chill for the first time. She'd need a jacket.

She turned an impish grin on Aaron. "You don't have a hot tub, by chance?"

Aaron laughed and shook his head. He pulled a tall stool from a bar she hadn't noticed and set it in front of the TV facing them. "Nope. Got a nice shower you can use, though. And a cot with clean sheets but no washing machine."

She turned to frown at Garrett.

"Hey, I didn't say a thing, angel. Remember what I told you about the audio around here?"

Ahhh, Aaron had heard her wishful thinking. She turned to the older man again. "No washing machine, huh?"

"Nope. Got something better."

"What's better than clean clothes?" she asked.

"I don't know … new clothes, maybe?"

Madman and two other men walked through the doorway.

"Derek! Kyle!" TJ jumped up and ran to embrace the two deputies from Hastings Bluff. "Thank you for coming to my rescue. Again."

They each dropped a bag on the floor and opened their

arms.

"Our pleasure, darling." Kyle gave her a squeeze but backed away when Garrett loomed at her side.

Derek tried to hide a smile. "You're looking good, sweetheart."

Garrett draped his arm around her shoulders before extending a hand to Kyle and Derek. "Glad you boys could make it."

A naughty smile lit Derek's green eyes. "So that's how it is."

"Yeah," Garrett said, pulling TJ flush against his side. "Is there a problem?"

Mimicking his buddy, Derek held his hands up with a laugh. "Not from me."

TJ looked up at Garrett and rolled her eyes, telltale heat rising up her neck. What was it with men? All about establishing boundaries and marking their territory. She elbowed his ribs.

He grunted but didn't let go.

Kyle picked up the two bulging shopping bags they'd dropped. "Lookee what we got you."

TJ squealed and reached for the sacks. "How did you know …?"

Derek grinned. "James had Mallory put a list together of everything you needed, so if it's not here, don't blame us. She gave us your sizes, too, even though we'd pretty much already guessed them."

Garrett made a sound that had Kyle backing up again.

Derek didn't seem to notice. "Me and Derek volunteered to do the shopping. Wait 'til you see the lacy little black—"

"That's it. Thanks for your help, boys." Garrett snatched the bags from Kyle and steered TJ to the sofa.

Derek and Kyle grinned as they settled in the two recliners.

Aaron shook his head like an indulgent grandpa. "Okay, kids. Time to get serious. I'll get you caught up, and then Ray's gonna give you a tour of the facility and subterranean level."

"Subterranean level... you mean a basement?" TJ asked.

"Hard to call it a basement when the darn thing's bigger than the warehouse with a maze of corridors." Aaron held up a hand as Garrett started to question him. "The lower level has four exit doors. All but one's been disabled. Ray's gonna make sure you learn the escape route. It's a bit of a mess."

Oh mercy. An abandoned basement. One that needed a map. "What do you mean ... a mess?"

"The original building was a shipping warehouse for the Southern Maryland Railroad. After it burned in 1922, they rebuilt it using iron and put the mechanicals below ground. All that equipment—generators, hydraulics, air handlers—are all located in a boiler room down there. When the building was modernized back in the eighties, they left all the outdated equipment, along with a century's worth of junk. Right before

the last owner went bankrupt he dumped a ton of shelving components in the storerooms and left a lot more in the hallways. You'll see."

Another voice spoke from behind TJ, making her jump.

"We'll need flashlights." Ray, a.k.a. Madman, met TJ's eyes. "You ready?"

This got better and better. Flashlights meant dark places. No, she wasn't ready. "Lead on."

Three hours later, she collected her toiletries, grabbed a brand new set of underwear and sweats from the dorm-like room they'd assigned her, and set off for the tiny little closet Aaron called a bathroom.

The only important thing now was hot water and soap— something to wash away the layers of grime and cobwebs she'd collected while crawling through the debris-laden maze. Aaron's "mess" was much worse. One wrong step could easily set off an avalanche of old metal shelving. So much for the Jonah in the belly of the whale parallel. This smacked of Alice down the weirdest rabbit hole ever. Without the mushrooms.

Aaron and Garrett were waiting in the hallway when she finished.

"Aaron wants to tell you about tomorrow's schedule before you head off to bed. I thought if you had an idea of what's on the docket you might actually get some sleep." Garrett brushed his knuckles against her cheek.

"Well, I'd invite you to my room ..." She raised her

eyebrows at them. "But you'd have to sit on the floor."

"Still got your sass, I see." Aaron laughed and turned away. "C'mon. We'll go to the family room. This won't take long." He led them past her room and the adjacent one assigned to Garrett.

Garrett flopped at one end of the sofa and pulled TJ down next to him. Aaron took the bar stool again.

"Breakfast is zero seven hundred. Two doors down." He jerked his thumb in the direction away from their rooms. "It's not much, but we got a small propane stove and fridge, so there's hot food if you want it. At zero nine hundred, you have a videoconference with the prosecutor, Dan Quigley. Knowing lawyers, the vidcon will likely take a few hours."

"A few hours? Is he planning to quiz me on the history of the world?"

Aaron shrugged. "They like all their i's dotted and t's crossed. Can't say as I blame them, considering how we're down to the wire here. Later, if you want, you can go jogging with me." When Garrett stirred, Aaron added, "Or him. A couple of the guys like to run so they strung some lights around the inside perimeter. Or you can watch TV. Take your mind off the case."

The long drive across the states, the warehouse, the living quarters—it all seemed unreal. But with mention of the pending court appearance, TJ's world came crashing in again. "You never explained why you chose this place. And how

many men are here? Will I get to meet them? I'd like to know the names and faces of men willing to risk their lives for me."

"Yeah, you'll meet them. We got a six-man perimeter team keeping outside watch. Three on while the other three sleep. Inside, we got four more men besides me, Garrett, Derek, and Kyle. We'll work in shifts, too. And then there's two more in the security bunker. They take turns monitoring video and audio surveillance."

TJ shook her head. "All this for one person? For only three or four days?"

"Castillo has D.C. saturated. He's drafted an army of lowlifes. He's also brought in his men and more than a few mercenaries. We can keep you safer outside the beltway for now and avoid civilian casualties if there is an incident. But it's close enough for backup to reach us within fifteen minutes. We also have an understanding with the local sheriff."

Garrett leaned forward, elbows resting on his knees. "Confidence is high that you can hold until backup arrives?"

Aaron nodded. "You saw the bunker and the arms room. We'll know if a squirrel squeaks from a mile away. Maestro and Buzzard will hit the red button if anything so much as makes them blink."

Leaning forward, eyes alight, Garrett said, "Maestro's here?"

"When word came down that you and TJ needed help, most of the guys from the Honduras task force wanted in."

TJ leaned her head against the sofa and closed her eyes. So many of the men from a mission gone wrong, looking for a chance to make it right, and all of them willing to risk their lives. She remembered Derek's words when she'd asked why he watched over her. "It's who we are and what we do."

If any of them got hurt, her heart would break a little more. But she couldn't refuse them a chance to finish the job. "It's who you are," she whispered.

Aaron leaned forward, elbows on knees and hands clasped. "It's who you are, too, TJ. You want justice, and it's finally within reach. What you say on Monday in front of the judge, jury, and the whole world is more important than you can possibly imagine. Your testimony will have repercussions for decades to come, a message that declares no one—not some slimy drug lord from south of the border, not a senator or a president—no one stands above our country's laws."

Imperfect Wings

Chapter Twenty-Seven

Garrett grabbed a bottle of water for TJ from the small fridge, unsure how much longer he could stand aside. Dennis Quigley, the prosecuting attorney on the Krieger case, had grilled TJ in what was supposed to be a mock run-through for the trial. They hadn't stopped for a break in almost four hours now. The man reminded Garrett of a blood-sucking tick—the more you tried to pry him loose, the deeper he dug in. And he was one of the good guys.

Garrett cocked his head and swore under his breath at the sound of muffled sobs coming from the family room. Not gone three minutes and the despicable jerk had reduced her to tears. If this was how he treated his own witness, what would he do to Krieger?

TJ sat on the same bar stool where he'd left her, facing Quigley's Skype image on the television screen. Her shoulders shook with the fierce emotion that wracked her body. "I s-s-saw soldiers pull a p-prisoner from one of the huts."

Her voice broke.

Garrett clenched his fists. It was all he could do not to

drag her out of there.

"Why do you say he was a prisoner?" Quigley prompted.

Quigley epitomized the modern urban male, fastidious, picky about his appearance, and focused on his upscale lifestyle. For crying out loud, he looked like a peacock in his pinstripe suit, lavender tie, and matching handkerchief. What kind of man wore lavender? On Saturday?

"T-they tied his hands behind his back and put a g-gag in his mouth. He stumbled and fell, s-so they dragged him."

On the screen, Quigley's beady eyes focused on TJ like a wolf going in for the kill. "Is this the man, the prisoner you saw?" Quigley fumbled with a piece of paper, finally raising it in front of the camera.

TJ gasped at the horrific image filling the screen. The room went silent.

The image showed two uniformed guards. A man's sagging body hung between them. They'd lifted their captive off the ground by his bound arms. A third guard had a fistful of the man's hair, holding the head upright. The camera zoomed in, revealing every detail—open eyes, vacant and staring. Slack mouth. Split lip. Bruises. And the small, neat hole in the center of his forehead.

"Oh, merciful Lord," TJ whispered, her face ashen. "They killed him. He was tied up and hurt. They shot him."

Garrett plunked the bottle of water on a table. What was wrong with the man? Why would Quigley put TJ through this mental torture? He wanted to hit something, preferably the weasel-faced lawyer. "That's it. We're done here."

He pulled TJ off the stool and into his arms, propelling her toward the doorway.

Quigley's irate countenance reappeared. "Wha—Who—Fowler, who is this guy? What's your name, soldier? I'll see you court-martialed for this. Who do you think—?"

Garrett jerked around and planted himself in front of the small camera. He leaned in close. "You pompous—" It took all his willpower to choke back the words he wanted to say. "She's your star witness, for crying out loud. And you treat her like ... like ..."

The prosecutor screamed in outrage. "You get her back in that chair! I'm not finished!"

Another man, thin and balding, appeared on screen for a split-second. He grabbed Quigley's arm, tugging him away from the camera. "Let it go, Dennis. You don't want to mess with him. TJ will do fine on the stand, now that she's dropped the emotional barriers. There won't be a dry eye in the place. We're done here."

The video feed went black.

Garrett nudged TJ to get her moving again. She needed privacy, and he needed to hold her while she cried the horror out of her system. Another step and she stumbled. Without a moment of hesitation, he slipped an arm beneath her knees and scooped her up.

Imperfect Wings

Aaron stepped aside and patted him on the shoulder as he strode out. "Take care of our girl. I'll deal with Fowler and Quigley."

With a curt nod, Garrett continued to her room. Inside, he sat on the narrow bed and held TJ on his lap. She slipped her arms around his waist and buried her face against his chest.

"Shhh. It's okay, angel. It's okay." He pulled her closer, rocking in slow, easy movements, his fingers running through her soft brown curls.

A long while later, after her tears dwindled to occasional sniffles, she sat up. "Why?"

Garrett understood what she meant. Why had Quigley focused on the horror? Why did he dig and dig until he'd stripped her of every defense, left her vulnerable and exposed?

"Quigley's a sadistic moron." TJ stirred him on so many levels. He'd never expected to have someone like her in his life. Desire played a large part of the fascination, but the attraction between them was so much more. He could get used to holding her in his arms like this.

When her breathing slowed, he eased her onto the cot and removed her shoes. Her reaction to the ghastly photograph revealed a boatload of unresolved grief. She'd been running for her life ever since seeing the DEA agent's murder. More than likely the memory got shoved aside in some dark, secluded corner of her mind. She'd never dealt with the trauma … until today.

11111111111111

Garrett tucked her blanket around, kissed her forehead, and left. Sleep would give her respite from the memories.

Outside, in the corridor, Aaron waited. "She okay?"

"She will be. TJ's tougher than she looks."

"Yeah, she is." Aaron nodded and turned to go. "But I'd still like five minutes alone with Quigley when this is over."

"Might not be anything left once I get finished."

Garrett hung out in his room for the rest of the afternoon. With the thin walls separating their adjacent rooms, he'd know when she stirred. TJ wouldn't want him watching while she slept, but he wanted to be there when she ventured out.

At ten past four, he heard her stirring and hurried out to the hallway. She must be starved. Quigley hadn't bothered to stop for lunch.

Derek and Kyle passed by while he waited in the corridor.

"Sleeping Beauty up yet?" Kyle asked. "We're having spaghetti tonight. Better hurry if you want any. These guys eat like it's their last meal."

TJ opened her door.

"Hey, darling. You okay?" Derek touched her arm.

"I'm fine. Thanks." Her mouth smiled, but her eyes looked haunted.

"We'll be along in a minute." Garrett turned to TJ as the other two men walked on. "You feel like something to eat, angel?"

She nodded, staring at the floor.

"Hey, look at me, TJ."

Her eyes lifted to the middle of his chest.

"Up here." He lifted her chin with one finger.

Those big blue eyes, still a little watery, locked with his.

Need slammed into Garrett like a mighty rushing wind. He had the overpowering urge to take her away, hide her where no one could ever hurt her again. The thought didn't even surprise him anymore.

He leaned down and let his lips lightly brush hers. "Better?"

Her lips curved up in a real smile this time. She leaned into him, took a deep breath, and released it. "Much."

"Good. Let's go get some of that spaghetti. I'm starved."

After supper, TJ declined Kyle's invitation for a movie. She pleaded a headache and went off to her room. The next morning, she showed up for breakfast with the others but said she didn't feel like doing anything more. She retreated to her room again.

At noon, Aaron banged on her door and threatened to drag her out by her toes if she didn't come out for lunch.

She ate the turkey sandwich in silence.

After everyone else had wandered away, Garrett caught TJ's hand. "Come for a jog around the building with me." He pulled her toward her room. "Let's go get your running shoes."

She shook her head and pulled back. "I don't feel like running. I'm going to lie down for a bit." Her voice came out so soft he had to lean down to make out her words.

Uh-uh. He wasn't having any more of that. And she sure didn't need pity. "Look TJ, I know Quigley doesn't play fair, but are you gonna keep wallowing in that woe is me mud hole?"

Her head snapped up. "Woe is me? You think I'm feeling sorry for myself?" Fire danced in her eyes.

Garrett lifted one eyebrow, fighting to hold back a grin. The self-pity comment sure lit her fuse.

Quigley had proven himself a masochistic devil who pushed ethical limits, but the lawyer also knew how to slice away layers to get to the truth. TJ hadn't liked being filleted like a trout, didn't care to have her defenses ripped away. Shoot, who would?

"I wouldn't call it feeling sorry—not exactly." He did grin this time. He couldn't stop it. Self-pity didn't suit TJ's personality. She needed another way to vent. Garrett sure hoped he could talk her into running, because he didn't relish being on the receiving end of her anger.

The look she gave him almost blistered his skin. "I need to change into sweats. Give me five minutes." She turned on her heel and stomped off.

"Better watch out." Aaron said behind him. "That's one dangerous little girl. She flips every protective switch a man has. It don't matter how old you are. And the darndest thing is, she don't even know it. All fire and innocence." He shook his

head. "Might as well dangle a pork chop in front of a starving hound dog."

A snarl got away from him before Garrett could stop it. He could actually feel his blood pressure kick up a notch.

"Settle your fur down, boy. TJ's like my daughter. Maybe if I was twenty years younger ..."

The admission surprised Garrett, except it didn't really. He'd seen the affection between TJ and Aaron. Crossing his arms over his chest, Garrett snorted. "More like thirty."

The older man laughed, a deep from-the-belly sound that made Garrett scowl.

"What's so funny?"

Aaron appraised him for several long moments. Finally, he nodded and grinned. "TJ's got some pretty sharp claws, boy. Take care she don't rip your heart out and keep it for herself."

"Too late."

"Thought so." The laughter faded, and Aaron's eyes turned to flint. "That little girl's had a lot of rejection in her young life. She needs a strong man, someone who'll stick by her for the long run. If you're not up to the challenge, you need to bail now."

"Not happening, old man."

Down the hallway, TJ opened her door and stepped out. She'd donned gray sweats and running shoes and strode by the two men without a word.

Aaron laughed. "Operation Pork Chop is underway. May

the strongest, fastest, meanest, most cussed hound dog win."

Garrett bumped fists with him and hurried after TJ.

He caught up with her at the far side of the warehouse and joined her as she did stretching lunges.

"What's the distance around?" she asked.

"Dunno." He glanced at the perimeter, calculating as he turned. "Maybe a quarter mile. Might take us a few laps to work up a sweat. Be good to move after being cooped up in the truck."

As they neared the end of the seventh lap, Derek came running up. "Aaron says we got company on the way."

Garrett and TJ hurried to the family room where Aaron handed them each a towel.

"I take it there's no threat." Garrett rubbed his face and tossed the towel aside.

"Fowler's on his way. Claims he has news."

TJ draped her towel around her neck and went still, eyes wide. "Fowler's coming? He's been so careful to stay away. Is it safe? Won't Castillo's men follow him?"

"Calm yourself, girl. Nothing is more important to Kevin Fowler than closing the book on this op. It's been his whole focus for more than five years. No way he'll mess up now."

Aaron's radio squawked. "Three people at the gate."

"Roger that." He turned to Garrett and TJ. "Let's go see what the boss man's got to say."

They waited in the vacant reception area as a black

Mercedes pulled up.

Garrett stood to one side of the front window, keeping TJ behind him. "I take it the driver is not Fowler."

"I forget you've never met him. The driver's Rocky Winston."

Garrett studied the two men as they got out of the car. Fowler was average height, thin build, with even thinner hair. Nothing remarkable. A man you wouldn't notice in a crowd.

The agent handling TJ's case adjusted his sunglasses, looked around, and then moved to the rear door of the car.

"Well, I'll be," Garrett said.

TJ peeked around his shoulder and gasped, her hands clasped to her mouth.

A little girl stepped out of the car and took Fowler's hand. Midnight black hair hung in a long ponytail over one shoulder.

"Gaby!"

Chapter Twenty-Eight

Garrett grabbed TJ before she could bolt out the door. "Hold on, angel. Let's wait here."

What was Fowler up to? Why would he bring the kid here? Garrett exchanged a look with Aaron.

TJ moved closer to the door, fidgeting with anticipation. "You said Fowler would get Gaby back." Twin spots of color stained her cheeks. The delight in her eyes when she looked up at him filled Garrett with satisfaction.

Ten feet from the door, Gaby spotted TJ. The little girl's face broke into a grin. "Tay Sjay!" She squealed, broke into a run, and threw herself into TJ's arms. "I am so happy to find you."

"Sweetie, you grew. I almost didn't recognize you. And your English …"

"*Sí.* I am in United States two years. In Atlanta, I attend school and speak English. But why you cut your hair?" Gaby patted TJ's short curls. "I like."

TJ's smile did funny things to Garrett's peace of mind. Her laughter reminded him of wind chimes on a breezy summer day.

"What is this place, Tay Sjay?"

Instead of answering, TJ extended a hand to the gray-eyed, sandy-haired man. "Agent Fowler, it's been a long time. How can I ever thank you for all you've done, especially for rescuing my little friend?"

Fowler surprised Garrett when he took TJ's hand and pulled her into a hug. From what he knew of the man, he didn't seem the touchy, feely type. Surprise edged into annoyance when the agent didn't release her right away.

"Are these bums taking good care of you?" Deep and raspy, the harsh timbre of Fowler's voice didn't seem suited to a man of such slight stature. He stood on the shorter side of six feet and would likely have a hard time making welter weight.

"Oh, yes. They've been wonderful. I believe you already know this guy." She held her hand out to Aaron who stood off to one side

Aaron extended his hand. "Fowler."

"Hanson."

The two men shook hands as TJ tugged on Garrett's arm.

"Garrett, this is Kevin Fowler. Agent Fowler, this is Garrett Cameron."

Garrett towered over Fowler, but the disparity didn't seem to faze the smaller man. From the way he stood with a stiff spine and shoulders squared, Fowler had to be former military. Army, most likely. The other branches had the same posture beaten into them, but that kick-you-in-the -teeth attitude only came from staring the enemy down in close combat. This man's stare held steel, his handshake firm.

"Why's she here?" Aaron's chin jutted toward Gaby.

Leave it to Farmboy to cut to the chase. Seems he didn't like Fowler bringing the kid here either.

Garrett turned to TJ. "Why don't you show Gaby around? Kyle hid some ice cream sandwiches in the freezer. She might like one."

TJ glared at him for an hour-long minute. From her frown, she didn't appreciate the thinly veiled attempt to get rid of her and Gaby.

"Fine." All five-feet nothing of annoyed female whirled around and took the little girl's hand to pull her along. "This is called a safe house, honey. It's a secret hiding place, but apparently only the men are allowed to know its secrets. C'mon and I'll show you where I'm staying."

By unspoken agreement, the men waited until TJ and Gaby moved out of earshot. Why'd you bring Gaby here?" Garrett asked.

The agent shrugged. "You said Gabriela's abduction distressed TJ. Since the child was also distraught, I brought her to TJ as a surprise. And now, they're both happy."

Garrett didn't buy Fowler's glib answer. "A phone call would have worked."

"How'd you find her so quick?" Aaron asked.

"Actually, she found us." Fowler chuckled. "Seems our little ten-year-old orphan outsmarted Castillo and his thugs. Gabriela climbed out a window and over a fence. She hid on the streets for two days, scrounging food from a garbage can behind a restaurant. The owner spotted her and called the police."

Aaron nodded but didn't seem convinced. "Well, since you're here, you might as well stay for supper. Hope you like your chili spicy."

After supper, Garrett followed Fowler, Aaron, and Madman back to the family room. The agent produced a map and spread it over the bar top. "Let's review the plan for getting TJ to the courthouse in the morning."

TJ and Gaby settled on the sofa behind them with a deck of cards, chuckling softly. He'd only had glimpses of TJ's lighthearted nature before today and now her playful laughter mesmerized him.

"Aaaagggh!"

The exaggerated exclamation coaxed a smile from Garrett. He stole a peek at the two and almost laughed out loud at the face she made. Gaby had been trying to explain the rules of a card game—something called *Burro Castigado*. It sounded an awful lot like a children's version of Five Card Draw.

"You're a card shark hiding in a sweet little girl's clothes, and I'm not playing with you anymore."

Wise decision. TJ wore her emotions like a neon sign. She didn't stand a chance against young Gaby's experienced poker face.

The little girl giggled.

Aaron cleared his throat, and Garrett yanked his attention back to the meeting. Kevlar or Spectra Fiber in flak vests. Yeah, that was fascinating. He fixed his eyes on the men, but his ears remained tuned to the girls.

"We'll take five vehicles." Aaron looked at Garrett for affirmation. "You have anything to add?"

Garrett shook his head and sneaked another quick look at the girls.

TJ tickled Gaby, who laughed with abandon. Their antics tricked a chuckle from him that he tried to cover with a cough. When he turned around, Aaron wore a look of amusement.

"What?" Garrett asked irritably. Man, he needed to get his head in the game.

"Fowler asked if you're carrying."

Madman snorted ... or was he laughing?

"Yeah. Sig Sauer, ankle holster-Beretta, and my Ka-Bar." The nasty looking, seven-inch knife had saved Garrett's hide on more than one occasion. "TJ also has a Sig."

"Not into the courthouse, you're not." Fowler typed a note into his phone.

Behind him, Garrett heard the soft musical score of a movie starting up. Did they have anything here suitable for a kid? He stole another peek at the sofa.

Gaby was stretched out on the couch, her head in TJ's lap.

TJ's fingers sifted through the little girl's hair. She'd catch a few locks with her nails and skim the length from scalp to tip. When the hair fell free, she flicked her fingers at a Styrofoam cup she held. Garrett wrinkled his nose. His mother had once done the same thing to him and his brothers when they were kids—lined them up on the porch, scrubbed their heads raw, and picked through their hair. Did Gaby have lice?

He frowned and tried to feign interest in the best route to the U.S. Eastern District Courthouse. He didn't know the city well enough to offer suggestions. A taxi or the Metro had always worked for him.

The next time he glanced over at the sofa, both girls had their eyes closed.

"Be right back," he told the men. He returned with the blanket from his bed and draped it over TJ and Gaby.

"All right. Recap. Task Force Tango-Juliet is a go." Fowler looked at each man. "Teams Bravo and Echo took control of the Albert Bryan Courthouse at twenty-two hundred hours. Teams Charlie, Foxtrot, and Delta simultaneously deployed in a two-block perimeter around the courthouse." The agent paused to let the information sink in.

"Headset communication is channel two." Fowler

drummed a pencil on the bar top. "You, Team Alpha, will depart the safe house at zero-eight hundred sharp. Use South Washington Street for a straight-in, full-throttle approach. Eagle Eye will monitor your route and vector you to safety should the need arise."

"How do we get TJ from the car to the courthouse?" Aaron asked.

"Delta will meet you at the curb and surround her with riot shields and then double-time her inside."

"I'm going with her," Garrett announced.

Fowler looked at him. "Of course, you are." He turned back to Aaron. "Delta will direct you and your team to support positions. Gabriela will remain with Maestro and Princeton."

Garrett rolled his neck, trying to ease the tension that had nagged him all day. His internal radar usually hit with a surge of wrongness before escalating into a full-blown call to arms. But not this time. The source of his worry remained elusive. Maybe he just didn't like handing over the reins of control to someone else.

"Okay. That's a wrap." Fowler paused in the doorway and pinned Garrett with a look. "I'll see you two in court in a few hours. Make sure TJ wears the body armor."

The hairs prickled on Garrett's neck. Those words sounded more like a warning than a reminder.

After the door shut behind Fowler, Garrett's eyes roamed back to the two sleeping figures on the sofa. Aaron came to stand beside him.

"Had a cot set up in TJ's room. You carry her. I'll get the girl."

"Nah. Leave 'em. They look like a couple of puppies all snuggled up." Garrett adjusted the blanket.

"What about you, Cowboy. Not much to do now but wait. Why don't you grab a few hours' sleep?"

Cocking an eyebrow at the older man, Garrett said. "You know good and well neither of us is gonna sleep tonight."

Aaron looked from Garrett's eyes to the hand rubbing his neck. "You're like a mouse in a barn full of cats. Something you want to share?"

Garrett lowered his hand. "When did you last check in with Maestro?"

"Been a few hours."

The nagging awareness had blossomed into a full-blown itch. And got stronger with each passing second. "Humor me. Call him."

"I told you ..."

"Do it, Aaron."

The seasoned old veteran might be the team leader on this op, but Garrett had no compunction about pushing him on this. With a nod, Aaron stepped into the hallway already speaking into his headset.

Garrett knelt by the sofa and watched TJ and Gaby as they slept. Their safety meant everything ... and he didn't like the bad feeling filling his gut.

Madman walked over to the bar carrying a black garbage bag. He scooped up trash left over from supper.

"You make the chili tonight?" Garrett asked quietly.

"Nope. I drew KP." He grabbed an orange-stained plastic spoon and bowl from the floor near the television, added some wadded up napkins, and stuffed it all in the bag.

"Pssst!"

Garrett turned to find Aaron motioning him over.

"I got Princeton on speaker. Go ahead."

"Fowler's departure was the last registered movement inside the complex. Nothing else since a plumbing truck this morning. They did some work at the furniture warehouse six blocks over."

"What about the main road outside the complex?" Aaron prompted.

"Light traffic all day, typical for a Sunday. Activity picked up between seventeen thirty and twenty hundred hours, but nothing suspicious. The vehicles all buzzed by without slowing. Our area of operations remains clear."

Garrett frowned. "Why the heavier traffic in our AO?"

"Sunday night church, maybe?" Aaron shrugged.

"Zoom in and check for side-mounted cameras," Garrett persisted.

Aaron frowned, his forehead wrinkling like a grizzled old Bloodhound's. "You thinking recon?"

Garrett had nothing to base his suspicions on but the roiling tension in his gut.

Aaron held his gaze. "Thanks, Princeton. Wake Maestro and run the traffic patterns through the zoom. Something's not right."

Every nerve in Garrett's body stood at attention now. Something was indeed wrong, very wrong. He went back to the sofa and shook TJ's arm. "TJ, Gaby, I need you to wake up. C'mon, girls. Open those beautiful eyes."

Behind him, Aaron muttered under his breath. "You got that weird ESP thing going on, don't you?" He spoke into his headset again. "Princeton, Ice, Romeo—get everyone up and armed. This is not a drill." He continued barking orders as he hurried down the hall.

TJ looked up at Garrett with sleep-drugged eyes. "What's going on?"

"Nothing to worry about, angel."

"Then … why?" She frowned in confusion.

"A precaution. I need you and Gaby to put your shoes on. We're moving out a little early."

"Boss!" Madman shouted from the other end of the sofa, his voice filled with alarmed urgency. "Get back here."

In seconds, Garrett reached Madman's side.

Aaron returned moments later.

Madman held out a Styrofoam cup. "Look."

Aaron peered in the cup. "An inch of Sprite with crumbs

in it. So?"

Madman shoved the cup under Garrett's nose. "What do you see?"

Garrett saw the same thing Aaron described. Black bits floating on what could have been Sprite or water. Except they didn't really look like crumbs. He handed the cup back to Madman. "Explain."

Taking the cup over to the bar, Madman switched on a gooseneck lamp. He stuck a finger in the cup, snared one of the black specks, and held it up under the lamplight. "Either of you know how these got here?"

A memory of TJ running her hands through Gaby's hair. Fingers pulling at long strands. "They're bugs."

"What?" Aaron demanded.

Swallowing hard, Madman told them. "I'm pretty sure they're Micro-trackers."

Bile filled Garrett's throat. "TJ was pulling at something in Gaby's hair earlier."

"What are Micro-trackers?" Aaron demanded.

"Microscopic transponders. When a parent transmitter signals a subordinate ..." He tipped the cup. "The transponder returns the ping."

"Wildfire! I repeat, Wildfire!"

Aaron, Madman, and Garrett all raised their hands to their ears at Princeton's yell.

Garrett's gut instinct had saved him so many times in the

past. Had he made a fatal mistake by not listening to it sooner?

Aaron spoke into the headset. "Talk to me, Princeton."

"Two panel vans turned into the complex. Three cars on their tail and slowing. Yep, they're coming in, too. Wait … there's another … oh man, we got a serious problem. They have a Bearcat."

Garrett locked eyes with Aaron and said, "A what?"

"What's a Bearcat, Princeton?" Aaron shouted.

"Lenco Bearcat. Biggest, baddest swat vehicle in service today. Got a ram on the front and holds a dozen men. Hold on … the other vehicles stopped … Oh yeah, the Bearcat's moving to the front. You better prepare for a breach."

A cold sweat broke out on Garrett's body. How had Castillo put his hands on one of the most coveted swat vehicles around? Had to be Senator Farleigh's doing. "My guess is they'll bust through the front gate and head straight for the building entrance. That's our weak point."

Aaron nodded, already shouting orders. "This is Six. Probability is high for frontal assault and infiltration. We are Zulu. I repeat, execute Plan Zulu. Two, respond."

"Two here."

"I want the driver of that swat vehicle taken out. Do you copy?"

"Copy. I'm in position."

Aaron turned to Garrett, jerking a thumb toward TJ and Gaby. "They're yours now."

Garrett nodded. Keep her out of the line of fire. Send her along the escape route below, if it came to that. Stand in the way of anybody who dared come after her.

"Fowler's been alerted. Backup is scrambling. Should arrive in …" He glanced at his watch. "Twenty-five minutes."

"I thought you said a fifteen-minute response time!"

"All the teams got moved to the courthouse, remember?" Aaron spoke into his headset again. "Princeton, ETA on targets."

"Two minutes and counting."

Imperfect Wings

Chapter Twenty-Nine

A switch flipped in Garrett's mind. Once a soldier, always a soldier—you never truly lose the mindset. His heartbeat sped up with the familiar rush of adrenalin.

He turned to TJ and Gaby, hating the fear on their faces. He had no time to ease them into this. "TJ, you and Gaby stay here. Do not move."

Gaby had both arms around TJ's waist. Her big black eyes looked like bottomless pools.

"You're not leaving us? Alone?" TJ looked close to panic.

"No, of course, not. You wouldn't do that."

He lifted one eyebrow. Had she finally gotten it? That he cared and would always be there for her. "I'm going for the flak vests and your gun. Be right back." Garrett raced from the room while Aaron's voice filled the headset.

"Princeton, status on the Bearcat."

More voices joined in. The updates and questions came so fast no one outside the team would make sense of what they said. Garrett listened, identifying the others using this channel—Aaron as Team Leader Six, Princeton on surveillance, Madman running the outside ops, Alamo and

Papa Bear running the east and west teams inside, and Two—the sniper on the roof. The others would use a sub-channel and report to Alamo, Papa Bear, or Madman.

He mentally located each position. They were seasoned veterans. A hush-hush group few knew about. A brotherhood he, James, Derek, and Kyle had belonged to. James would hate not being here.

Derek and Kyle, a.k.a. Iceman and Romeo, worked for Papa Bear on this op. Good. Their team stood directly between Castillo's men and TJ.

"Bearcat approaching."

"Two, you copy?"

"Roger. On the roof. Target is a can't-miss."

Memories of Garrett's own early assignments as a sniper gave him a mental picture of Two's over-watch position. He'd likely be crouched behind his rifle looking out through a blue scope over the approach. His spotter would be close by, using a souped up Barska night scope to search out and follow the target's route.

"Madman, are you ready?" Six called over the airways.

"In position."

Garrett rushed into his room, snatched up one of the flak vests from the corner and put it on. He pulled boxes of ammunition from the duffle and jammed them in the pockets of his camo pants and then cinched a wide belt around his waist. The Ka-Bar went into the knife sheath strapped to his leg. His pistol slid into its holster. He slipped on a pair of night vision goggles, letting them rest against his forehead. Slinging the sniper rifle over one shoulder, he grabbed two more vests and hurried to TJ's room.

"Bearcat just made the turn. He's speeding up. The other five vehicles are on his tail."

Her Sig Sauer P-238 was in her backpack along with several clips of ammunition. He snatched the pack up and raced back to the family room.

"Bearcat is at the gate. Engine revving. This is it."

"Got him in my sights. Oh, yeah. Direct hit. Uh-oh … uh-oh. Brace for impact. Bearcat is a dead stick and still coming."

A resounding crash of grating metal drowned out the running commentaries for a moment, followed by a sizzling screech, and then … kaboom! The concussion rocked the building. Bursts of machinegun fire erupted outside.

"We have a breach. Hit the lights."

Garrett reached the family room where TJ and Gaby huddled on the floor as the lights went out. Pitch darkness surrounded them but did nothing to deaden the sound of gunfire inside the building.

When Gaby cried out, TJ shushed her with soothing whispers.

"I'm back. TJ, don't move. I'll come to you." He pulled the night vision goggles on and waited for his eyes to refocus. There!

"Here I am," he said a second before he touched TJ's cheek and Gaby's arm.

"I can't see anything, Garrett."

"It's okay, baby. I can see. Keep Gaby close and do what I say. Understand?"

"You have night vision goggles? Can I have a pair?"

He chuckled softly. "I got something better." He pushed the backpack to her side and put her hand on it. "Your gun and holster are in here. Let's get the body armor on you and Gaby first. You okay, squirt?" He rubbed the little girl's arm as the headset crackled to life again.

"Enemy targets have penetrated. I count nineteen from the Bearcat. Could be more. They scattered like roaches."

"Madman, this is Six. What is your situation?"

"We count fourteen tangos outside the building."

"Eliminate outside targets and move inside."

"Six, this is Alamo. I got two men down. I repeat, Lucky and Roadrunner are down. Wait … Lucky's crawling to cover. Four tangos converging on him."

"You and Outlaw offer support if you can."

"Hoo-whee. Lucky might be down, but he ain't out! He just blew one of those suckers away. The others are bugging out. Outlaw's going for Roadrunner."

"Six, this is Madman."

"Go ahead, Madman."

"It's like target practice out here. Two and Ghost are

picking the tangos off from the roof one by one. Only five still standing."

"Leave two of your men to clean up the rest and sweep the area. Alamo is down two men in the east sector. Enter by the rear door on that side. Alamo, you hearing this?"

"Roger, Six."

With the warehouse infiltrated, Garrett had to take up his own defensive position. "I'm going to high ground where I can see what's coming. I'll be right above you, able to see you the whole time. Stay put."

TJ clutched his sleeve for a moment.

Rather than pull away, he waited for her to let go.

"Okay." Reluctance filled her voice.

Garrett brushed his fingers down her cheek before turning away. He went to the kitchen and the makeshift ladder Aaron's men had built into the side of the six-foot-wide support column and scrambled up the rungs. A box-shaped perch sat a few feet higher than the walls they'd constructed. His very own sniper's nest. He settled on his belly, legs splayed wide, and slid open the small ten-by-sixty-inch aperture near the floor of the perch. The opening provided a one-hundred-eighty degree view of the warehouse. After making sure his handgun was within easy reach, he settled the rifle in its brace and peered through the scope.

"Six, this is Cowboy."

"Roger. You in position?"

Garrett looked around the warehouse as he spoke. "Yep. I count four targets in east sector. Alamo, they've regrouped. Looks like they got headphones. They're sneaking around, trying to get to your flank."

"Roger that, Cowboy. We're good here. The cavalry has arrived. Glad to see ya, Madman."

Activity near the annihilated swat vehicle drew Garrett's attention. "Four targets still hovering at the rear of the Bearcat. Looks like they're working awful hard to offload something. You might want to punch a hole in that plan."

"Roger that. Papa Bear, this is Six. Did you copy?"

"Papa Bear, here. Got two men on it."

"Cowboy, what else you got?"

"Two targets. Ten o'clock. Huddled behind a column. One more behind your truck. Uh, you're gonna need a new windshield."

Aaron muttered something under his breath. "Keep looking, Cowboy. We got eight unaccounted."

"Five ... no, seven ... eight! Far left. Moving low and fast and heading this way. They just ducked out of my line of sight. Can you see them?"

"I see them. Madman, I need you in the kitchen. They're heading for TJ. Cowboy, send the girls to ground. Now!"

Garrett frowned. Eight coming meant Castillo's men knew TJ's location. "Negative, Six. We need to send Gaby in a different direction. They're tracking the bugs."

"Papa Bear, go to Plan Yankee. I repeat Plan Yankee. Send Iceman to the kitchen. He can take the kid and book out through the east rear entrance. You copy, Alamo? Madman?"

"Roger," they both replied.

"Maestro—Six."

"Maestro here. Go ahead."

"Double-time it over here. Provide cover for Ice. He'll be coming out the rear east door with the kid."

"Roger."

Garrett slung the rifle over his shoulder and slid in a fireman's drop, feet hugging the outside of the ladder. Iceman reached the family room at the same time he did.

"TJ," he whispered. "We gotta move, angel. Derek is here. He's gonna take Gaby and head out in a different direction."

"No!" The little girl cried out, clinging to TJ.

"Listen, honey." Garrett knelt beside them and brushed Gaby's cheek. "You have to go so the bad guys don't find TJ. Derek's really fast. All you have to do is be quiet."

TJ squeezed Gaby. "We have to do what Garrett says, Gaby."

Iceman grabbed the little girl up with whispered shushes and disappeared seconds later.

"Let's go, TJ. We're heading downstairs."

She held her hand out, fumbling for his.

Aaaggh. He hated doing this to her. She hadn't conquered her fear of dark places, and here she'd been left alone in the

pitch black, responsible for a scared kid. And now he was shoving her into the poorly lit basement. Garrett took her hand, kissed it, and placed it at his back. "Hang on to my belt. I'll move slow and warn you of any obstacles. The lights will be on down there, so you'll see again in a minute."

Gunfire erupted outside the flimsy walls. Too close.

Garrett yanked the door open and pushed TJ through. "Grab the handrail." He eased the door closed behind them and slammed home the deadbolt. It wouldn't stop whoever followed, but it might slow them down.

"Cowboy, you copy?" Aaron's voice sputtered over the headset.

"Cowboy, here."

"We got six of those last eight tangos. The other two are on your tail. We're coming."

"We're in the basement and proceeding to the exit point. No sign of pursuit yet."

"Move fast. Outside, head east along the building. Madman is there."

"Roger."

Garrett looked up to find TJ watching him. "Keep moving. Don't wait for me. He tumbled a broken shelving unit into the aisle behind him and then toppled a second one.

When the clanging died away, she was there in his face. "You're using Gaby as a decoy. To draw them away from me."

He looked into her accusing eyes. "What I'm doing is

trying to save both your lives. Castillo's got a bigger force and a boatload of firepower. By splitting you and Gaby up, we force them to divide. Now move."

A crash came from the stairwell.

TJ froze, staring back the way they'd come.

He hated seeing fear on her face. "Run, TJ. Fast as you can. I'll lag twenty yards behind. Do not look back. When you reach the exit door, look around first. Stay low and hug the building. Head east—that'll be to your left. Madman's team will meet you."

The terror didn't leave her eyes, but she lifted her chin and did what TJ did best. She took her gun from the holster and pulled the slide to check the load. Slamming it back in her holster, she whirled and sprinted down the debris-littered hallway.

He laughed, no more than a soft chuckle. They might be in a tight situation, but he couldn't help a flare of pride. Angel or fairy, TJ McKendrick was one amazing woman.

A second crash rang out. On the third, he knew they'd breached the stairwell. Loud footsteps raced down the steps. Garrett pulled his rifle into position and took aim. *Ping. Ping…ping…ping.* Four overhead lights went out. He re-slung the rifle and ran after TJ. A little extra darkness for the new arrivals might gain TJ some extra time.

Imperfect Wings

Chapter Thirty

The harsh *brrrrttt* of machine gun fire grew fainter with each step. Did they have enough of a head start?

TJ took a ragged breath and cast an anxious glance over her shoulder. Her heart pounded with another spike of adrenalin.

A sense of déjà vu fell over her in a dizzying wave. This time, instead of one unarmed woman fleeing with six little girls through the jungle, TJ had an army of battle-hardened soldiers standing between her and Castillo's men.

Echoes of the war raged above, giving a bizarre feel to the moment. She shuddered, unable to fathom why men pitted themselves against other men. Why they wanted to kill and maim each other. The toll from this battle would be terrible.

The long hallway stretched before her, the end in shadow. Thankfully, the junk cluttering the way didn't reach far beyond the first dozen yards or so. But if she could move faster so could her pursuers. She and Garrett had to get off this wide-open bowling alley.

TJ breathed a soft sigh and kicked up her pace. She looked back to see Garrett tossing some of the junk into the aisle.

The hall seemed dimmer in this section. Some fifty paces ahead, one of the fluorescents flickered and buzzed, went dark for a few seconds and then flared to life again.

As TJ neared the first turn, the schizophrenic light gave up the ghost and plunged the new hallway into near darkness. She checked to be sure Garrett followed.

He passed the last debris field a few seconds later, shoved a bulky metal contraption into the path, and sprinted toward her. "Why are you stopping? Go!"

TJ grabbed her bag and bolted down the new hall.

This new corridor seemed longer. Too many lights were out here. The feeble beam of the tiny flashlight she carried helped enough so she didn't trip.

At the end of the hall, TJ glanced back again and saw Garrett crouched at the far turn, peering back the way they'd come.

"It's clear," she whisper-shouted to him. When he waved for her to go on, TJ turned right and ran.

Gunfire erupted behind her, the answering fire too close. Heart pounding, TJ barely managed to quell a scream. *Garrett*!

Another gunshot echoed through the concrete walls, and then another. Unable to tell who had fired, TJ crept back to the intersection to peek around the corner.

Garrett was running full out this time, but his stride seemed off-kilter. Her flashlight skimmed down his body and honed in on the black stain spreading over his thigh. "You're hurt!"

"Cut the light!"

He reached the end of the hall, barely slowed to navigate the corner, and careened into TJ. His momentum knocked her down.

Scrabbling to the near wall, Garrett leaned against it and reloaded. His hands moved too fast to follow as he ejected the clip from his gun and snapped a new one home. "I told you to keep moving."

He held the gun barrel up by his face, took a split-second look around the corner, and fired two quick shots before retreating behind the wall again. "They're too close. You gotta go. Now!"

"You're bleeding."

The wound in his leg had soaked his pants leg and now dripped in a steady stream to the floor.

"A lucky ricochet. You gotta go, TJ. I can hold them until you get out."

"I can't leave you like this, Garrett. The bullet nicked something. You're losing too much blood. We need a tourniquet." TJ fumbled in her rucksack and found a thermal undershirt. "Give me your knife."

He handed her the wicked weapon without argument and fired two more shots at their stalkers.

A scream reverberated through the basement.

"One down, one to go. Hurry up. Do what you can, but

then you're leaving."

The knife made a soft snick as she sliced off the arms of the shirt. Holding the tiny flashlight in her mouth, TJ cut two long strips from the sleeve. "This will hurt." She slipped one strip of cloth around his rock-hard thigh, a few inches above the wound. "Relax your leg so I can tighten the knot."

He complied and grunted when she cinched it.

Hacking another swatch from the shirt, she folded it into a pad and covered the wound and used a second long strip to secure it. She made a third compression bandage and tied it in place.

The blood flow stopped.

"You need medical attention."

"Not until you're safe. Now get outta here."

"I can help, Garrett." She handed the knife to him and reached for the gun at her waist. "You know I can shoot."

"TJ. Please. Listen to me. What you say to that jury is important. You have to leave and let me protect you. It's what I do. Now go while I can still help."

She heard his words and watched him sway. He was weak from blood loss. Without medical attention, his chances of survival were slim. Leave him? Everything in her screamed at the wrongness of it. Why did he always have to be right?

He slipped to one knee and dared another quick look. Another quick shot brought a string of curses and return fire.

"Think I winged him. That should slow things down. Now

go."

TJ placed her hand on his chest over his heart. "You said you would always come for me. Swear to me now that you'll find me."

Garrett gripped the nape of her neck and dragged her to him. His kiss, hard and fierce, lasted only seconds. He thrust her away saying, "I'll find you."

Leaving her pack where it sat on the floor, TJ took off.

The light improved with the next left bend. Her legs pumped hard, the strides in sync with her thudding heart. At the next turn, she broke into a sprint. Two more changes of direction and there it was—the exit sign. Big red letters hung from the ceiling, no more than twenty yards ahead.

Too late, she saw the wet patch on the floor. The ceiling leak she'd seen when Madman had shown her the emergency route.

Her feet slipped. She twisted, arms wind-milling in an effort to correct her balance. She fell in a sprawl and lay without moving, afraid to even breathe. To come so far only to falter with the end in reach ... Why?

Gritting her teeth, TJ said a silent prayer for strength and courage. She pushed to her feet, her knee throbbing, and hobbled toward the exit.

A furious barrage of gunfire shattered the unnatural silence. Many more than two. Had help arrived? Or more of the enemy? She prayed through the tears, asking protection for

Garrett and Gaby. For the others.

She couldn't wait around to find out. Eighteen more steps and she reached the exterior door. Garrett's words came back—look around first. Her lungs burned. With another plea for Garrett's safety, TJ eased the door and took a quick look.

Okay. This could go either way. If she couldn't see Castillo's men, they couldn't see her. Could they? She slipped outside. S*tay low. Follow the building to the end. Find Madman.* How far to the end of the building?

The night mist swirled. The hair on her neck prickled as though a ghost lover pressed a kiss to her skin. The sense of foreboding intensified.

A shadow materialized in front of her, paralleling her every step.

Her walk became a slow jog.

The shadow stayed with her.

Not good, not good. Could she outrun him?

The shadow lunged for her.

TJ screamed and ran.

The monster, a giant of a man, caught her right arm before she'd gone three steps. He yanked her backward and wrapped a beefy arm around her neck. "*Cállate!* Shut up!"

One of Castillo's men.

She struggled, but he only squeezed harder. Black dots swam at the periphery of her vision. A buzzing sound filled her ears.

The vise-like grip eased when she stopped struggling. But then a second figure materialized out of the fog, pointing a pistol at her.

"*Señorita* McKendrick. At last."

The too-smooth Latin accent made her stomach roil. Why would Castillo risk coming here?

"Bring her. Quickly!" he instructed the giant.

Why didn't he kill her?

TJ's captor kept his chokehold and forced her away from the building.

She squirmed, pummeling him with her free hand. The ineffective blows had no impact.

A well-placed kick to her captor's shin drew a grunt, but then his arm tightened and her vision dimmed again.

Help was close, here near the building. If Castillo took her away, they might not find her. TJ twisted in the giant's grip— and felt the Sig Sauer Garrett had given her dig into her belly. She reached for the handgun, freed the snap on the holster. Men of Castillo's ilk held little respect for females. He hadn't bothered to check her for a weapon.

She'd rather die here than face a life of unimaginable torture at Castillo's hands. She kicked at the giant's other leg and wrenched again. The weapon slid free. She thumbed the safety off. The grip felt awkward, but at such close range, aim wouldn't be necessary.

Her lungs burned now. She wouldn't last much longer. TJ

jabbed the barrel into the man's belly and pressed the trigger.

The giant stiffened. His arms fell away and then he keeled over.

Behind her, Castillo cursed.

She was tired of running away, being forced to hide. But she turned and ran.

Pffft! Pffft!

Fire slammed into her back, the impact sending her airborne. The first hit punched low on her left side and drove the air from her lungs. The second struck between her shoulder blades.

The ground rose up too fast. She crashed to the pavement and curled into a ball of pain. Darkness crowded in.

"TJ!"

"Garrett?" He was alive. Others crowded around. Aaron. Kyle.

More gunfire filled the night. Voices yelled. Another scream—all a backdrop to the searing pain.

"TJ, baby, I came for you. I kept my promise. Now talk to me."

Calloused hands touched her cheek. He said he would come for her. TJ smiled and let the void embrace her.

Chapter Thirty-One

"How is she?"

The raspy voice sounded close. Familiar, but not Garrett.

"Alive. Thanks to the flak vest."

This voice didn't belong to Garrett either. TJ groaned, trying to decide what hurt the most.

"Yes or no," Raspy Voice said. "In your professional medical opinion, will the patient die or be permanently disabled if we delay transport to the hospital by a few hours?"

Were they talking about her? Images rushed in—the man with python-like arms choking her. The gun—oh dear Lord, no!—she'd killed him. And Castillo. He'd come for her. Shot her.

She groaned, feeling the slugs hit again. No wonder her body hurt.

"She's coming around," Sweet Voice said. "Let me assess her responses."

"I need a decision, Ronkowski. You know how important this is. You got ten minutes."

Ten minutes for what? Who were these men?

Someone touched her shoulder.

"TJ, my name's Ben. I'm a doctor. Agent Fowler's here, too."

Fowler. No wonder his raspy voice seemed familiar. She opened her eyes.

Two men knelt by her side, backlit by the gray morning. They wore uniforms similar to Aaron's. "Garrett," she managed to say. "He's hurt."

Fowler leaned closer. "We got him out, TJ. He caught a bullet and lost some blood, but he's okay. Your field bandage probably saved his life."

Thank You, Lord. "Where is he? I thought … I heard…"

"Doc Ronkowski here knocked him out so we could load him on a helicopter. He didn't want to leave you. Right now, he's on his way to Walter Reed."

He had come for her.

"Help me get this flak vest off her."

Fowler produced a knife as big and as lethal-looking as the one Garrett carried. He sawed through the Kevlar's front closure and shoulder seams and, together, he and Ben peeled away the heavy material.

"Help me turn her over. Cut the shirt, too." They rolled TJ onto her side and Fowler crawled behind her.

"What happened to Castillo?" TJ asked.

Ssssnnnnit. Cool air brushed the bare skin of her back.

Fowler choked back an exclamation. "He's lucky to be dead. Otherwise, I'd have to kill him all over again for this."

Ben took Fowler's place and continued his methodical examination.

"Where's Gaby."

Fowler brushed the hair from her face. "She's safe. Ice got her away. My wife's taking care of her."

"Your wife?"

A dry chuckle. "Surprised? Well, my Margaret is a saint. She has a weakness for strays."

"Almost done. Ben's hands probed along her ribs. "Does this hurt?"

He must have interpreted her groan as a 'yes,' because he stopped poking.

"Everything hurts. I'm cold."

He tucked a blanket around her.

"Well?" Fowler growled.

"Lung sounds are good. The flak vest did its job, but she's bruised pretty badly. I'd like to get X-rays of her chest and ribs."

"Yes or no, Ronkowski."

"Yes, Agent Fowler." Ben growled. "She'll survive three hours without treatment, but she'll be in a great deal of pain. I can give ibuprofen, but anything stronger will negate her testimony. You keep her a minute longer, and I'll drag her out myself. Now, let me go find a stretcher."

"TJ?" Fowler took her hand. "You need to listen to me, this is important. It's almost seven in the morning. The trial

starts in two hours. You can still finish this. Doc here says you're okay to testify, but he can't give you anything strong for the pain. It's your decision. We can go to the hospital or the courthouse. There is no right or wrong. Only your choice."

He waited in silence while she digested his words.

"If I go to the hospital, what happens with the case?"

"They'll go on without you."

"And if I don't testify?"

"Krieger will likely still be convicted but probably won't get the death penalty."

"Then he won't turn state's evidence."

The agent's steely gaze held hers, but he said nothing.

Could she find the courage one more time to do the right thing? "You knew Gaby had those micro-things in her hair."

He nodded.

"You brought her here so Castillo would find me."

He nodded again.

"Why?"

"Because Castillo needed to be neutralized."

There was more, she could tell from the way his jaw clenched. She waited, not letting him look away.

"My real name is Kevin Flores. My mother was an American missionary. She married my father, the leader of a small village in Honduras. They wanted more for me and my sister, so we lived in Alexandria during the school year and spent our summers in Honduras. I was fourteen when Castillo came to the village. When he murdered my parents."

TJ waited for him to go on.

"My chance to put him away came when I got assigned to the Honduras task force. I've hunted Castillo for the last five years. Almost had him, too, until you came along." His mouth twisted in a gruesome smile. "I was ready to settle for a lesser drug conviction, but as it turned out, you got the proof we needed. Evidence we spent twelve months trying to ferret out."

"You risked Gaby's life and mine for vengeance?"

"You were never supposed to be in danger. I had Team Delta in a warehouse three minutes away. They've been there since the day you arrived. No one knew."

She waited, wondering what more Fowler might reveal.

"When the attack came, I ordered Delta to engage ... but then we caught sight of Castillo lurking on the periphery. I knew the coward would run if Delta approached. Forgive me, but I couldn't let him slither away this time. I instructed Delta to hold back but to hem him in. I swear, TJ, I never thought Castillo would come after you himself."

She studied the agent for several long moments. To his credit, Fowler didn't shy from her stare.

The unrepentant man walked a lonely knife's edge. He faced a daily choice to do what was right without falling prey to "whatever it took." She understood his motives and forgave his actions, but she'd never fully trust him again.

"I'll need a ride to the courthouse. Probably someone to

lean on, too."

A sad smile lit the agent's face. "Get that stretcher over here, Doc. We got a deadline to make."

"Is he really a doctor?" she whispered.

"Ben spent three tours with a SEAL team in Afghanistan before heading to medical school. You, my dear, have been treated by one of the most decorated medics in the Army, who just happens to now be one of the finest gynecologists in the northeast."

An armored vehicle, tricked out like an ambulance on the inside, transported TJ to the U.S. Eastern District Courthouse in Alexandria. Aaron and Madman accompanied her, along with Dr. Benjamin Ronkowski. The rest of the team—some wounded, several limping—rode in vehicles in front and behind hers. TJ had no idea where Fowler went.

The men from Delta, who'd arrived in time to clean up the stragglers from Castillo's army, fanned out around the small motorcade and led the parade through downtown Alexandria.

Team Bravo met them at the loading dock in back of the courthouse where eight pairs of hands lifted her stretcher and carried her inside. Fowler met her with a wheelchair padded with pillows.

"Your chariot, milady." His eyes twinkled.

Aaron helped her to the chair. "Slow and easy, girl."

Fowler rolled her to the courtroom, escorted by Aaron and Madman. When the court officer whisked the big double doors open, she stood, refusing help.

Murmurs followed her slow progress down the aisle. One woman pointed a cell phone at TJ.

The judge, an older woman with iron gray hair pulled back in a bun, banged her gavel. "Bailiff, remove that woman. Detain her and confiscate that phone."

She turned to Prosecuting Attorney Dennis Quigley and said, "Counselor, your witness appears a bit unsteady. Is she capable of testifying?"

"Your honor, I have a signed affidavit from Dr. Benjamin Ronkowski stating that he has examined Ms. McKendrick and found her mentally competent to testify."

"Ms. Kendrick? Is this your wish?"

"Yes, Your Honor."

"Very well. Mr. Quigley, you may proceed."

Quigley faced the judge and announced in a sonorous voice, "The prosecution calls Trevian Jane McKendrick to the stand."

TJ breathed a sigh of relief. By the clock at the back of the courtroom, she'd been on the stand for a little more than thirty minutes. So far, the proceedings had gone exactly as Quigley expected, right down to the questions the defense attorney asked. Could it be this easy?

The defense attorney returned to his table. "I have no more questions, Your Honor."

"Mr. Quigley, please call your next witness."

Fowler hurried forward to help her from the stand. "You did great, TJ."

Chapter Thirty-Two

Forty thousand feet below, an earthen patchwork flowed by in slow motion. Green squares abutted gold and brown rectangles, a beautiful, asymmetrical hodgepodge of fields squeezed into wherever free space the shifting topography allowed. Kind of how her life had unfolded.

"Ladies and gentlemen, this is your captain speaking. We are currently cruising at forty thousand feet with smooth skies and a tail wind that should get us into Idaho Falls on schedule. Our current ETA is five minutes past one local time."

TJ looked away from the window and met Aaron's knowing look.

"You okay?" He covered her white-knuckled hand with his much larger one and squeezed.

"Yes. No. Maybe a little edgy. I never cared for flying." Liar. The butterflies in her stomach had nothing to do with being suspended five miles above the earth.

Aaron rolled his eyes "You think too much, girl."

TJ turned back to the window where the eastern rim of the Rockies smudged the distant horizon. She'd once heard the craggy peaks described as 'the rugged stairway to heaven.'

Would she find heaven waiting for her in Hastings Bluff? Or a cowboy who'd had a change of heart?

That would explain why she hadn't heard from Garrett in three long weeks. No phone call, no text. The last e-mail he sent, the day she flew to Atlanta to deal with her former life, had been almost brotherly. With nothing since.

Her business in Atlanta took longer than expected. Thankfully, Fowler had the wherewithal to freeze her bank accounts when she'd gone into hiding. He'd also terminated her apartment lease and arranged to store her belongings. Even so, she'd faced a time-consuming process working through all the legal tangles. Time she could've spent in Idaho.

"You know, TJ," Aaron said. "You made your decision. The ball's in his court now. Let it play out."

Aaron was right. Worry wouldn't make Garrett return her feelings. All she could do now was trust God to work things out the way He wanted.

"What about you, Aaron? Will you return to Mississippi once you're done babysitting me?"

"Nah. I don't think so."

"What about Stella? The diner?"

"Stella's good. She's got Virgil to look after her."

"Did Virgil know about me?"

He nodded. "Virgil's and old friend of mine. After Fowler put me on your detail, I called him up. He got the gig at the diner for you. That town might be small and beyond rural, with everybody getting all up in everybody else's business, but what better place to hide? Castillo and his boys would stick out like bachelors at a baby shower there. And they did."

TJ's attempts to hold back a giggle resulted in a snort instead. Why hadn't she realized how funny Aaron was?

"I just didn't expect Phyllis Hempfling, queen of the Nosy Nellies, to snap your picture at the diner and submit it to *The Bachelor*. I don't know what shocked me more, that the old biddy is eighty years old and knows how to use an iPhone and all its apps, or that she picked up four thousand avid Twitter followers voting for you." His shoulders shook when he laughed.

"That's how he found me? From Phyllis's tweets? And the chief knew about me the whole time?"

Aaron nodded.

"Stella, too?"

"Nah, not Stella. She's a bigger gossip than Miz Hempfling."

TJ remembered well how the middle-aged, but gorgeous, woman loved to share information. "Who'd Stella get to replace you?"

"Her brother and co-owner. Teddy was the cook before me but seems he took my arrival as a sign to retire. Claimed his pigs made better conversation than the town folk. Apparently though, the good life wasn't as good as he hoped 'cause Teddy came running when Stella called."

"She still leading the sheriff around by his ear?"

Aaron laughed again. "Not anymore."

"Okay, I'll bite. What happened?"

"He arrested her."

TJ's eyebrows arched. "Arrested Stella? Whatever for?"

"Virgil caught her speeding and gave her a ticket. Must've been one of his short-fuse days 'cause when she sassed him and called him a name I won't repeat, he whipped out the handcuffs, tossed her pretty little fanny—his words, not mine—in the backseat of the cruiser, and hauled her off to jail. Man, I'd give a month's pay to have seen that."

TJ laughed until tears leaked from her eyes. She could almost see an outraged Stella blistering the sheriff.

Aaron grinned. "Took a day and a night, and half another day in the cell for Stella to figure out Virgil meant business. That woman's needed a firm hand for a long time, and now she's got one.

"A firm hand?" TJ sputtered.

"Now don't go getting your female hissy fit on. You watched those two same as I did. She ran Virgil ragged, pushed him around and tied him in so many knots a sailor couldn't get him loose. 'Bout time he stepped up. Now they're engaged, and she's got a rock on her finger that could outshine Las Vegas. Here, let me show you. Stella texted a picture yesterday." He pulled his cell phone out and found the picture.

"Yikes! That's some serious bling!" The diamond had to

be three carats minimum. It sparkled atop small pavé-set chips in a diamond-encrusted band. "She needs a sling to hold her arm up."

"That ring, hands down, has to be the ugliest thing I've ever seen."

TJ covered her mouth and silently agreed with him. She pictured another ring, one more to her liking—a small, pear-shaped stone on a plain gold band. Elegant and simple.

Whoa! Not a good train of thought. If you stick your hand in the fire, you get burned. The solution? Don't stick your hand in the fire. Yet, somehow Garrett Cameron had pulled her into his flame.

The airplane dipped, jerking her back to the moment. "So, if not Mississippi, where?"

"Interesting you ask. Fowler always said he'd retire once Castillo was out of commission. Knocked us all off kilter when he did. Except now he's got his finger in a private security shop. I'll probably hang out in Alexandria with him for a bit."

TJ nudged him with her shoulder. "You want to stay in Virginia? Why?"

A furious red swept up the grizzled veteran's neck and spread north to flame his cheeks.

"It's a woman, isn't it?"

She stared in open-mouthed delight as his color rose even higher. A direct hit. "Aaron, that's wonderful. It's about time you found someone to settle you down."

"It's not like that. Amelia's a friend." He clamped his lips together and looked away.

"A friend, huh? Amelia who?"

He mumbled something undecipherable, cleared his throat, and then stated very clearly, "Fowler. Amelia Fowler. Okay?"

Fowler's sister? Choking back a grin, TJ took pity on him and changed the subject. She understood his reticence. New attractions were fragile things, and often didn't bear up under the close scrutiny of others. "I have another question for you. Can I trust the Fowlers to keep Gaby safe? Margaret says they want to adopt her."

He took so long to speak TJ began to think he wouldn't answer.

"Those two have a lot to offer. I know you thought Gaby would go with you, but you have to think about what's best for her."

"Well, yeah ... but ..."

"Kevin Fowler has been forced into some terrible decisions in his life. He's done things best not spoken of. Same as me, same as Garrett, and anyone else who's sworn to protect and serve. But know this—Kevin is one of the finest and most honorable men I've ever known. He's got a steady compass in his head and heart and a good woman to keep him anchored. I trust him with my life, my mother's life, and with any child I might have spawned along the way. That man would die to protect his family. He and Margaret are perfect for Gaby."

Disappointment turned into relief, tainted by a touch of guilt. "Okaaaay."

"There you go again. Don't over analyze this. There's no reason why you can't still be a part of Gaby's life. You two made a connection that won't fade with time or distance."

Was he talking about her relationship with Gaby? Or with Garrett?

She'd seen her wounded cowboy exactly twice since the bloodbath at the warehouse, once after he woke up from surgery, still groggy, and again when he came to visit the Fowlers where she'd been staying. They talked about the verdict, how Krieger had given up the senator as expected, and how Fowler's final job was dismantling the crippled distribution pipeline. They mourned the two men from Team Alpha who died in the attack on the warehouse. And then Garrett surprised her.

"I'm heading back to the ranch tomorrow. Dad, Wade, and Jonas have been carrying my slack for too long. Mom wants you to come back to the Triple C soon as you get on your feet." A kiss on her forehead, a promise to stay in touch, and poof—he left. A handful of phone calls and a few text messages were all that kept her hopes alive.

His mom wanted her to visit, but did he?

Aaron broke into her reverie. "You know you're one lucky woman, don't you?"

The warmth in his eyes wrung a smile from TJ. "What do you mean?"

"Well, let's see, you survived two years on the run, with my help, of course." He gave her a wink. "You walked away from a gun battle with nothing worse than a bunch of bruises. You turned the U.S. District Court on its ear and sank the winning shot for the prosecutor. There's a crooked senator on the ropes who's gonna have a close encounter with justice because of you. Six little orphan girls have homes and bright futures, a bunch of traumatized old soldiers finally got closure on a busted case, and you shut down a drug pipeline that would've ruined thousands of young lives. I can't count the number of fans you've made, and now you got a good friend in Margaret. You get to spend time with Gaby, there's a home waiting for you in Idaho, and more important, you got some much needed breathing room with Garrett."

So many blessings, and yet all she could focus on was his last words. "What do mean … breathing room?"

"All I'm saying is that in combat situations, emotions run high. Bonds are forged and your mind gets all tangled up. Your survival becomes entwined with your buddy's, like if he doesn't make it you won't either. Some of these links go soul-deep and stick for life. Similar to what you have with Gaby. It might slip away with time, but the memory never forgets. What I'm trying to say is that you and Garrett needed this time apart. To see if what the two of you feel for each other is gonna stick."

"Do you think he'll meet our plane? I e-mailed my flight information but never got a response."

"Did you call him? Did you call anyone?"

When she dropped her eyes, he burst out laughing. "That's what I figured. You're waiting on him, and he's probably waiting on you, both too scared to take a risk."

"I'm terrified he's moved on."

Aaron's laughter died away. "Garrett Cameron would be a fool to not meet you at that airport, and one thing I know for a fact is that cowboy is nobody's fool. Besides," he chuckled again, "if he don't show, we'll rent a car and chase him down."

Idaho Falls International might be small, but security remained as tight as the rest of the American airports. She searched the crowd as they followed the signs to baggage claim.

"If you don't breathe, you're gonna pass out." Aaron leaned down to whisper.

"What if ..."

"Hush. Don't go there."

Beyond the security doors, a mob of people had gathered to welcome the arriving flight. TJ and Aaron followed the other passengers into the terminal...and there he was. Wide

shoulders, hands in the pockets of his form-hugging jeans, black Stetson. Wearing a smile both wicked and welcoming, Garrett towered over the rest of the people.

His gaze met hers and locked, those ocean deep, midnight blue eyes saying things she couldn't name. He pushed away from the wall and ambled toward her, a slow and confident gait that only a cowboy could pull off.

TJ took a risk. She ran to him, tears slipping free. "Oh, Garr—"

He stole his name from her mouth with a kiss that consumed her.

Sometime later, hours or minutes, TJ couldn't say, Garrett pulled back. "Angel, you slay me."

Once again he'd come for her, keeping his promise. "And I've been wanting you to kiss me like that for a long time, cowboy." She tilted her head up inviting another kiss, but they were thrust apart by the Cameron horde.

Cate and Cody, Wade, Jonas, Mallory, and Cassidy. James was there, too. TJ found herself hauled in tight against Garrett's side with his arm cinched around her waist. Awkward when the rest of his family tried to pull her into hugs, but she didn't care. Her laughter and tears mixed freely. She'd come home.

"Well, I think you did a pretty good job of staking your claim, son. Now, how about we get this circus on the road. I got a ranch down the road that needs tending. Let's get this little filly's suitcases and get outta here." Cody herded them toward baggage claim.

TJ tugged at Garrett's sleeve until he leaned down. "Did your father just call me a horse?" she whispered.

Garrett threw his head back in a hearty laugh. "I guess he did. That means you're one of the family now, so get used to it. You should hear what he calls me."

TJ sighed. She would have Garrett alone for the drive to Hastings Bluff.

In the truck, he reached across the console and took her hand. "Have you given any thought to what's next in your life? I'm hoping you'll settle in Hastings Bluff. It wouldn't take much to get your CPA in Idaho, and mercy knows Wade can use all the financial help he can get."

"I'm happy to help Wade out, but I was thinking something else."

She felt him tense. "You don't want to stay?" He let go of her hand.

"That's not what I said. Before my life fell apart, I used to teach adult education in Atlanta on the weekends. I've been thinking about teaching school instead." She reached over and entwined her fingers with his again.

His frown disappeared, replaced by a blazing smile.

"That's a great plan, angel. You should visit Miz Tilberry. If anybody can help, it's her."

The Hastings Bluff town limits sign appeared ahead. She recognized Sidewinders, the local watering hole, on the outskirts. They passed the Taste-T Pig Restaurant, the sheriff's office and the combination library and post office next door. Further down was the office building where Wade had his business, right next door to the bakery with the small apartment above. It didn't take long to breeze through town and then she spotted the little white church where she'd attended services with Garrett and Mallory. The turnoff to the ranch wasn't far now.

When the Triple C sign loomed ahead, Garrett didn't slow down. They whizzed right on by the turn.

TJ turned in her seat to look back. "Uh, Garrett. Did we miss the turn for the ranch?"

"Yep."

Uh-oh. They were back to the monosyllables.

"So, are you gonna tell me where we're going?"

"Nope."

Definitely something underfoot. Well, she could play his game.

Another mile passed before he slowed down. TJ searched both sides of the road but didn't see anything that resembled a road—only a rough trail that looked recently cleared.

He slowed some more and flicked on the right turn signal.

"Garrett?"

"Not far now." Tree branches scraped against the sides of the truck.

"The woods? Really?" TJ wanted to be alone with him, but sheesh. What if they had a flat? Or got stranded? She looked in dismay at the strappy sandals on her feet. She wasn't exactly dressed for hiking. And with the sun sinking low on the horizon, what if they had to walk back to the highway?

Garrett chuckled. "I can hear the gears in your brain churning. Relax, angel.

Like he'd snapped his fingers, all her worries slipped away. "You're right. If we get stuck out here, you'll give me a piggyback ride."

The sound of his laughter made her heart beat faster.

"I'll carry you anywhere you want to go."

They bounced along the track a few minutes more until the wooded area opened onto a clearing. He stopped at the edge and reached in the backseat to retrieve a bandana. "The next part is the surprise, so I'm gonna blindfold you for a few minutes. Okay?"

TJ nodded.

He covered her eyes with the scarf and tied it behind her head. A second later, he pulled her from the truck and led her by the hand up a slight incline.

"Wait here. Don't move and don't peek."

His deep voice sounded even huskier. She schooled her

thoughts, determined to love whatever the crazy man had in mind.

Garrett returned and swept her up in his arms. "What …?"

"Shhhh. We're not going far."

A half dozen steps and he set her back down. "I spread the blanket out. Sit down, and I'll take off the blindfold.

The view that greeted her left her speechless. They sat on a raised knoll, a sweeping panorama spread out before them. She saw the Salmon River in the distance…and the Triple C. Behind it all, the sun hung above the horizon, a fiery orb set amidst a watercolor sky.

"I'm always reminding you to breathe, angel." He sat beside her on the blanket and pulled her into his arms.

The fragrance of the open range and the wildflowers dotting the hills beguiled the senses. "It's beautiful. I love it."

"Mom and Dad ceded a parcel of land to each of us kids. This is the one I chose."

"It's perfect." She turned in his embrace and pressed her cheek against his chest, feeling his heart thud in a steady rhythm.

"I want to build a home here. For you."

She looked into his eyes and melted. He hadn't said those precious words, but his feeling showed nonetheless. He'd proved himself again and again with his actions.

She touched his face, remembering Aaron's words from the plane. "I know it's too soon, that we don't know each other very well. But I'm willing to take a chance. I love you, Garrett Cameron. I think I fell for you when you threw me off that cliff."

His mouth hovered over hers. "I want to do it right this time." He pulled away and helped her stand.

TJ stopped breathing when he pulled something from his pocket. And then he got down on one knee. "Trevian Jane McKendrick, our new home will be ready in about a year. During that time I want to learn everything about you—why you have nightmares, how good your aim is, what your tickle spots are, what makes you angry and happy, your favorite things. In return, I intend to bare my soul and pray you won't run away screaming. I've never said this before, not to any woman, but I love you, angel. More than I can say. Will you wear my ring? Will you marry me?" He flicked the black velvet box open.

A two-carat, pear-shaped diamond sparkled on a slim gold band, catching the light of the late afternoon sun.

"Breathe, baby."

Her life lay before her, the whole fairytale. Her eyes fluttered, trying to hold back the rush of tears.

"Don't torture me, TJ. I need to hear the words."

She held her left hand out to him and whispered, "Oh yes, Garrett. I will marry you."

Imperfect Wings

About the Author

Elizabeth Noyes, by day, works as a professional writer and editor of business and technical documents for a privately held corporation in Atlanta, Georgia, where she also teaches basic business writing skills. She lives in the

northeast suburbs of Atlanta with husband of 40 years, and is blessed to have her two children, their spouses, and three grandchildren close by.

By night, she pounds away on a computer keyboard, having authored numerous manuscripts, a women's monthly devotional, and more than thirty inspirational vignettes. While entertainment is a primary goal of her writing, she also seeks to scatter seeds of her faith in hopes that some will fall on fertile soil.

She is an avid reader across many genres including suspense, science fiction, thrillers, how-to books, westerns, biographies, mysteries, and what she terms hysterical (lighthearted historical) romance. With two writing conferences under her belt, a growing library of books on the craft of writing, and having attended several writing classes, Elizabeth

Imperfect Wings

is driven to reach the next level.

Elizabeth also participates in a weekly Bible Study with a group of Octogenarians who keep her on her toes and teach her how to stay young. She has a special affinity for the aged and for those with special needs, and enjoys volunteering with the Special Olympics program in Atlanta. As the wife of a retired Army officer, the military men and women serving today hold a particular place in her heart, as do their families.

Other Books by the Author

A Dozen Apologies

Mara Adkins, a promising fashion designer, has fallen off the ladder of success, and she can't seem to get up. In college, Mara and her sorority sisters played an ugly game, and Mara was usually the winner. She'd date men she considered geeks, win their confidence, and then she'd dump them publicly.

When Mara begins work for a prestigious clothing designer in New York, she gets her comeuppance. Her boyfriend steals her designs and wins a coveted position. He fires her, and she returns in shame to her home in Spartanburg, South Carolina, where life for others has changed for the better.

Mara's parents, always seemingly one step from a divorce, have rediscovered their love for each other, but more importantly they have placed Christ in the center of that love. The changes Mara sees in their lives cause her to seek Christ. Mara's heart is pierced by her actions toward the twelve men she'd wronged in college, and she sets out to apologize to each of them. A girl with that many amends to make, though, needs money for travel, and Mara finds more ways to lose a job that she ever thought possible.

Mara stumbles, bumbles, and humbles her way toward employment and toward possible reconciliation with the twelve men she humiliated to find that God truly does look upon the heart, and that He has chosen the heart of one of the men for her to have and to hold.

Available on Kindle.

Look for other books

published by

www.WriteIntegrity.com

and

Pix-N-Pens Publishing

www.PixNPens.com

31973198R00220

Made in the USA
Charleston, SC
03 August 2014